RESET

by

Rebecca Xibalba and Tim Greaves

(from an original idea by Rebecca Xibalba)

Reset
Copyright © 2022 Rebecca Xibalba and Tim Greaves
TimBex Productions

'Obedience is not enough. Unless he is suffering, how can you be sure he is obeying your will and not his own? Power is in inflicting pain and humiliation. Power is in tearing humans minds to pieces and putting them together again in new shapes of your choosing.'

George Orwell – "1984"

CHAPTER 1

'Oh poop!'

It was the third time that morning the office printer had played up. Only this time when Frances had attempted to free up the multiple sheets of paper that had become jammed between the feed tray and the rollers, just to add insult to injury the damned thing had decided to vomit toner all over her.

As she looked down in despair at the black powder peppering her formerly spotless white blouse and beige knee-length skirt, she noticed to her dismay that she had also somehow managed to ladder her tights too. That would have been a few minutes earlier, she thought, when she'd been down on her knees gathering up the myriad of multi-coloured paperclips scattered across the floor, the container for which she'd knocked off her desk while mopping up her spilt cup of tea.

It never rains but it pours.

It wouldn't be unreasonable to surmise that Frances Stade was having one of *those* days.

'Poop and poop again,' she muttered to herself as she hurried out of the office and down the hallway, ignoring the unconcealed amusement on Simon Reynolds's face as he passed her going the opposite way. Pleased to find the ladies' washroom empty, she crossed to the basin and spent the next five minutes trying to clean up.

Satisfied that she had done the best she could, she stepped away from the mirror to examine herself. The sight didn't make her feel any better. I look like a walking version of one of those awful abstract paintings, she thought; the ones that anyone sane would swear a 3-year-old had created, yet mind-bogglingly manage to sell for millions at auction.

There was a smudge of toner on the bridge of her nose – how it had got there she had no idea – so she held a finger under the cold tap and gently rubbed it off.

Sighing, she turned away from the mirror and went into the end stall of three. Locking the door, she pulled down her tights and underpants and dropped her generous posterior down heavily on the seat. She heard a cracking sound and felt a wave of pain in the underside of her plump left thigh. She let out a little squeal. Quickly rising again, she twisted and looked down to inspect the damage. There was a bright red welt across the pink flesh where the skin had momentarily got pinched by the crack in the seat. She gently ran her fingers across it and the responding sting made her wince. She looked down at the seat, which, to use one of her ex-husband Vernon's favourite sayings, was absolutely buggered; it had split right across from the inner to the outer rim.

'I don't think this day could get any poopier if it tried,' she sighed.

Things had got off to a bad start when she had been woken by the sound of an argument coming from the overhead flat. Again.

The Horleys had moved in a year earlier and at first Frances had been delighted, although anyone would have been preferable to the former occupants in her opinion. She had been relieved beyond words when that awful Hazelwood woman, her objectionable partner and their constantly squabbling girls had mysteriously disappeared. Their very presence had made living in her flat absolute purgatory. Although Paul Horley was a bit standoffish from the outset, the wife, Jean, had initially been polite and friendly whenever Frances crossed paths with her. But it hadn't been long before it became obvious that they were as equally unpleasant as their predecessors, just in a different way. The arguments – regardless of the time, day or night – were incessant and Frances could hear every single word.

The subject of this morning's row was one she bore witness to with alarming regularity; Jean was haranguing Paul over his unwillingness to lift a finger to help with the housework. For most couples that would probably amount to a five-minute spat, but whenever the Horleys got started, no matter how trivial the impetus, it never failed to escalate to aural Armageddon.

When Frances had gone to prepare breakfast she had realised she'd forgotten to pick up a pint of milk on the way home the previous day. So she had been forced to eat her Shredded Wheat dry.

When she left for work, she had only got halfway down the street when the heavens opened. Miscalculating how long it would take her to return to the flat to fetch an umbrella and get back to the bus stop in time had cost her dearly; she'd been unable to find the brolly and, realising she must have left it at work, had to get her raincoat out of the wardrobe instead. Then she had to run as fast as her legs could carry her 17-stone, only to end up ruddy-faced and panting for breath as she watched the number 47A bus recede into the distance. During the half hour wait for the next one, a passing car had hit a puddle beside the kerb at speed and doused her in a wave of dirty water, so she'd had to return home to change and ended up catching the one after that.

Her late arrival at the office had resulted in a dressing down from Martin Lindley. What compounded the humiliation was the fact Frances knew only too well he was filing away all her little transgressions until the day he found a really good excuse to be rid of her. He'd then lumped a pile of paperwork on her that she had no hope of getting through before the end of the day, even if she worked through her lunch.

Yes, indeed. Frances Stade was without question having one of *those* days.

With tears brimming in her eyes, she carefully positioned herself back on the broken toilet seat and felt the sense of relief as the pressure eased in her bladder.

The rest of the day actually passed without incident and Frances had been quietly pleased that, contrary to her own expectation, by five o'clock she had managed to complete all the typing, printing and filing Martin had assigned her.

The sense of jubilation didn't last very long.

On the way out through the revolving door at the front of the office block, her heel got caught in the deep-ribbed rubber matting. Slipping her foot out of the trapped shoe and bending to retrieve it kept the man on his way out behind her waiting – yes, it was Simon Reynolds again, and this time he openly laughed at her predicament. Then the heel had snapped off. She was left with no option but to remove the other one, tuck both shoes and the errant heel into her shoulder bag and walk barefoot through the rain to the bus stop, feeling the cold, icky wetness as water seeped up from the pavement, creeping between her toes and saturating her tights.

The bus, which arrived 10-minutes late, was as rammed as it always was at that time of the day. This meant Frances spent the journey home standing, wedged between a man intent on reading his broadsheet newspaper, regardless of how awkward it was in the restricted space, and a young couple – both of them greasy-haired and suffering from unsightly outbreaks of acne – whose mouths remained locked together in a passionate clinch for the entire 20-minutes the bus took to reach Frances's stop.

She crossed the road to Baddi's and went inside. Kabir, the owner of the little convenience store, greeted her with the usual display of exuberance he reserved for his regulars.

'Good afternoon to you, Mrs Stade. How are you today?'

'Hello, Kabir,' Frances said, pushing several strands of wet hair away from her face and reaching for a pint of milk in the refrigerator. 'What an awful, awful day.'

'Yes, very much so. I am not seeing this much water since Chelsea are losing the Cup for second year running and my brother-in-law, he be crying all the way home.' Kabir chuckled and grinned at her. 'Have you heard the most magnificent news?'

Frances looked at him blankly. 'No.'

'One of my customers, he is winning much money on the lottery. And he bought the ticket here at Baddi's! I have been talking to television camera this afternoon!'

'Who won?' Frances asked.

'Mr Reginald Avery, a very fine customer and good friend to me. You must be knowing him, he has a flat in the Hamlets.'

Frances shook her head. 'I don't *know* him exactly, but I know who you mean. How much did he win?'

'Half of a million pounds!'

Frances had been doing the National Lottery every week since it started in 1994 and her numbers had yielded nothing, not so much as a £10 note. She tried to look pleased. 'That's amazing,' she said, thinking that it was anything *but* amazing; it's always someone else, never *you*. And why, of all people, Reg Avery?

'It is indeed the most wonderful thing,' Kabir said, smiling broadly.

Seeing his face lit up like that made Frances feel a little better. She reached for two cans of Kitti-Chunx from the shelf and set them down on the counter along with the milk. 'Oh, just a moment.'

Kabir watched as Frances went across to the shelf of canned goods and picked up a couple of tins of baked beans.

On the way back over to the counter she grabbed up a packet of lemon puff biscuits and placed everything down beside the other items. 'And can I have a scratchcard too, please?'

'Of course! Your usual?'

'Hang on...' Frances pulled out her purse and scanned the contents. 'Actually I'm feeling lucky. Can I have two £5 ones please? If Reg can win on the lottery, I reckon I've got a good chance with these.'

The shopkeeper grinned at her again. 'If you are winning big monies like Mr Reginald I hope that you are remembering your very good friend Kabir.' He handed Frances the scratchcards.

She laughed. 'I might see my way clear to buying you a pint.'

'But I do not drink. I think you are knowing this.'

Frances tucked the cards into her purse, picked up the carton of milk and waggled it at him. 'I meant a pint of milk.'

Kabir burst out laughing. 'In that case I am wishing you much luck, pretty lady.'

Frances smiled and held up her crossed fingers. 'Thank you.'

She paid for the goods and bid him a pleasant evening.

As she left the shop, Kabir called after her. 'Don't be forgetting to watch the television news tonight to be seeing Kabir!'

Churchill Hamlets, the towering concrete eyesore where Frances had lived since her divorce seven years earlier looked even more unwelcoming than usual in the unrelenting early evening rain. By the time she reached the entrance the wind had whipped up too, reducing the day to something even more unforgivingly bleak.

She wasn't surprised to find the lift out of order; it was always hit and miss whether it was working, and more often than not miss. Averting her eyes as she always did from the crude words and images bedecking the walls, she trudged wearily up the steps to the second floor. As she got to the top, there was a loud barking sound away to her left and a large German Shepherd came bounding along the corridor towards her.

Startled, Frances let go of her shopping and took a step back. The milk carton hit the floor and promptly split. The tins rolled towards the top step and clattered off down the stairwell. The biscuits would undoubtedly have been crushed.

As the dog jumped up and set its large paws on her, an angry shout came from off down the corridor – 'Atticus!' – and a burly man carrying a leash appeared in an open doorway. 'Down, Atticus! Get down!'

The dog completely ignored the order and started to lick Frances's face enthusiastically. Suddenly becoming aware of the familiar wetness in her underwear as she started to pee, Frances clenched her pelvic floor muscles as tightly as she could before she completely humiliated herself in front of the dog's owner. Frances looked at him angrily. 'You promised me faithfully you'd keep him on a lead, Mr Pearson.'

'I know, I'm sorry. Little fucker did a runner on me.' The man hooked the leash onto the dog's collar and yanked him away. The animal didn't put up any resistance and lay down at his master's feet. 'He don't mean no harm.'

'You know I don't like dogs.'

The man looked at her with evident disinterest. 'C'mon, Fran. A big old bird like you, afraid of a harmless little dog like Atticus?'

'That's the problem,' Frances said, letting the jibe about her size go unchallenged, but still unable and unwilling to disguise her ire. 'He's *not* little.'

'Come.' The man pulled hard on the lead and the dog obediently stood up. 'Yeah, well, like I said, sorry.'

With the dog trotting submissively behind him, Mr Pearson set off down the steps, kicking aside one of the cans as he went. 'You dropped your shopping, Fran,' he called out. His laughter echoed back up the stairwell.

Making a mental note never again to challenge a day not to get worse, so as to steady herself Frances took hold of the handrail coated in the grime of a thousand hands and bent to pick up the cans. Then she collected up the split milk carton and made her way slowly down the corridor to her flat, dripping milk behind her.

She opened the door and, alerted by the rattle of keys in the lock, Marmalade – her fluffball of a ginger tabby cat – sauntered lazily down the hall to greet her. As Frances put down her shopping on the little table inside the door and dropped her shoulder bag to the floor, Marmalade circled her legs once and then padded away into the living room where he settled back down in his basket.

Frances took off her sodden coat, dropped it on the floor, and walked down the hall and through the living room to her bedroom. She picked up the TV remote from the glass top coffee table as she passed and turned on the television.

Removing her ruined blouse and skirt she laid them on the bed. They *might* wash out, she thought, although she was pretty sure they would end up in the dustbin. Stripping off her tights – they were *definitely* no longer fit for purpose – and underwear, she went through to the bathroom and had a shower. The warm water improved her mood and 10-minutes later she stepped out of the bathroom wearing the favourite baggy knee-length T-shirt she'd bought on holiday in Madrid two years earlier.

The local news had just come on and she stopped in front of the TV as Kabir's face appeared on the screen.

'Mr Reginald Avery is very good customer here at Baddi's. He has been coming here often for many, many years and I am delighted for him to be winning with a ticket that he buy here.'

The camera cut away to an exterior glimpse of Churchill Hamlets and then Reg appeared on the screen. Frances scowled. She didn't know much about him beyond the fact he lived on the ground floor of the block and was pretty much disliked by the other residents, not leastways because he was so indiscriminately objectionable to everyone. Now, here on the television, he was looking understandably pleased with himself and, contrary to his usual disheveled state, remarkably well groomed.

10

As Reg started to speak, Frances hit the power button on the remote and the screen went black. 'That's quite enough of that I think.' She looked down at Marmalade, who was peering up at her with mild interest. 'How in a fair world does a grumpy old bugger like him win half a million quid?' Marmalade mewed at her. 'Yeah. I guess you're right, Marms. It *isn't* a fair world, is it?' Frances sighed. 'Our turn one day though, eh?'

She went out into the hall and collected her shopping, took the two scratchcards out of her purse, then walked through to the kitchen and set everything down on the worktop. Marmalade followed her and sat in the doorway looking up at his mistress expectantly.

'Come on then,' Frances said. She disposed of the milk carton in the waste bin, opened one of the cans of Kitti-Chunx – 'Chicken tonight!' – and spooned the contents into a dish bearing the legend *The Boss.*

As Marmalade padded over, Frances set the dish down on the floor by the skirting board, but the cat took one quick sniff at it, turned away, and disappeared back into the living room.

'Come on, fussy!' Frances called after him. 'It smells delish.' She picked up the bowl and sniffed the dollops of food. 'Ugh! No it doesn't,' she muttered to herself.

She put the bowl back on the floor and set about preparing her own meal. She placed a Cathedral City Mac'n'Cheese into the microwave, set the timer and hit the start button.

While she waited for the food to heat up she filled a pint glass with cold water and set it down on the little kitchen table where she ate alone every morning and evening. Using her thumbnail, she carefully scraped away the silver coating from the scratchcards, which a minute later – accompanied by a sigh of disappointment – were consigned to the rubbish bin.

'Let's have some music,' Frances called through to Marmalade. She switched on the transistor radio that was sitting on the worktop and the upbeat refrain of Ray Frost singing "Lucky To Be Me" filled the kitchen. Frances raised her eyebrows. '*Really?*' She loved the song to bits, but talk about irony. 'Lucky to be *me*? You want to try having the mega-poopy day I just had, Mr Frost!'

She switched it off and went back through to the living room where she selected a CD from the extensive collection on the shelf behind the TV set. She popped it into the player and moments later the sound of Bach's "Air on a G String" enveloped her in calm. Pumping up the volume, she picked up her subscription copy of the celebrity gossip magazine "Hi There!" from the coffee table and returned to the kitchen just as the microwave pinged.

Ladling a generous serving of the steaming pasta onto a plate, she took a fork from the cutlery drawer and sat down at the table. While she ate she browsed through the pages of the magazine, only occasionally stopping to look at anything in detail, and even then only for a few fleeting seconds. However, when she came across a double-page spread featuring paparazzi snapshots of Kim Kardashian sunning herself on a beach in Nassau, she stopped to inspect the images more closely. The woman was wearing the skimpiest bikini imaginable and her bronzed body glistened with tanning lotion. Frances ran her forefinger over a full-length shot that showed Kim striding out of the surf. Oh, to have a body like that, she thought wistfully.

A blob of cheese sauce dripped from the corner of her mouth and landed on the open page. Frances hastily wiped it away and sucked the residue off her fingers.

Finishing the mac'n'cheese in another three loaded forkfuls, she reached over to the worktop and picked up the packet of lemon puffs. She tore the end off the wrapper and a crumbled biscuit scattered over her magazine.

'For God's sake!' Frances picked up the pieces and hastily consumed them. 'Oh well, waste not, want not.' Then she pulled out two more that – given the fact they'd been dropped earlier – were remarkably intact and greedily pushed them both into her mouth, one straight after the other. As she crunched she heard a mewing noise and looked down to see that Marmalade had snuck up on her and was sitting beside the chair watching her intently.

Frances smiled at him. 'Nothing like a lemon puff to help you forget a terrible day,' she said through a mouthful of flaky pastry.

Lemon puffs had been Frances's favourite since childhood. As far as she was concerned you could keep your chocolate digestives and your custard creams and your ginger snaps; as long as she had a couple of lemon puffs to hand, she was happy, and it was seldom that a day went by without one.

The cat was looking up at her with those imploring eyes that Frances was never able to ignore. 'You should have eaten your dinner,' she said sternly, taking another biscuit out of the packet. 'But Mummy loves you very, very much, so go on with you.' As she bent to give Marmalade his treat, a crumb lodged in her throat and made her cough. She dropped the biscuit on the floor and sat upright. The cat quickly snatched it up and retreated to the living room.

Frances reached for the glass of water and took a large gulp, and clearing her throat followed up with a smaller sip. Then she returned her attention to the magazine, idly reaching out for another lemon puff. As she opened her mouth to pop it in she felt the crumb catch at the back of her throat again. She coughed hard to try to dislodge it, but it only made matters worse. With her eyes beginning to water, she picked up the glass and took another large swig.

Possibly hoping to coax another of the delicious morsels out of his mistress, Marmalade reappeared and sat himself in the kitchen doorway.

Frances coughed again – harder this time – and a blob of phlegm shot out of her mouth and landed on the magazine. Now stuck in a rotation of coughing and clearing her throat, she stood up, pulled a piece of kitchen towel from the roll on the worktop, dabbed away the tears from her eyes and wiped her mouth. She reseated herself and, as she went to wipe the slimy mess from the magazine, she frowned; the thick yellow mucus was streaked with red threads. She looked at the paper towel in her hand and her stomach turned. There was a large splotch of blood on it.

Almost immediately she felt her throat constrict and her breathing became laboured. She began coughing again and within seconds it turned into full-on convulsions. Her face scarlet, she tried to stand up, but her head began to swim and her vision blurred. Then her knees gave out beneath her and she dropped to the linoleum like a sack of potatoes, splitting open her forehead on the table leg as she fell. She rolled over onto her back, her chest heaving as she tried desperately to breathe. But her whole abdomen felt like it was clamped in a vice and she was unable to inhale. Her eyes bugged out and her mouth opened and closed rhythmically, just like that of a fish in those heart-stopping moments between finding itself caught and being mercifully returned to the water.

Then abruptly the strangled gasping sound stopped and Frances fell still.

Marmalade stood up and padded over to his mistress's lifeless body. He licked her face once and waited for a response. He got none. He waited for a moment, then turned away and returned to his basket.

CHAPTER 2

Hazel Cooke stared up over the top of the shower cubicle door. The sun was beating down outside and she smiled as her eyes followed a Red Admiral butterfly that was lazily flitting about on the breeze.

She turned off the shower, grabbed her wet hair between both hands and wrung the water out. Opening the cubicle door just wide enough to reach her arm out, she reached round and grabbed hold of her dressing gown from the hook on the outside. She whipped it inside and slid the bolt back across.

Emerging from the cubicle, Hazel made a quick dash across the campsite to her Volkswagen camper van, which was parked underneath an oak tree on the far side of the field. She reached into the pocket of her gown and pulled out a bunch of keys. As she inserted a key into the lock on the side door, she heard a voice from two vans down calling out.

'Oooh, Heather!'

Wincing, Hazel spun round, checking her gown was done up tightly before turning to face the man. She forced a smile and replied, 'Morning Neville – and it's Hazel.'

'Oh yes, of course. Hazel.' The man eyed her up and down. 'I see you've just been to the shower. How was it?'

'Wet,' Hazel answered sarcastically.

Neville frowned. 'Eh?'

'It was hot, Neville. Nice and hot.'

Hazel turned back to face the van and slid open the side door.

'This is a lovely camper you've got here,' Neville said, edging closer.

Hazel hopped up inside. 'Yeah, it does me,' she replied, slowly pulling the door closed.

Neville stuck his head inside, forcing Hazel to abruptly hold back the door.

'What you got then? Twin hob? Sink?'

Hazel sighed inwardly. 'Yeah, all mod cons in here. Look, I don't mean to be rude but…'

'Oh yes, I'm sorry, you'll be wanting to get dressed,' Neville said, cutting her off. 'Why not pop by later? I've got some lovely cold lemonade in my van and if you're really lucky I might drop a tot of gin in for you,' he continued.

Hazel smiled. 'Oh, I'd love to, but I'll be hitting the road later. Places to go, people to see.'

'Oh that's a shame.' Neville patted the side of the van. 'Well, safe journey, Heather. Maybe our paths will cross again some time.' He turned and walked briskly back to his own van.

Hazel let out a sigh of relief and slid the door shut.

*

As the clock on the wall behind him struck seven, the British Prime Minister, Cameron Stirling picked up a black folder from the table just inside the door of Number 10 Downing Street, possibly the most famous and – in the eyes of many in recent years – *in*famous addresses in the British Isles.

He took a deep breath, adopted his most stoic expression and then stepped outside. Following in his wake, each with a similar black folder tucked underneath their arm, were two of his closest colleagues and advisors; on the left was Health Secretary David Simpson and to the right Chief Medical Advisor Sir Malcolm Stone.

A popping of flashbulbs and a low mumble of apprehension from the large assembly of journalists greeted them. There were upwards of 40 or 50 media representatives on the opposite side of the street, all penned behind interlocked barriers, which were policed at regular intervals along their length by armed security staff.

The three men stepped up to the lecterns that had been arranged in a line, spaced exactly – almost purposefully – two metres apart, and surveyed their audience; newspapers, radio and television were all represented in the sea of expectant faces.

'About bloody time too,' a man's voice shouted angrily. 'Call this six o'clock?'

Stirling ignored the jibe over the tardiness of his address. He stood in silence behind the middle lectern patiently waiting for the hubbub and random insults being hurled at him to die down. He had turned 57-years-old the previous day and his bouffant hair – still as thick and luxuriant as it had been when he was young, only now almost completely white – rippled in the gentle evening breeze.

A minute passed, by which time the assembly finally appeared to realise they themselves were exacerbating the delay and a complete silence fell in the street.

Steely-eyed, the Prime Minister stepped up close to the microphone and spoke. 'Good evening,' he said solemnly. 'I would like to thank you all for coming this evening. I only wish I were able to impart better news. I shall be taking questions shortly, but first...'

'Just get on with it!' a woman's voice cried out.

Stirling took no notice. 'But first,' he repeated, opening his folder and setting it down on the lectern in front of him, 'as I explained in my briefing yesterday, the virus responsible for the virulent outbreak of illness across our capital is spreading swiftly and the number of identified infections has escalated at a frightening rate. The number of identified cases has already far exceeded our predictions earlier this week and I very much regret to have to inform you that the death toll has now exceeded 700.' He paused to allow the gravity of his words to sink in. 'We are, of course, continuing to monitor the situation very closely and naturally every resource at our disposal is being employed to analyse the nature of the virus and identify its source. For the short term, however, measures to stem transmission rates are being drawn up as I speak and these will be explained and implemented very soon. Nevertheless, our health service is rapidly approaching a crisis situation wherein it will no longer be able to cope with the influx of emergency cases. Now...'

'Turn the volume down a bit, would you?' Gary Parsons didn't even look up from his newspaper.

His wife, Abi was nursing a mug of tea and staring intently at the television screen, on which she was watching Cameron Stirling address the nation. She picked up the remote control and dipped the sound until it was almost inaudible. 'I still can't quite believe it,' she said, taking a sip of her tea.

Gary glanced up at her. 'Believe what?'

'How fast this has all happened.' She emptied her mug, set it down and turned to face her husband. 'This time last week no-one had even heard of this virus, now there are 700 people dead!'

'Nothing surprises me any more.' Gary sighed and returned his attention to the paper. 'Especially with that cretin in charge.' He gestured towards the TV, on which the Prime Minister had started to field questions. 'Anyway, it's probably all the fault of the Chinese again. I wonder what garbage they've been eating this time?' He rolled his eyes.

'It's not bloody funny, love. People are dying.'

Gary peered at her over the top of his paper. 'Yeah, okay, I know. But come on, how many times have we heard all this before, eh? Bird Flu, SARS, Foot and Mouth, BSE, Ebola – and let's not forget COVID, the gift that keeps on killing – they're all flippin' lethal.' He folded the newspaper, put it down on the arm of his chair and took off his glasses. 'I'll grant you this virus thingy seems to have come out of nowhere, but you mark my words, it'll all blow over in a week or two and by Christmas everyone will have forgotten all about it. These nightly updates are your typical knee-jerk over-reaction by a spineless, clueless, indolent bunch of self-serving jokers who haven't got the nous to organise an orgy in a brothel, let alone run a country. It's scare mongering, I tell you, and like everything else it's all fuelled by the irresponsible media. It happens time and again and all it serves to do is incite panic and fear. Yet as soon as something more interesting grabs their attention for five minutes, they'll lose all interest in this COVID variant, or whatever the hell it is.'

'It's worse than that,' Abi interjected. 'And we suffered over two years of COVID.'

'Whatever, it doesn't make any difference,' Gary continued. 'They'll slide it onto the back burner and you'll not hear anything more about it. It'll just quietly go away.'

Abi frowned. She loved her husband to bits, but his laissez-faire attitude to everything in life irked her more than she would ever admit. 'I hope you're right. I really do. But they said the hospitals are getting overcrowded.'

'Yeah, well, we've heard *that* before too. If they'd invested all that taxpayers' money into keeping the health services buoyant instead of leeching it to live in swanky hotels and buy new toasters and install wrought iron fireplaces and have their effing moats cleaned out, understaffed and overcrowded hospitals would never be an issue.'

'Please don't turn this into another political rant,' Abi said tetchily.

'I'm not. But facts are facts. They've systematically undermined...' Gary trailed off as the living room door behind Abi silently opened and a little boy clad in *Star Wars* pyjamas appeared.

Rubbing his eyes sleepily, he coughed. 'Mummy, I don't feel well.'

Abi stood up and went over to him. 'What's wrong, Harrison, love?' She squatted down in front of the boy, who was rubbing his stomach.

'My tummy hurts. I feel sick.'

Abi put a hand on his forehead and glanced back at Gary. 'He's burning up.'

Gary tutted. 'He's probably just angling for another day off school, you know what he's like when it's football day.' He sat forward in his chair and smiled at his son. 'Is that it?'

The boy shook his head wearily.

Abi's face was now etched with concern. She was feeling the back of Harrison's neck. 'No, he's *really* burning up, Gary.' She stood up. 'Come on, sweetie, let's get you…'

The boy appeared to wobble for a second and then his legs gave way beneath him. Abi just managed to grab hold of him before he crumpled to the floor. 'Harrison!' she cried, as her son slumped into her arms unconscious. 'Oh, God, Gary, call an ambulance quickly!' She turned her head to see that her husband was already on his feet.

He snatched up his mobile phone as Abi cradled their son in her arms. 'It's alright, baby,' she was saying softly. 'Mummy's here.'

'It's a recorded message!' Gary exclaimed, disconnecting the call.

Abi looked at him with exasperation. 'Call 999, for God's sake!'

'What the hell do you *think* I called? This *is* 999. Listen.'

He tapped in the number again and switched the phone to speaker mode. After two rings there was a click and a monotone recorded voice said: 'Sorry. Due to the current unprecedented demand on our emergency services we are currently unable to take your call. Please keep trying. We ask that you please be aware you should only do so in the case of a genuine emergency. For all non-emergency medical enquiries call the helpline on…'

Gary tapped the screen and the voice was cut off. 'What do we do?'

Abi was staring at him in disbelief. 'Just try that.'

Gary looked at her blankly. 'Try *what*?'

'For crying out loud, the fucking helpline!' Her voice was trembling and there were tears in her eyes.

'I'll have to listen to the message through again.'

Abi carefully lifted Harrison into her arms and carried him over to the sofa. As soon as she lay him down he began to twitch violently. 'Hurry!' she shouted. 'I think he's having a seizure!'

Gary grabbed up a piece of paper and a pen from the sideboard and as he listened he scribbled down the helpline number. As soon as he had it, he ended the call and punched the number into the keypad. After a few seconds, he said, 'It's not connecting.' He ended the call and tried again. 'Nothing. It just goes dead. I don't know what to do, Abs!' His voice was filled with fear. 'What the hell do we *do*?!'

Harrison had ceased jerking around and beneath the closed lids there was evidence of REM. Abi put an ear

23

to his mouth and a wave of relief swept over her. 'I think he's asleep. Go start the car,' she said, taking control of the situation. 'I'll get some blankets.'

Exactly 17-minutes later, carrying his son's limp, sweat-sodden body in his arms, Gary barged past two hospital porters who were making a pig's ear of manoeuvring a large trolley filled with medical equipment through the twin sliding doors of St Marks Hospital.

'Easy, pal,' one of the porters snapped shirtily. 'You can push as much as you like, it won't get you seen any quicker.' Gary didn't even hear him; he was already half way across the deserted foyer with Abi, her face streaked with tears, right behind him. That sterile hospital smell filled their nostrils as they followed a sign on the wall down a short corridor, at the far end of which was another set of double doors, above which was a sign: **Accident & Emergency Department**.

As they stepped through into the waiting room the sight that greeted them was the embodiment of Hell on Earth. It was absolute chaos. Masked nurses and doctors wearing full face visors, scrubs and rubber gloves were jostling to move around a room packed to capacity with the sick, all of them uniformly soaked in sweat, while many had splashes of vomit and blood on their clothing. All the seats were occupied and every available area of floor space was filled with people standing, most of them looking as if they were on the verge of collapse. Some *had* collapsed and were laying where they fell, left to flounder in their own feculence.

Others were slumped with their backs to the wall, hunched over, heads hung low. Perhaps most distressing of all, the bodies splayed out on the floor were being trodden on by the hospital staff as they moved around struggling to cope with the sheer volume of patients. They were possibly dead, possibly not, Gary wasn't sure, but he could see that one of them was wearing a nurse's uniform.

'Jesus Christ!' Gary hissed in disbelief. He had never seen commotion quite like it – and he'd served two tours of duty in Afghanistan.

The acrid stench of vomit was overwhelming. Abi almost retched and quickly cupped her hand over her mouth and nose.

With Abi following in his wake, as quickly, but as carefully as he could – and even then he managed to tread on someone's arm – Gary moved forward, shuffling between the littering of bodies alive, dead and almost dead, until he reached the admissions desk in the corner where a woman wearing a visor was sat talking on the phone.

Gary turned to Abi – 'Here, take him for a moment, would you? – and passed over Harrison's limp little body to her.

The boy's eyes were open. He had regained consciousness, but his breathing was irregular. Gently tucking the blanket up under his chin, Abi held him close. 'It's alright, baby, you're going to be fine.' She looked at Gary, her eyes filled with doubt. 'He will, won't he?'

'Absolutely,' Gary said. He ran a hand lightly through Harrison's blonde curls, then, as much as anything to hide his own tears, he turned back to face the woman on the desk. She looked flustered and tired and was still talking on the phone, but she acknowledged him by holding up a "just one moment" finger.

'Keep your fuckin' hands off me!'

Gary and Abi turned to see two security men grappling with a bare-chested man over near the doors. Those that were lucid enough to have even noticed were watching the spat with indifference.

'I'll have you fuckers dragged into court for assault!' the man screamed as he was wrestled through the swing doors and out into the corridor. His anger morphed into a not quite sane laugh. 'You're goin' down, man, all the fuckin' way down!'

Gary turned back to the desk. 'I'm really sorry to interrupt,' he said impatiently. 'But we have to see a doctor.'

The woman glared at him and held up her finger again. 'Okay, I'll get that seen to,' she said into the phone.' A pause, then she nodded. 'Give me ten minutes.' She put down the receiver and looked wearily up at Gary. 'How can I help you, sir?' Her slightly unmoved tone suggested that although she could see what the situation was, there was no sign of urgency, nor so much as a hint of compassion.

As calmly as he could, Gary said, 'We need to see a doctor immediately.'

'As does everyone else here, sir.' The woman gestured to the room. 'As I'm sure you can see, we're extremely busy this evening. What *specifically* can I help you with?'

Gary felt his anger rising. He motioned to Abi and Harrison. 'Isn't it obvious, woman? Our son is really sick, he has a burning temperature and he passed out. He's only…'

'One moment.' She spun her swivel chair away from him and tapped the return key on her computer keyboard. The screen lit up. 'Name?'

There was a groaning sound to their left and a man who had been leaning up against the wall – perhaps only a year or two older than Gary –dropped to the floor.

Gary brought his fist down angrily on the desk. 'My son is sick, God dammit. I demand to see a doctor right *now*!'

The woman spun back in her chair to face him. 'And I'm trying to facilitate that for you, sir,' she said curtly. Gary opened his mouth to speak, but she held up a finger again. 'But I need to take some details first and we will get this done a lot quicker if you retain a civil tongue. I won't help you if you're going to be rude. If you persist with your abusive and threatening tone I shall have no other choice but to have you forcibly removed from the premises.'

Gary looked suitably contrite. 'I'm sorry. I'm… we're just scared.'

The woman wasn't interested. 'Your name please.'

Gary glanced at Abi, his eyes filled with anger and frustration. She shook her head. 'Don't cause a scene,' she whispered.

He looked back at the woman at the desk. 'Gary Parsons.'

She turned back and tapped his name into the computer. 'Home address and date of birth?'

'11 Coppice Road, Ealing. 23rd June 1995.'

The keys rattled.

'And your son's name and birth date?'

Harrison. Harrison Parsons. Er...' He looked to Abi for help.

'26th October 2015,' she said.

Gary gave her a half-smile of thanks.

'26th October's my birthday too,' the woman said. Her tone had softened. She tapped the information into the computer. 'And you say he has a temperature and he fainted?' She glanced at Harrison, observing that he was now conscious. 'How long ago was this?'

Abi moved forward. 'Please, I know all this is necessary, but when can we see a doctor?'

The woman looked at her. 'And you are?'

'Harrison's Mum. We...'

'If you'd like to take a seat, someone will be with you as soon as possible.'

Gary glanced round the room. *Where*?

'Have you any idea how long we'll have to wait?' Abi said, close to tears again.

The woman turned her attention back to the computer screen. 'Sorry, no,' she said flatly.

'None at all?' Gary asked desperately. 'We...'

'Some of these people have been here since this morning. You're just going to have to wait your turn.'

Abi carefully passed Harrison back into Gary's arms. 'Where are the toilets please?'

Without looking up, the woman gestured towards a small door on the right. 'Through there, down the corridor and turn left.'

'I won't be a minute,' Abi said, and made her way out to the ladies' toilet.

When she got there she closed the door behind her and broke down and sobbed.

CHAPTER 3

As the door opened and the Prime Minister entered, the garbled chatter among the dozen men and women seated around the circular, polished walnut table in one of Downing Street's boardrooms ceased abruptly.

Carrying a black folder and a newspaper, Stirling marched purposefully over to the one empty seat and, rather than sitting down, pushed it in neatly and assumed a standing position behind it.

'I won't keep you long this morning, ladies and gentlemen,' he said. His expression was grave. Placing the folder on the table, he unfolded the newspaper and held it aloft for the assembly to see. The bold headline read:

VIRUS CLAIMS FIRST CHILD VICTIM!

'I think you'll concur that this is a significant development.' He dropped the paper on the table.

One of the women at the table raised a hand and spoke. 'Who was the child?' Her tone conveyed interest, but no discernible hint of concern.

'Harrison Parsons.' Stirling replied. 'He died in his parents' arms at St Marks hospital late last night,' he added solemnly. 'Undeniably sad, of course, but hardly unexpected. We knew it was only going to be a matter of time. Understandably, the parents want answers.'

The slightly effeminate looking man seated opposite flicked his hand in the air. 'The press are going to have a field day with this. How do we deal with it?'

'Beyond extending our condolences to the parents, we don't,' Stirling said firmly. 'We haven't the time to dwell on individual cases, nor must they be permitted to influence our strategy. We cannot and *must* not deviate. Things are as under control as they can be at this stage, but I cannot stress strongly enough how imperative it is that we enforce our message to the nation, and in a way that leaves no room whatsoever for doubt. The rules we're about to implement are never going to work unless people are willing to comply.'

There was a nodding of heads and a murmur of general agreement.

'As from noon today we shall be commandeering every TV, satellite and radio channel and our message will be broadcast every hour on the hour. It's vital that the public sits up and takes notice. And this means *everyone*! No exceptions. People are inherently complacent. They think the rules don't apply to them. Dissension needs to be nipped in the bud.'

Stirling looked at the man opposite him. 'Peter. I want you to inform the media that I shall be making another announcement at 8.30 pm this evening.'

*

The roar of a passing car rudely roused Hazel from her slumber. Momentarily disoriented, she looked around her. The last she remembered, she had been laying on the bed in her PJs looking at her tablet and struggling with a tenacious case of eyelid-droop. Clearly she had lost the battle.

31

She squinted at the little travel alarm clock on the small shelf beside the bed; it showed 20:37. She realised she had been dozing for the best part of half an hour.

'Life on the road always takes it out of me,' she said aloud, sitting up and stretching.

Another vehicle passed by at speed – a big lorry by the sound of it, Hazel thought – dousing her VW camper van with a cloud of roadside detritus.

She threw aside the soft, cosy blanket, which had been responsible for prompting her unintended nap, and stood up. Stepping over a large bag full of clothes, she pulled aside the curtain on the window and peered out. The daylight was almost gone, but she could just about see up to the end of the lane and the taillights of an ASDA delivery lorry that was negotiating a bend, which curved sharply away to the right.

She pulled the curtain shut again and, shivering, crossed to the chemical porta-potti and relieved herself. It took up more of the already limited space in the van than she had calculated when she'd first bought it, but it had proven an absolute Godsend, especially during the harsh cold snap at the beginning of the year. Prior to that her lavatorial options had been limited: a handy bush in the great outdoors – provided the weather was fair, that is – or, if she happened to be near one, a public convenience.

She washed her hands. Then, yawning and rubbing her eyes, she went over to the fridge. She took out a bottle of still spring water and filled the kettle to the halfway mark. She put it down on the compact gas hob and waited for it to boil, then made herself a mug of tea.

She put the mug on the worktop and, before getting back into the pull-out bed, she knelt on the duvet and inspected herself in the mirror mounted on the wall above.

She had been lucky. Although she was approaching 40-years-old, her soft features, which were currently benefiting from a healthy tan, hadn't really changed a great deal since her late teens. Of course, if she looked really closely she could see evidence of crow's feet at the corners of her eyes, but they didn't worry her too much; she preferred to think of them as mirth lines anyway, proud scars of a life filled with laughter and happiness. But her wavy locks – currently swept back and held in place with a purple scrunchy – had retained their rich golden brown hue, with not a single grey hair in evidence.

Hazel pulled off the scrunchy and tossed it onto the worktop, then snuggled down under the duvet and pulled the blanket up around her. She picked up the mug and took a sip of tea, then set it back down.

Her tablet, which had switched itself to standby mode, was lying on the bed where she'd dropped it when she dozed off. She tapped the screen and as it returned to life Cameron Stirling's face appeared on the screen. Across the bottom was a scrolling line of text that read: **...PM extends deepest sympathy to Parsons family over the loss of their son... New measures to defeat viral outbreak to be announced soon...**

Stirling was midway through a rallying speech: '…and provided that we stand strong together, look out for each other and follow the rules, we *will* defeat this terrible outbreak of…'

Hazel hit the mute option and shook her head. 'Bollocks, man. You haven't got a clue what's going on, have you? Everyone can see it in your face.'

Suddenly, her mobile phone, which was lying on the pillow, started buzzing. Hazel set aside the tablet, picked up the phone and looked at the screen. She smiled as she saw the name Julie and tapped the green Accept icon. 'Hello, lovey!'

Like Hazel, Julie Morrison had changed into her pyjamas early and she was sitting on the sofa with her legs tucked up beneath her. A pair of reading glasses was sitting on her head, holding her long hair out of her face and there was an open newspaper on the coffee table in front of her. 'Hi. I hope you don't mind me calling so late,' she said, her tone typically – but, as usual, unnecessarily – apologetic.

'Late?' Hazel laughed. 'Don't be daft, it's not even nine yet!'

'Oh, well, I wasn't too sure what time you usually go to bed.'

'Actually, I *am* in bed. I'm in the van tonight. It's a bit chilly, so I thought I'd hop under the covers. Anyway, it's lovely to hear from you. How are you?'

'I'm fine,' Julie replied. 'I was just ringing to check that *you're* okay. I haven't heard from you for a few days.' She frowned. 'You say you're in the van?'

'Yeah,' Hazel said. 'I've got my cuppa and I'm snug as a bug in a rug.'

Julie looked doubtful. 'Whereabouts are you?'

Hazel winced. She hated fibbing to Julie. They had been best friends for more years than she could remember, but Julie was a natural born worrier and sometimes it was easier to be economical with the truth than to trigger unnecessary anxiety.

Deciding that under the circumstances a little white lie was excusable, Hazel crossed her fingers. 'Oh, I'm parked up on a little campsite in the New Forest.'

It wasn't so far from the truth. She had, after all, only left the site that morning. Besides which, the lay-by she'd settled on was almost as good as many of the camps she had stayed on and moreover it was free.

'What's it like?'

'Er… small.'

No sooner had the words left her mouth than an articulated lorry thundered past, and the sudden rush of wind in its wake rocked the little camper van. Hazel gritted her teeth.

'What was that?' Julie said.

Was there a hint of suspicion in her friend's voice or was Hazel just being paranoid now? She winced again. 'What was what?'

'I thought I heard a noise…'

'Oh, that.' Hazel crossed her fingers again. 'It's another van parking up. He's making a meal of it.'

'Okay.' Julie didn't sound convinced, but she let it go. 'Well, I guess that means you haven't seen the news today then?'

'The blob's speech? Yeah, I just caught a bit of it on the tablet. I saw all I needed to see.'

Julie made a little tutting noise. 'All you *needed* to see? What does *that* mean?'

'About ten seconds.' Hazel laughed. 'And that was easily nine seconds too much.'

Julie harrumphed. 'You really should have listened to it all. It's important. Things are getting very worrying.'

Hazel shook her head. 'It's all being blown out of proportion if you ask me,' she said, picking up her mug and swallowing a mouthful of tea.

Julie tutted again. 'You would say that, wouldn't you? But it sounds to me like it's getting out of control. Almost a thousand dead already – almost three hundred up on yesterday. And they said the first case outside London has been identified.'

'You worry too much,' Hazel said.

'You don't worry enough,' Julie responded with a note of sternness.

Hazel rolled her eyes. 'I don't really need to, do I? You do enough worrying for the both of us.'

'Well one of us has to, Hazel! You're far too insouciant for your own good, young lady.'

There was a pregnant pause. Hazel struggled not to snigger at the supercilious tone. Julie was almost 20-years her senior and her little reprimands could often be more like a mother scolding her daughter than a friend to a friend. And although she couldn't help but be amused by it, Hazel was secretly pleased that her friend looked out for her with maternal concern.

Both of them burst out laughing.

'Hey, listen,' Julie said, all trace of annoyance gone. 'How long are you planning on staying at the site?'

Hazel crossed her fingers for the third time. 'To be honest I've had enough of it already. I was thinking about moving on tomorrow, or maybe the next day.'

'Well why don't you swing by here? It would be lovely to see you and I could certainly use the company.'

Hazel finished her tea. 'That would be nice. I haven't seen you for ages.' She smiled. 'Actually, I have a bag full of washing that needs doing too, so if you're offering the use of your laundry facilities…'

'Oh I see!' Julie tried to sound piqued, but she couldn't hide the humour in her voice. 'You only want me for my washing machine.'

'Of course not!' Hazel exclaimed. 'But no-one has a Hotpoint as reliable as yours.'

Julie laughed. 'It's agreed then. I'll see you tomorrow evening?'

'You will. I'll text you when I'm on my way.' The line went quiet. Then Hazel remembered. 'Oh, sorry, you don't like texting, do you?'

'It's not that I don't *like* texting,' Julie said indignantly. 'It's this phone, I get messages come in and the bloomin' thing loses them before I can read them. It's exasperating.'

Hazel chuckled. 'It's okay. I'll call first.'

*

Stirling frowned. 'You're sweating, man. And you look nervous.'

It was the following morning and the Prime Minister was preparing to once again speak to the press. 'And straighten your tie, for God's sake,' he continued. 'I need my Chief Medical Advisor to appear calm and confident. Now, are you up to the job, or do I need to think about replacing you with somebody else who is?'

The question could have been rhetorical, were it not for the fact that Stirling was staring fixedly at Malcolm Stone, waiting for a response.

Looking suitably apologetic, Stone loosened his tie and re-knotted it. He withdrew a handkerchief from his breast pocket and wiped it across his brow. 'Sorry, Prime Minister. I don't know why, I just feel abnormally twitchy about this one. I'll be fine. I won't let you down.'

Stirling appeared to consider the reply. He nodded. 'Very well. Just remember, you mustn't let anything or anyone distract you, and under no circumstances deviate from what we've discussed. The buggers are putting us through the wringer as it is. I'll introduce you, you say your piece – keep it concise – then leave the rest to me. We'll have to open up for questions, but you just stay quiet, I'll handle them. We'll give the bottom-feeding tabloids a little nibble today, and everything released after this will be through our approved newsreaders and journalists only.'

Outside the general mood among the gathering of reporters, all bundled up against the unpredicted shower of light rain, was rapidly deteriorating from impatience to annoyance.

'Twenty past bloody nine,' one of them grumbled. 'You'd think the least thing the useless sod could do is get his lazy arse out of bed and show up on time.'

'Par for the course though,' the man next to him replied breezily. 'It's always the same, ain't it? They call these damned things, we all dutifully show up at the time we're expected to and they keep us standing around in the rain like a bunch of spare pricks at a wedding.' To his left there was a tall woman dressed in an immaculate pinstripe suit. He noticed she was giving him a filthy look. 'Sorry.' He grinned at her sheepishly. It seemed for a moment as if the woman was about to give him a piece of her mind, but before she could actually say anything the door of Number 10 opened and the policeman on the step moved aside. 'Oh, here we go,' the man said, turning away from the woman as the Prime Minister and his Chief Medical Advisor appeared.

Stirling stepped over to the lefthand lectern of the two that had been set up for the morning's briefing. Stone faltered in the doorway for a moment, then took up position at the one on the right and stood playing with his tie. It suddenly felt extremely tight and he longed to remove it completely.

'Good morning, everyone. As always I'd like to thank you for coming.' Stirling cleared his throat. 'I apologise that we're running a little late, but we've only just received and had time to assess the overnight figures on casualties. I'm extremely sorry to have to report that the situation is worsening. As of 7am this morning we have registered in excess of 1200 deaths. 1207 to be specific.' He paused and let his message of doom hang in the air. His face darkened. '1207,' he repeated for full effect. 'It has become very clear that this dreadful epidemic isn't going to go away any time

39

soon and the strain on the health service is now bordering on untenable. We shall be taking questions in a moment, but right now, however, for a slightly more specific analytical report on the death toll, I want to hand you over to our Chief Medical Advisor, Malcolm Stone.'

Stirling looked at his colleague and noticed to his annoyance that the man's tie was slightly askew again.

Stone fished a pair of spectacles out of his top pocket and put them on. 'Er…'

Stirling prickled. You don't ever start a speech with "Er", he thought. It shows indecisiveness – and indecisiveness translates as weakness.

'As you are aware,' Stone said, 'in a bid to understand both the nature of the virus and determine its source of origin, we have been tirelessly undertaking an extensive regime of exploratory assessments on both the sick and those who have sadly passed away. Whilst it remains something of an enigma at this time and we have reached no firm conclusions yet, we have managed to ascertain that it preys most virulently upon those with pre-existing underlying health conditions. There is a direct correlation between the health of those who contract symptoms and the speed and severity with which it attacks. Now, er…'

Again with the "er"! Stirling was incensed. He was going to have to address this later.

'98 percent of the deaths registered thus far have been among the elderly and the infirm,' Stone continued. 'The other two percent fall outside the 70 plus age bracket and it is those that we are particularly keen to understand. There is a common denominator and we shall find it. We will of course continue to keep everyone closely apprised of our findings. Er…'

Stirling leaned in to his microphone, turning his head slightly to cast a disapproving look at his colleague. 'Thank you, Mr Stone.' He looked out at the assembly. 'We have to be brief this morning, I'm afraid, but as I said just now we do have a few minutes to answer questions.'

The woman wearing the pinstripe suit raised her hand. 'Sarah Martindale, TLB News. The situation is getting worse very quickly. Yesterday you mentioned that there are measures the Government plans to take. Things are getting worse and worse. Do you have a solid plan of action and if so when will we be informed of what that plan is?'

Stirling nodded his head. 'That's a very good question, thank you. These things take time, I'm afraid, I'm sure you appreciate that. We must remember what we're dealing with here is a contagion that the world has never encountered before. Now, when…'

Moving forward, right up against the barrier, the woman persisted. 'Do you or do you not have a plan of action, Prime Minister? It's a simple question.'

'If you listen, I shall answer you. We do indeed have a plan of action, the structure of which will be revealed later today and put into place nationwide within the next 12-hours.'

'That's fine. But can you…'

'Thank you.' Stirling cut her off and pointed to a man who had his hand raised. 'The gentleman in the leather jacket.'

'Ed Morris, "The Sun". People are saying that simple measures like taking paracetamol can have a positive effect. Can you confirm that?'

Stirling glanced at Stone. 'That's more Mr Stone's field, but I don't think he'll mind me answering this one for him?'

Removing his glasses, Stone shook his head. He was painfully aware that his nerves had got the better of him and he could detect Stirling was far from impressed. 'Of course not, Prime Minister.'

'It's impossible to say at this stage whether paracetamol or any products of its ilk actually serve to alleviate any of the effects of the virus. Eating healthily and drinking plenty of water is paramount, however. Given that the virus appears to thrive upon those less healthy than others, the best advice we can give everyone right now is keep fit.' Stirling pointed to a shabbily-dressed man standing on the far left of the throng.

'Colin Parsons, SW Radio. The vaccine program proved invaluable in eradicating the last viral outbreak. Do you think this will be implemented as rapidly in this instance?'

Stirling chuckled. 'The short answer to that is no. We're barely more than a week into dealing with this epidemic and it may well be that once we learn more about the virus we'll discover we already have the solution at our fingertips. But as far as developing a brand new vaccine, that would obviously be some way off yet.'

As Stirling was about to point to someone else, a young man who had been standing at the back pushed his way forward and spoke. 'Isaac Owusu, freelance vlogger.'

Stirling eyed him up. He was black with close-cropped hair; maybe 25-years-old and his eyes sparkled in the sunlight from behind a pair of steel-rimmed spectacles. He was holding a compact dictaphone.

'If you wait a moment, Mr Owusu, I'll get to you,' Stirling said, without the least intention of allowing the man to speak again.

Isaac wasn't about to be fobbed off. 'The one question everyone wants answered – and one that has been asked before and systematically ignored – is precisely how long the Government has known about this virus.'

Stirling looked momentarily out of sorts. He composed himself. 'Not an unreasonable question, Mr...?'

'Owusu.'

'Yes, of course.' Stirling spoke slowly as he scoured his memory. 'Mr Owusu. I believe we've encountered one another before, haven't we?'

'Once,' Isaac replied. 'Please answer the question, Prime Minister.'

With the trace of a sneer on his face Stirling peered at the young man. 'You wrote that piece about...'

'The question, Sir. Please. Just answer it.'

Stirling suddenly became aware that a deathly silence had fallen in the street and everyone was watching him intently, hanging on his response. He cleared his throat. 'Very well, although I'm sure it's not the answer you're fishing for. Barely a day longer than anyone else.'

43

'Actually that was *exactly* the answer I expected,' Isaac said. 'But it seems to me…'

'Thank you for your attention this morning, ladies and gentlemen.' Stirling nodded at the crowd. 'I shall see you all later today when we announce our plans for dealing with this virus as swiftly and efficiently as possible.'

He stepped away from the lectern and, to the slight astonishment of everyone present, spun on his heels and crossed back to the door of Number 10.

Even Stone was slightly taken aback by the abruptness with which things had concluded. But as Stirling disappeared through the door, he glimpsed the look of thunder on his superior's face. Acknowledging the crowd with a perfunctory nod, Stone scuttled inside after him.

A thin smile formed on Isaac Owusu's lips. Blue touch paper successfully lit. Time to grab a late breakfast. Singing quietly to himself, he turned away and set off along Downing Street towards Whitehall. 'Run rabbit, run rabbit, run, run, run…'

CHAPTER 4

Isaac got home just after 11. No sooner had he removed his jacket and gone into the spare room that he'd converted into a small office than the front door opened and Keisha came in, looking exhausted from her midnight to 10am shift at Parrish's All Night Convenience.

'You're up and about early,' she said suspiciously. It wasn't unusual for her to return home and find her boyfriend fast asleep.

Isaac stuck his head out of the door of his office. 'I told you yesterday, I blagged a press pass to Stirling's address this morning. Not that the incompetent blimp had anything much to say.'

'Oh yeah, sorry, I forgot.' Keisha hung up her bag and took off her coat. 'Have you eaten?'

'Yeah, I grabbed something in town on the way home.' Keisha, who was taking something out of her bag, had her back to him Isaac walked over and gently slipped his arms around her waist. 'Come here, beautiful lady.'

She turned to face him and they kissed.

Isaac peppered her warm neck with soft butterfly kisses. 'Missed you,' he whispered.

At the feel of his warm breath beside her ear, Keisha felt goosebumps rise on her arms. She laughed. 'You only saw me last night.'

'Yeah, but I need my baby.'

'And I need something to eat.' She unhooked his arms from around her waist.

'Awww, come on, baby.' He took her in his arms again. 'I need a little bit of your luvvin'.'

They kissed again, more passionately this time, and Keisha cupped his ear with her hand.

Isaac slid his hand down the back of her jeans and squeezed her left buttock. 'Come to bed with me.'

Although they had only moved in together fourteen months earlier, Keisha and Isaac had actually been a couple for almost three years. They had met when he came to the university to canvas students' opinions on the upcoming election. Keisha's friend Anni, who had agreed to do it, went down with flu and asked her to stand in. Although she had been reluctant at first – politics didn't interest her one bit – agreeing to do so turned out to be the best decision Keisha had ever made. As she later admitted to Isaac, having been told a vlogger was coming to interview the students, she had expected some nerdy kid with specs and acne to show up. She couldn't have been more wrong.

Keisha fancied Isaac the moment she had set eyes on him. Who wouldn't have? That tall, muscular, broad-shouldered physique; the way he moved, with a panther-like grace; the boyish good looks with a smile that could charm the birds out of the trees; the dark satin skin; those almond-shaped eyes, burning with passion; his earthy scent. They had started dating a week later and when Anni found out what she had missed out on she'd been fuming. Much to Keisha's amusement.

They made love for the first time exactly one month later. That was the day she had fallen in love with him.

The alarm on Isaac's smartwatch beeped. He and Keisha were nestled naked on the sheets, both of them basking in the languorous afterglow of their passionate lovemaking.

'I'm gonna have to get up. I've got today's broadcast to deal with.' Isaac sighed. Despite his declaration he was making zero effort to move. Instead he lay staring sleepily at the ceiling.

'Penny for them.' Keisha propped herself up on one elbow and ran her fingers across his smooth, hairless chest.

He rolled onto his side and kissed her on the nose. 'I *could* tell you, but I'd have to kill you.'

Keisha laughed. 'I suppose I'm gonna have to watch your broadcast to find out.'

'Yep.'

She stretched and yawned. 'I'm knackered. I'm gonna hop in the shower, grab something to eat and then go get me some sleep.' She rose from the bed and Isaac watched her cross the room, musing upon how she managed to move so gracefully; it was almost as if she were floating.

She stopped in the doorway. 'Don't spend too long chained to that damned computer today.'

Isaac grinned at her. 'I won't, baby.'

As soon as she had disappeared into the bathroom, he threw on some clothes, collected the dictaphone from his jacket pocket and went through to his office in the spare room. He sat down, pushed the play button and started listening to his recording from earlier that day. He frowned. It was inexplicably muffled and he couldn't clearly make out everything that was being said. Not that it mattered too much. He had pre-recorded today's five-minute episode before he'd set foot out the door, with the intention of editing it in a postscript if anything of value had come out of Stirling's address; unsurprisingly, the suspected lie he'd told Isaac aside, it hadn't.

Isaac had been vlogging professionally now for more than five years. He occasionally varied the topic when something arose that he felt particularly passionate about voicing an opinion on. But his primary focus throughout all that time had been the incompetence of the UK's Governmental body. Was he outspoken? Yes. Controversial? Without question. But he considered himself fair, and although they were few and far between there had actually been a handful of episodes in which he'd been glad to acknowledge a positive Government resolution. Over time he'd cultivated a format that was both immensely entertaining – the swathe of positive feedback he received was testimony to that – and, most crucially, got his message across. "Owusu's Eye" had built an impressive number of followers. He'd lost count of how many short videos he'd created throughout the years, but he never neglected to read through the comments section on each new post and respond wherever appropriate. There was little he enjoyed more than tugging the tiger's tail, and Stirling and his circus of clowns had provided him with ample opportunities.

Having been able to get in a little dig first hand that morning had been a real thrill.

He heard the sound of the toilet flush and a minute later the rattle of the cutlery drawer. He turned his attention to the laptop screen and double-clicked a folder entitled "OE Week 277". It opened and he dragged the .MOV file with today's date on it across to the desktop. He always gave his recordings a final watch before he passed them to Rory Hopkins, his go-to web guru, to upload them to the NuTube video hosting platform. He double-clicked on the file and it opened and started to play.

At six-minutes and 37-seconds the episode exceeded the usual length by about 60-seconds, but there wasn't really anything in it he felt he could sacrifice.

As he was about to upload the file, Keisha called out, 'Goodnight then.'

It never failed to amuse him that she said goodnight when it was only ever just after lunch; a vagary of shift-working unsociable hours, he thought. 'Love you, baby,' he called back. 'See you in your dreams.'

'Love you too.'

Isaac heard the bedroom door shut. He uploaded his video to WeTransfer and selected the option to send an email notification. Then, swiftly keying in Rory's email address, he clicked the Start Transfer icon.

*

Hazel switched off the ignition and sat for a moment looking at the large, semi-detached house in front of her. She felt a pang of guilt. How long had it been since she was last here? It had been quite a while. And one thing was for sure: she'd forgotten what a tight squeeze it was to park her camper van on the narrow drive.

Picking up her shoulder bag from the passenger seat, she climbed out and cast a look along the twin rows of pretty properties with their impeccably maintained gardens that lined the cul-de-sac. Julie was very lucky, Hazel thought. This really was a pleasant spot to live.

She walked over to the gate at the side of the house and pushed it open. It made a loud creaking noise.

The back door was slightly ajar. Hazel stuck her head round the corner. 'Hellooo?'

There was no sign of anyone in the kitchen, but there was a portable television on the worktop and it was switched on with the sound turned low. It was displaying a close-up of Cameron Stirling with his lips flapping. Hazel poked out her tongue at the screen.

'Helloooo?' she called again, louder this time.

A reply sounded from somewhere off in the house. 'Come on in, I'm in the utility room. Won't be a minute.'

As Hazel stepped inside and crossed to the little room that annexed the kitchen, a dog started barking in the house next door. She stopped in the doorway.

Inside, Julie was on her knees, removing clothing from a washing machine and dropping it into the large plastic basket beside her.

Hazel grinned. 'Say one for me while you're down there, will you, Jules?'

Julie turned her head and her face lit up. 'Hello, you! Well, aren't you a sight for sore eyes?' Her knees made a little cracking sound as she stood up and pressed her hands into the small of her back. 'I tell you,' she said, 'these old bones of mine have a good future behind them. How are you?'

'I'm good. All the better for seeing you.' Hazel moved forward and stretched out her arms to give her friend a hug.

Julie took a swift step back. 'Better not.'

Hazel stopped. 'What's up?'

Julie looked slightly awkward. 'Sorry, I think it's best that we don't... well, you know, touch each other. The virus and all that.'

Hazel pouted playfully. 'So I come all this way and I don't even get a hug from my best friend?'

'Sorry,' Julie repeated. 'I think it's just prudent to be careful at the moment.'

'Well, it's really good to see you.' Hazel smiled. 'And speaking of being careful, you really shouldn't leave your back door open like that, especially if you're not in the kitchen. Anyone could come in while you've got your back turned and nick something.'

Julie shook her head. 'I was only in here and I heard the gate squeak.'

Hazel laughed. 'I was going to suggest you put some oil on that!'

Next door the sound of the dog barking intensified.

'No, no,' Julie said. 'I purposely haven't. Like I say, I can hear when someone's coming up the side of the house. That gate is my little guard dog.'

'You've got a real one of those too.' Hazel pointed to the wall. 'Persistent little bugger, isn't he?'

'He's a she. Mrs Parkinson's dog, Pip. She's a lovely little thing, but I tell you, when she goes off on one she can bark for England.'

They walked out to the kitchen. Hazel pointed at the television on which the Prime Minister was still talking. 'I think we've seen this one before,' she said sarcastically.

Julie tutted. 'I know. I've been trying to keep up with it all, but to be honest they do waffle on so, and I find it all very confusing. It actually terrifies me if I'm being honest. Sometimes I wonder if we'd all be better off not knowing anything at all.'

'The Government clearly don't, that's for sure,' Hazel scoffed. 'It's pretty obvious to everyone that they're up the creek without a paddle. *And* they know it. They haven't even managed to come up with a name for this virus yet. That's usually the *first* thing they waste taxpayers' money on, sitting round for hours on end, drinking tea and eating cake, trying to come up with a snappy name.'

Julie shook her head sorrowfully. 'That's very cynical, Hazel. I agree it's all pretty grim. But how can we ignore it?'

'I can.'

'But surely there has to be some good news soon,' Julie said. '*Surely.*'

'Don't hold your breath.' Hazel noticed the tears in Julie's eyes; she was genuinely frightened. She took a step towards her. 'C'mon, can't I even have one ikkle hug?'

Julie swiftly positioned herself on the opposite side of the kitchen table. 'No!' she exclaimed emphatically.

Hazel chuckled. 'Don't worry, I'm only teasing. I'll stick to the rules of the house.' She made a little gesture in the shape of a cross on her chest. 'Honest.'

Eyeing Hazel warily, Julie crossed to the stove. 'I wasn't expecting you for a few minutes yet. I was going to put the kettle on and have a cuppa ready for you when you arrived. Would you like one?'

Hazel shook her head. 'No thanks. I'd love a glass of water though, my mouth's as dry as…'

Julie held up a finger. 'Don't say it!'

'Say what?' Hazel replied, adopting an expression of innocence.

'Don't you look at me like that,' Julie said, her tone admonishing. 'You know very well what.'

'Gandhi's flip-flop?'

Julie laughed. 'Oh, alright. Sorry, I thought you were going to say something rude.'

'You thought I was going to say a nun's crotch, didn't you?'

Julie gasped. 'Hazel! You're awful. That's *exactly* the sort of remark I'd expect from you!'

Hazel burst out laughing at the note of sanctimony in her friend's voice. 'I won't say it then.'

Julie smiled. She knew she came across as prim and proper sometimes, but although she'd never admit it she rather enjoyed Hazel's slightly naughty sense of humour. 'It's okay. I guess I should be used to it by now.'

'So about that water…'

'Oh, yes.' Julie reached a glass out of the cupboard and went to the sink.

'Actually, I don't suppose you have any bottled water, do you?'

Julie frowned. 'Why would I waste money on that when I have a perfectly good tap?' She glanced at the dripping spout. 'Well, perfectly good once I put a new washer in it.'

Hazel looked at her doubtfully. 'Perfectly good tap? There's a contradiction in terms if ever I heard one.'

'What do you mean?'

'Well,' Hazel said, frowning, 'tap water might have been good enough to drink once upon a time, but not any more. They put fluoride and all sorts of God-knows-what shite in it now. I stopped drinking from the tap years ago.'

'That's okay,' Julie said. She crossed to the fridge and opened the door. 'I have a filter jug chilling.' She held the jug aloft.

Hazel shook her head. 'Thanks, but no. If you don't mind I have some in the van.' She walked over to the back door. 'Back in a jiffy.'

Julie rolled her eyes and returned the jug to the fridge. 'Bring your washing in while you're at it,' she called after Hazel. 'I'm going to be putting another load on later.'

*

With a grateful smile, Professor David Walsh accompanied the Prime Minister and his Chief Medical Advisor to the exit. They walked down the flight of

54

stairs, across the small lobby and stopped at the set of glass doors that fronted S&P Research, the unobtrusive Cambridge-based laboratories that had been seconded to assist the Government.

Walsh was tired and his sallow complexion and thinning, whispy hair did little to hide the fatigue. Nevertheless, despite the fact the two men had caught him off guard by arriving unannounced a day early, he was feeling confident and very pleased with himself. The impromptu meeting with his guests and the ensuing whistle-stop tour of the laboratories had gone as well as could be expected.

'I applaud you for everything you and your team are doing for us here, Professor,' Stirling said. 'You've been a vital element in our plan and the results of your work so far have been exceptional.'

Walsh adjusted the rimless spectacles that were perched on the end of his nose. 'Merely doing my duty, Prime Minister. I have to reiterate though, the pathogen is proving to be extremely efficient, far more so than any of us here could have predicted. Obviously we'll continue to work tirelessly on your solution.'

Stirling nodded appreciatively. 'Excellent.' He turned to Stone. 'I don't think the public is paying heed.'

Stone, who was looking just as uncomfortable as he had at the morning's address, nodded. 'I tend to agree, Prime Minister.'

'I think it's about time that we made it abundantly clear that things are going to have to change if they want to get through this.' He turned back to Walsh and extended his hand. 'We'll speak again soon.'

55

Walsh looked momentarily uncertain. He glanced around and saw that there was no-one else in the lobby, then turned back to face Stirling. There was a pregnant pause as the two of them looked at each other and then, simultaneously, they broke into a smile. Walsh gripped the Prime Minister's hand and shook it firmly, then repeated the gesture with Stone.

Stirling chuckled. 'Good man. I'll be in touch.'

CHAPTER 5

Paul and Sarah Porter's living room was frightfully shabby. The wallpaper was peeling in several spots, revealing ugly patches of poorly rendered plaster. The remaining wallpaper had succumbed to the assault of thousands of cigarettes and was stained with unsightly nicotine stains, most prominent right behind Paul's favourite chair. The carpet too had seen better days, worn to a thread in front of the matching armchairs that Sarah had picked up second hand from a charity shop.

It was only a small room and it wouldn't have taken much effort to redecorate and lay a new carpet, but although their bank balance would have taken a bit of a hit, the real reason was that Paul simply couldn't be bothered. Sarah had always thought her father was idle, but Paul took indolence to a whole new level. He had no excuse either. He'd been out of work since he lost his job as a builder six months earlier and had systematically managed to shirk employment ever since. As he reminded her often, 'Why would I bother to go out to work when I can claim almost as much as I was earning by doing fuck all?'

They had married in their late teens. Twelve years had passed since then and it was a remarkable feat that they had remained together. Sarah must have loved him once, but if she had done then whatever love she'd felt had long since evaporated. What was it that had made her say yes when he'd proposed? It wasn't as if she'd been up the duff or anything like that. It was all a bit of an enigma to her now, but she supposed it had to have been love.

In any event, whatever feelings she may have had for him back then certainly hadn't lasted long. Within weeks of tying the knot Paul had cheated on Sarah with the spotty girl who worked at the local chippy. The night she found out he'd come home drunk. She'd challenged him over the dalliance and he'd responded with his fists, telling her if she didn't want it to happen again she ought to learn to be a bit more considerate about his "needs" in bed. The next morning he had apologised to her profusely and sworn he'd never raise a hand to her in anger again. And, of course, she had forgiven him and promised to try harder to please him. That was the only time he'd ever shown any remorse for his actions and, unsurprisingly, he would resort to violence with alarming frequency.

Sarah was 30 years old now and she was still as petite and pretty as the day Paul had met her. Except that most of the time there was a sadness about her and the beautiful green eyes that once sparkled were often muted and filled with an unspoken plea for help.

Not that Paul ever noticed, and nor would he have cared if he had. He was either too stupid or too drunk. He was a year older than her, but he didn't look anywhere near as youthful. The excessive alcohol intake was undoubtedly responsible for that.

This afternoon, as they were most days, they were in the living room together watching a quiz show on the TV. Sarah was dressed in her PJs and idly curling her blonde hair around her finger as she stared vacantly at the screen. Paul – who was slumped in his armchair with a bent roll-up hanging lazily from his bottom lip – was wearing grubby tracksuit bottoms and a Manchester United football shirt. He was a slim man, but the shirt, his favourite, was barely substantial enough to cover his swollen beer belly, which, when he slouched the way he was now, gave the amusing impression that he was pregnant. Not that Sarah would have ever dared to remark upon it.

The end credits on the programme they were watching began to roll.

Paul removed the cigarette from between his lips and emptied the last of the can of beer down his throat. 'Well that was a fuckin' waste of time,' he slurred. 'Prick deserved to lose. Even I knew the answer was Dominican Republic.' He dropped the can on the floor and returned the withered fag butt to his mouth.

Sarah looked at her husband. The expression on her face said it all. 'You didn't shout it out though.'

'Didn't need to. It was fuckin' obvious.'

Sarah was pretty good at solving anagrams and quick with it, but even she would have struggled to arrange NICE LAND, OPIUM CRIB into the name of a Caribbean country in 30 seconds. Paul wouldn't have been able to do it if he'd had 30 years.

'I liked the guy,' she said. 'I wanted him to win.'

'He was a worthless fuckin' dildo.'

As Sarah reached for the remote to turn off the set, the words **Breaking News** flashed up on the screen and then a newsreader appeared. 'Within the last half an hour, Downing Street have confirmed that the measures that are to be implemented in order to stem the rapid spread of the virus will be delineated by the

Prime Minister, Mr Stirling, in an address to the nation at six o'clock this evening.'

'Oh, for fuck's sake, that's the match cancelled then.' Paul coughed – a real hacker – and reaching out he snatched the remote from Sarah's hand. 'Gimme that.' He hit the standby button and the screen went blank.

'Never mind the football. We need to know what they're gonna do,' Sarah said firmly. As soon as the words left her mouth she regretted the terseness in her tone.

Paul glared at her. 'Who the fuck asked for your opinion?'

Sarah felt herself blush. She was 30 years old and she still coloured up like a rebuked schoolchild when Paul had a go at her. 'I just think…'

His eyes were filled with contempt. 'No-one gives a flyin' fuck what you think. Why don't you just get your lazy arse off that chair, get some fuckin' clothes on and go get me some beers.'

Sarah nodded. 'Sorry. Yes, of course.' She got up and crossed to the door.

Paul's eyes followed her. Her mousey subservience always amused him. 'That's right, run along now.' He waggled his fingers at her. 'Quick as you like, you skanky bitch.'

*

Julie sighed. 'So that was about it really. Not much else I could have done about it. But I tried.' She was sitting on the sofa in the living room with her legs tucked up

60

underneath her. 'Anyway, enough about me, I want to hear about you. What have you been doing with yourself?'

Hazel was occupying an armchair on the opposite side of the room. She was still aware of the sound of next door's dog yapping, and although they had the television on in the background, the sound was muted.

'Nothing very exciting, I assure you,' Hazel said. She hitched a thumb at the wall. 'How *do* you put up with that all day?'

'Pip?' Julie smiled. 'I don't even really notice it that much to be honest.'

'*Really*?' Hazel said with a note of disbelief. 'It's been making that infernal racket since I arrived.'

Julie laughed. 'I can assure you she was building up a head of steam long before you arrived. She's pretty excitable today though. She's not normally quite as bad as this. But like I said before, she's very sweet and Mrs P dotes on her, treats her like a princess.'

Hazel raised her eyebrows. 'Hmm, well the princess is clearly in a bit of a strop.'

Julie chuckled. 'So come on then. What *have* you been doing with yourself?'

'Just enjoying life on the road really. I had a lovely drive down to the coast last week. Parked up late on Friday night and bedded down. Then I was up with the lark and I got to see the most beautiful sunrise. It was stunning, Jules. I wish you could have been there with me to see it. I was thinking...'

Julie raised a hand to hush her. 'Hang on.' While Hazel had been talking Julie had been keeping one eye on the television. 'They're about to make the

61

announcement.' She reached for the remote control and unmuted the sound.

Hazel shook her head resignedly and rolled her eyes.

The Prime Minister was standing at his lectern, on the front of which was a brightly-coloured banner that read **Keep Hydrated :: Stay Healthy**.

To his left was the ever-present Malcolm Stone – who was actually looking tidier and a tad more confident than usual – and to the right stood the Health Secretary, Michael Simpson. Perhaps it was Simpson's general casual demeanour that made Stone look comparatively smart. He was attired in an ill-fitting suit, at least one size too big, and his short blonde hair was uncombed. He was scratching nervously at a full beard that was crying out for a trim.

There was a very noticeable difference to the evening's address, however. There were no people in attendance and each of the men was facing an unmanned, remotely-operated television camera.

Stirling began to speak. The almost imperceptible movement of his eyes from left to right made it evident he was reading from an autocue. 'I appreciate that there has been immense anticipation for this broadcast. We have in fact been working extremely hard to formulate an interventionary course of action, which we are now confident is ready to be activated immediately. Whereas I realise that our slight tardiness in doing so may have suggested indecision, I can only stress that a plan such as this takes extensive coordination and we are completely satisfied that we have done everything that *could* possibly have been done to facilitate its rollout as early as it was feasible to do so. Regrettably the situation has worsened dramatically since I spoke to you this morning and the virus – or ORACULTE as it shall henceforth be referred to – has spread beyond London, with a number of deaths across the Home Counties and the South East being identified as directly linked to ORACULTE. We now expect that it will move rapidly into the Midlands and the far north. As such, what we are about to implement applies not only to London as we initially intended, but to the country as a whole.'

He paused and cleared his throat. 'We now have no choice but to sanction every household across England with vital instruction – instruction that *must* be adhered to if we are to defeat the dreadful epidemic that has blighted our great nation. From extensive research by the best scientific minds available to us we have ascertained what we must do to control the spread of ORACULTE and prevent our health service from becoming irreparably overwhelmed.'

He stopped for a moment and took a sip of water. 'Firstly, the only way that we can hope to stop ORACULTE from spreading is if people have no contact with anyone outside of their own households. This means that as of 8:00 pm this evening nobody will be permitted to leave their home for the next 14 days. As we have previously explained, it has become evident from our research that ORACULTE is primarily thriving among the elderly and those with pre-existing health issues. Therefore, those who fall

63

into either of those categories will be rated as high priority in terms of medical needs and food supplies. We have the requisite information from last year's general census and all applicable households will receive the appropriate level of extra attention and special measures will be put in place. Now, there are of course exemptions from the 14-day period of isolation, specifically those who fall into the category of key workers. This includes medical staff, emergency services, care workers, food suppliers – *not* vendors, I shall come to that in a moment – and the transportation sector. All households will be means tested and those currently receiving benefits will continue to do so. Those who are able to work from home will be expected to do so. Those who are *unable* to work will have any loss of income upheld by the Government. Details of this scheme will be forthcoming.'

He took another sip of water. There was a discernible glaze of sweat forming on his brow. 'As a further precautionary measure, as from midnight tonight we will be indefinitely suspending all travel in and out of the country. It will be a difficult and trying period for us all. We *will* get through it as we have done before, but I cannot stress strongly enough at this stage how absolutely vital it is that everyone stays healthy and keeps drinking plenty of water.'

Somewhat condescendingly Stirling leant forward and pointed over the top of his lectern at the banner. 'Keep healthy, stay hydrated.'

Stone and Simpson both nodded their approval.

'Food supplies then. All shops will close this evening and shall *remain* closed throughout the 14-day isolation period. Everybody will be issued with a Government-funded weekly allocation of the basic essentials, which will be delivered to you by the British Army. These deliveries will commence tonight. Medication will also be provided where requirements have been identified. Now, as I say, there is no question that there are difficult days ahead. But these are difficult times. As I'm sure you appreciate these decisions have not been made lightly, and I hope that everyone understands the potentially disastrous situation we would be facing *without* taking action and, ergo, the necessity of these drastic measures. Their implementation is for the greater good and we expect everyone to comply. We shall be closely monitoring the situation throughout the two-week period of isolation and if the evidence shows that contagion levels of ORACULTE are being satisfactorily contained then these measures will of course be revised. In the meantime I implore everyone to act sensibly and responsibly and I can only reiterate that you all remain thoroughly hydrated. Thank you.'

Stirling glanced quickly at Stone and Simpson. In unison the three men raised up their glasses of water and drained them.

'Wow. I certainly wasn't expecting *that*.' Hazel looked at Julie. 'What d'ya reckon?'

Julie said nothing. She was staring at the television with a look of dismay on her face.

'I wonder if that's actually water or gin?' Hazel mused aloud as the picture on the screen switched from a shot of Stirling and his ministers stepping down from their lecterns back to the BBC news anchor. 'Oh well, I suppose I have to take back what I said earlier anyway. They *have* come up with a name for the virus.' She looked over at Julie again, who was still staring at the television in silence. 'You're very quiet.'

'I... I just don't understand,' Julie said, muting the sound on the TV. 'How's it all going to work?'

'It isn't,' Hazel said. 'It can't. I'd be doubtful of the feasibility even if we had someone trustworthy in charge, but this lot couldn't organise...'

Julie cut her off. 'I've hardly got any food in. I was going to go shopping tomorrow.' She started to cry.

Hazel got up from the armchair, walked over and sat down on the sofa beside her. 'Come here.' She took Julie in her arms and moved forward to give her a hug. Rather than pulling away, Julie buried her face in her friend's shoulder and sobbed.

CHAPTER 6

'Are they havin' a fuckin' laugh?'

Paul Porter put the television onto standby and took a swig from his can of beer. 'If they think I'm staying in this bastard flat for two weeks they've got another fink coming.'

'You never go anywhere anyway,' Sarah said under her breath.

'What did you say?' Paul sat forward suddenly as if he was about to get up.

Sarah saw the tightly balled fist and flinched. 'Nothing. I was just…'

'You was just *what*?' Paul slumped back into his chair.

'I was just thinking that I was going to visit Mum tomorrow,' Sarah said, her eyes watering up. 'I promised her. I haven't been to see her for almost two weeks what with one thing and another and she's *so* unhappy in that home. This is awful.'

'Oh fuck off, would you? That senile old cow doesn't even know you're there half the time.'

Sarah looked inconsolable and a tear ran down her cheek. She wiped it away on the sleeve of her cardigan. 'Yes, I know. But…'

'Fuck me, if I'm gonna have to sit here lookin' at your pathetic phizog for two whole weeks I'm gonna have to be seriously bladdered,' Paul snapped.

'Why don't we make good use of the time and decorate the flat? We've already got the wallpaper in the cupboard.' Sarah forced a smile. 'It could be fun.'

Paul belched loudly, threw back his head and laughed. 'Fun? Fuckin' *fun*? Are you havin' a laugh? I can think of plenty of words to describe decoratin' and fun sure as shit ain't one of them.'

'I was just trying to be positive.'

'Oh, you're fuckin' tryin' alright.' He grinned at her cruelly, revealing several broken and yellowed teeth and a gap where one was missing at the front.

'Why are you so horrible to me all the time?' Sarah whimpered, wiping away another tear. 'I don't deserve to be treated like this.'

Paul looked at her with abject contempt. 'If you have to ask me that then you're thicker than you look. Well, don't just sit there fuckin' moping. Go on with you, you miserable skank. Make yourself useful and get me another beer.'

Sarah sighed and stood up.

Paul belched again. 'Oh,' he added. 'And you can shove this one in the bin while you're at it.' He drained the can in his hand, crumpled it effortlessly and hurled it at her. It missed her face by a few inches and bounced off the back of the chair onto the floor.

He laughed spitefully as Sarah dutifully bent down and picked it up.

*

Four minutes into recording his second vlog of the day, Isaac was looking earnestly into the lens of the Sony

68

ZV-1 camera fitted to his laptop. The red light on the top was blinking.

'Never mind that they've clearly known about this virus – or as they're now calling it, ORACULTE – for far longer than they're letting on. And incidentally, I wonder how many hours of fraught debate it took them to come up with ORACULTE? How abstruse is that? Are they suggesting they regard themselves as oracles now? What a bunch of...' – he paused – '...cults. Outstanding work, guys, absolutely first class. I'm in awe. But if there was *ever* any doubt about what's really going on here, I think this evening's address made it abundantly clear. George Orwell, anyone? "1984"? The words draconian measures don't even begin to cover it.'

He sat back in his chair. 'Make no mistake, people. It may or may not have started out as an epidemic – history will have the final say on that one, trust me – but this is irrefutably going to end up being all about control. What better excuse could they hope for than a situation like this to tighten their grip on the masses? You can only begin to imagine how badly it vexes them in the corridors of Whitehall that they don't have more control over the daily lives of the people. It must give the Prime Minister and his cronies sleepless nights. Control, that's what it's all about.'

He leant forward again. 'Control of me...' – he pointed to himself and then at the camera – '...Control of *you*. Control of *everyone*. It's coming, people. You know I'm right.'

He eased back in his chair. 'Until next time, be strong.' He waved a clenched fist in the air. 'This is Isaac Owusu signing off.'

He reached down and tapped a key on the laptop and the light on the camera stopped blinking.

'Great,' he said aloud to himself. 'That should get them thinking.'

*

Cameron Stirling stood looking at the ministers gathered around the circular table in the boardroom at Number 10.

Stone and Simpson were seated on either side of him. Standing behind him alongside a widescreen monitor mounted on the wall was a clean-shaven man with a crew cut, immaculately dressed in military attire, the breast of his jacket decorated with an impressive array of ribbons and medals.

'When faced with a national crisis in the past,' Stirling was saying, 'the public have proven apathetic when it comes to compliance. We need to come down hard and fast if this plan is to bear fruit. What do we think about introducing some incentive?' He looked hopefully at the assembled faces. 'What if we were to offer the public a small reward to play turncoat, eh? To squeal on their neighbours. To engage in a healthy dose of social shaming. Inevitably they'd turn on each other and make the job less arduous for us.'

One of the ministers raised his hand. 'I think that's an excellent idea, Prime Minister. What sort of reward did you have in mind?'

70

'*What* is of no importance. People are inherently backbiters. They don't show it of course, but deep down behind the sycophantic smiles they afford their neighbours they detest them. They'll be champing at the bit for an opportunity to line their pockets with ill-gotten gains. Insurrection cannot and *will* not be tolerated. This little idea of mine will ensure that it's kept to the bare minimum. Dissenters will soon fall into line when they realise the people they classed as friends have – to use the vernacular of the great unwashed...' – He held up his hands and made little quotation marks in the air – "...dobbed them in".'

'Inspired, Prime Minister,' Simpson said.

'Excellent,' Stirling looked at another of the ministers seated at the table. 'I want a media release to that effect prepped post-haste, Nigel. Keep it concise, but make sure there's no margin for dubiety. We need to ensure our little whistleblowers squeal with confidence that they'll be reimbursed.'

The man nodded. 'Yes, Prime Minister.' He scribbled a note on the pad in front of him.

Stone raised his hand. 'Speaking of whistleblowers,' he said, 'I'm sure everyone here is aware of that irksome little rat and his conspiracy theory broadcasts. What's his name again?

'Owusu,' one of the women at the table said. 'Cocky little shit.'

'Owusu. That's it,' Stone said. 'How much longer are we going to let him carry on shooting his mouth off, Prime Minister?'

'He'll be taken care of,' Stirling said flatly. 'Getting back to business, as things stand, Phase 1 of our control

71

measures is now underway. The Home Office – along with the Department for the Environment, Food and Rural Affairs – has been working closely with the British Army for the past few days to devise a strategy for the national supply of food and medication. There will be no deviation from what has been decided. It is a colossal task, but distribution will commence tomorrow morning and within 48 hours every household will have sufficient supplies to carry them through the 14-day isolation period. I'll let General Mathers fill you in on the specifics.'

Stirling turned and nodded at the military officer who was standing behind him. 'Philip. If you please.' He took a seat.

'Good evening,' Mathers said. He clicked a button on the small remote control in his hand and the monitor on the wall lit up. A map of England appeared on the screen. Mathers clicked the button again and London and its outer boroughs turned red. 'The rollout of supplies will begin in London at midnight and all army personnel from every regimental division across the country will be deployed – along with the Territorial Army – in the distribution process. As the Prime Minister said, everyone will have all the basics they require to see them through the two-week isolation period.'

'Sorry to interrupt.' It was Simpson. 'But how can we really be sure that people will do as they're told and stay at home? With all due respect to your excellent address this evening, Prime Minister...' – he smiled obsequiously at Stirling – '...even with the planned supply package delivered free of charge to their doorsteps, no matter how hard we've worked to give them everything they need, there will always be those who think the rules don't apply to them. We saw the alarming level of apathy just a few years ago with COVID-19. As you yourself said, Prime Minister, the general public have an irksome problem with the notion of compliance.'

Stirling chuckled. 'I did indeed say that, Michael. However, COVID-19 played out under a different regime. My little incentive scheme will take care of those that breach the rules. But with the extensive military presence that will be out on the streets 24-7, I doubt that there will be many plebs who'll dare to step outside.'

Stirling looked at General Mathers. They smiled at each other in a manner that could only be described as conspiratorial. 'Please continue, General.'

Mathers clicked the remote and the image on the screen changed to show a graph displaying all the regions across England.

'We estimate that when this is all over the numbers in all sectors of the community will be considerably more manageable,' Mathers said.

*

As the clock on the living room wall ticked to a minute past nine, Julie was sitting on the sofa watching Hazel pace back and forth, muttering under her breath.

'They can't do this to us,' Hazel was saying. 'We're human beings, not robots. We have rights!'

'Just sit down, would you? You're making me dizzy. Nobody said anything about robots. It's obvious this ORACULTE is out of control and far more deadly than anyone first thought. If it wasn't they wouldn't be doing this.'

Hazel frowned at her friend. 'You've sure changed your tune. A couple of hours ago you were panicking about not having any shopping.'

'I've had time to think. And talk about me changing my tune. You were the one making light of it all.'

'Yeah, well, I've had time to think too,' Hazel snapped. 'And it stinks.'

'I know it's going to be hard, but I'm sure these new rules have got to be for the best.'

Hazel was getting more irritable by the minute. 'You think they're for the best, do you? Wake up, Jules. This isn't about a bloody virus. It's about control!'

The two women stared at each other. The moment of silence was shattered by the sound of Pip barking again.

Hazel scowled. 'Doesn't that bloody dog *ever* give it a rest?'

'Please don't get angry,' Julie said softly, trying to mollify her friend. 'They're only doing what they think is best. What choice do we have?'

Hazel looked bemused. She shook her head. 'So you're just going to sit there like a good little girl and wait with your hand out for our generous leaders to deliver a box of God knows what that has to last you for… what? A whole week?' A frown crossed her face. 'Hang on a second. They don't even know I'm here.

I'm practically off the grid. How am *I* going to get food?' With a sigh she dropped heavily into the armchair. 'We're all screwed.'

Julie got up and came over. She put a comforting hand on Hazel's shoulder. 'We'll share whatever they deliver here. Don't worry about it any more tonight. Let's have some supper and then we'll sleep on it. We can figure out what we're going to do in the morning.'

*

Sarah turned over and looked at the bedside clock. The red numbers on the digital display showed 4:09. What was it that had woken her? She was sure it had been the sound of a door slamming. She lay listening, her breathing shallow.

Beside her, Paul was sound asleep, snoring loudly, as he always did when he was laid on his back.

'Did you hear that?' Sarah whispered, knowing full well that he hadn't.

Paul grunted and rolled over onto his side. 'What fuckin' time is it?' he muttered sleepily. He had heard her after all.

'It's only just turned four. But I'm sure I heard something.'

'Well if you heard somethin', get your skinny arse outta bed and go fuckin' check it out. Jesus, woman.' Even half asleep he knew how to hurt her. He kicked out with his foot and caught her a glancing blow on the shin. His unclipped big toenail drew blood.

'Alright, alright, I'm going.'

Sarah slipped out of bed and scampered naked across the bare floorboards to the door. She flicked on the light and Paul put up a hand to shield his eyes. 'Fuck's sake, Turn the light off!'

Sarah flipped the switch and the room fell back into darkness.

'What's the fuckin' matter with you?' Paul growled. 'Are you *tryin'* to make me lose my rag?'

'No, of course not.' Sarah whispered. 'Sorry.'

She took her dressing gown off the hook on the back of the door and shivered. 'God, it's freezing in here.'

Paul yawned. 'Once you've checked we ain't got burglars or nuffin' like that – not that there's fuck all worth nickin' in this shithole anyway – grab my fags while you're up.'

'I will.'

Sarah walked out of the bedroom into the hall. Still shivering, she was about put on her gown when she was startled by a movement outside the front door at the end of the hall. Through the frosted glass, silhouetted by the streetlamp across the way, she could see the figure of a man bending to set something down on the step outside. She was just about to cry out to Paul when the doorbell rang.

Sarah almost jumped out of her skin. Fastening her gown, she tiptoed quickly down the hall, but the figure stepped away and disappeared from sight. When she reached the door, Sarah pressed her face up against the glass. It was a pointless thing to do; the frosting was completely opaque. She slipped the safety chain on, turned the latch and opened the door a couple of inches.

She peered out. 'Hello?' There was no reply. 'Hello?' she said again. Still no reply.

'Who is it?' Paul shouted from the bedroom.

'No-one.'

'What the fuck are you talkin' about, no-one? I heard the fuckin' bell.'

'There's no-one here.' Sarah was about to close the door again when her eyes dropped down and she saw the box on the doorstep. She immediately realised what it must be. 'Oh!' she cried excitedly. 'I think it might be our supplies.'

Closing the door and removing the safety chain, she opened it wide and leaned out. She looked up and down the walkway outside the ground floor flats. There wasn't a soul about, but all the neighbouring doors had a similar box sat on the step in front of them.

She bent down to inspect the box more closely. There was a printed label stuck to the top that simply said **PORTER (2)**, with their flat number and postcode beneath it. She tried to lift the box but it was ridiculously heavy. Squatting down in the open doorway she used a thumbnail to slit open the tape on the top and peered inside.

In the poor light she could see several tins of beans and pasta, corned beef and Spam – she winced with revulsion – some cooking sauces, other assorted groceries she couldn't quite make out and a few loose vegetables. Whatever else might be lurking in the box, it was obvious to Sarah that these really were the barest of essentials on which she and Paul were expected to survive for a week.

'Well?' Paul shouted again impatiently. 'Is it our grub, or isn't it?'

Sarah picked up a tinned steak and kidney pudding and pulled a face of disgust. She dropped it back in the box. 'It is.'

'Well fuckin' sort it out and bring me my fags! Jesus, how many times do I have to fuckin' ask?'

Sarah pulled out the solitary, forlorn-looking toilet roll that she could see and peered hopefully into the box. No, there was just the one. 'I hope we don't get the shits,' she muttered, dropping it back in.

As she bent to try to lift the box again, the neighbouring front door opened and John Goodley stuck his head out. 'Mornin'.' Sarah didn't like him much, but she acknowledged him with a smile. Without another word, he bent and effortlessly picked up his box, stepped back inside and slammed the door shut.

Try as she might, Sarah couldn't lift the box. She glanced back over her shoulder in the vain hope that Paul might actually have got out of bed and come to help her. She should have known better.

Exasperated – and with great difficulty – she managed to drag it inside and then elbowed the front door shut.

CHAPTER 7

At a little after 6 am, the large green MAN SV 4x4 army truck rumbled to a stop kerbside.

The driver turned to the man in the seat next to him and pointed through the windscreen at the VW camper van parked on the driveway across the road.

'I promised the missus we'll get ourselves one of those little beauties when I retire next year. Take ourselves off to the coast, or the countryside, or wherever the wind blows us.'

'Nice, Colin,' his colleague said without so much as a hint of interest.

'Yeah. Sun, sea and sand. And our own little mobile retreat when we want to get away from the crowds. Absolute bliss.'

'Yeah,' the second man echoed indifferently.

The truck rocked slightly as six men and women dressed in army fatigues jumped out of the back. While three of them began unloading boxes of supplies onto the tarmac, the other three scooped them up and began to hurry back and forth, distributing them to the doorsteps around the crescent, ringing doorbells and then hurrying away without waiting for anyone to answer.

One of the soldiers was just squeezing up between the camper van and the laurel hedging on Julie's driveway when the front door opened and Hazel appeared. She stepped outside and, seeing the approaching man, she called out, 'Good morning.'

He halted in his tracks. 'Stop right there!'

Slightly confused, Hazel stopped. 'What's the problem?'

'You're not allowed to leave your property, m'am. There's a lockdown in force.'

Hazel smiled. 'Oh, yes, I know. It's okay, I was…'

'No exceptions.'

Hazel frowned. 'No exceptions? How do you know I'm not classed as a key worker?'

The man hesitated. 'Are you?'

She smiled. 'Well, no, I'm not, but…'

'Then you're not allowed out,' the soldier said firmly.

'I was only going to fetch something from my van. Surely…'

'Like I said, no exceptions. Not for any reason. I'm going to have to ask you to return to your house please.'

Hazel couldn't help but laugh. 'This is ridiculous,' she said. She started to walk forward and in a flash the soldier dropped the box of supplies he was carrying to the ground and rested his hand on his hip… no, wait, *not* his hip. Hazel hadn't noticed before, but her eyes widened as she saw that the soldier had a holster fitted to his belt and his fingers were now curled around the butt of a gun. She stopped.

'I'm going to have to insist, m'am.' The fingers tightened on the gun.

A woman dressed in army uniform and also carrying a box suddenly appeared behind him. 'Everything okay here, Kev?'

Without taking his eyes off Hazel, the soldier now identified as Kev called back over his shoulder. 'All in hand, Sally. The lady's just going back inside.'

'Hurry it up then, mate,' the woman said. 'We've got thousands of these things to deliver today.'

'Be right with you.'

The woman hurried over to the door of the house that adjoined Julie's and dropped her load on the step. Ringing the bell, she turned and hurried back towards the truck.

Kev was still staring Hazel out. 'Well?'

Hazel turned and walked back to the house. As Kev let go of the gun and bent to pick up the box, she stopped in the doorway and spun round. 'You can't threaten people like this, you know.'

'I can actually.' Kev walked up to the doorway and Hazel took a step back inside. 'Sorry. It's Government rules.'

'It's legalised bullying is what it is,' Hazel snapped. 'I want your name. I'm going to report you.'

'Private Kevin Reynolds.' He bent to set the box down on the step and stood upright. 'You're perfectly at liberty to report me, m'am, but it won't get you anywhere. We're just following orders.' With that, he turned and walked back in the direction of the truck.

As Hazel stood watching him go, Julie appeared behind her. 'Ooh, is that our box of goodies?'

Hazel jumped. 'You gave me a start. I thought you were still in bed.'

'No, I was probably awake before you were. I heard you moving about. I like to have a little read before I get up. I'm in the middle of a really good one at the moment. It's about…' She trailed off as she noticed that Hazel wasn't listening. She was watching the people over by the truck. 'You okay?'

'Not really,' Hazel said. 'I was just going to get my tablet from the van and one of those soldiers as good as threatened me with a gun.'

'You're kidding!' Julie looked aghast. 'Which one?'

'The one pointing at us,' Hazel said.

Julie looked. Kev was standing beside the truck talking to one of the other soldiers and he was indeed gesturing in their direction.

'He can't do that, surely.'

'Apparently he can. Claimed it's orders.'

'Don't let it get to you,' Julie said. 'He was abusing his remit. He looks like the sort who would. It wouldn't surprise me if it happens a lot over the next few weeks.' She rested a consoling hand on Hazel's shoulder. 'Come on, help me get this box inside.'

Julie leant forward and looked at the label. It read **MORRISON (1)** and her house number and postcode were printed neatly underneath.

'It's fine,' Hazel said. 'I'll manage.' She bent down and lifted the box. 'It's not very heavy. I don't think our leaders have exactly been generous.'

A worried look crossed Julie's face. 'Oh dear. I was hoping we'd be able to eke it out between the two of us. At least they delivered it promptly, I suppose, I'll give them that.' She stepped aside to let Hazel through.

'Almost too promptly, wouldn't you say?' Hazel mused aloud, turning sideways and pushing the door shut with her foot.

Julie frowned. 'How do you mean?'

82

'Well, think about it. Delivering boxes of food to *every* household in the country isn't something you could organize overnight, is it? And remember, each one has to be tailored specifically for the number of people in each house, never mind all the medications and whatnot. Think about the sheer logistics of that.'

'It's a huge undertaking,' Julie agreed, nodding.

'Exactly. Kind of suggests to me that they were orchestrating it *weeks* ago.'

Julie rolled her eyes and followed Hazel along the hall. When they got to the kitchen, Hazel put down the box on the table.

'Let's have a look and see what we've got,' Julie said excitedly.

Hazel cast her a doubtful look. 'I wouldn't get my hopes up if I were you.'

Julie laughed. But as they picked through the contents of the box her face got longer and longer. 'I can't eat even *half* of that,' she sighed. 'I wouldn't feed some of that to a starving dog.'

As if on cue, Pip's barking from the house next door resumed, only something about it was different now; it seemed less vociferous and was punctuated by infrequent little whimpering noises.

'Poor little Pip,' Julie said. 'Listen to her. She sounds really upset.'

'Tell me about it. She woke me up in the night with that infernal yapping.'

Julie sighed. 'She woke me too. Sorry.'

'It's not *your* fault,' Hazel said. 'She's obviously just very excitable.'

'Like I say, I don't tend to notice it most of the time, it's just background. Mrs P lost her husband a few years back and Pip has been her constant companion since. She's always full of beans, but I will say she's been exceptionally persistent since yesterday. You know what? I think I'm going to knock next door and check everything's okay.'

'Good luck getting past Action Man out there,' Hazel said, pulling a mock stern face.

'Easy,' Julie grinned. 'I'll go round the back. Won't be a mo.'

She walked over and peered out of the back door. Glancing down the side of the house towards the front, and satisfied she couldn't be seen from the road, she nipped through the door, up towards the garden and disappeared round the corner.

She went across the garden, stepped between the bushes that divided the two semi-detached properties and walked over to Mrs Parkinson's back door. As she tapped lightly on the glass, the sound of Pip barking inside became a little more frantic.

Hazel appeared in the garden and stopped beside the bushes.

Julie tapped the glass again, a little harder. There was a scrabbling sound on the other side of the door and Pip's barking became even more hysterical. But no-one answered. Julie looked at Hazel and shrugged.

'Try the door,' Hazel said.

'I don't know if I ought to.'

Hazel rolled her eyes. 'How long are you going to stand there waiting for someone to come then?'

Looking uncertain, Julie pushed down on the door handle but it moved barely half an inch before it stopped. 'It's locked. This is no good, Mrs P's pretty hard of hearing nowadays, it's likely she just can't hear me. I'm going to try round the front and ring the bell.'

Surely, if her own dog is going bananas she would investigate why, Hazel thought. But she said nothing.

Checking to ensure that there was no-one out on the road who could see them, they walked stealthily back along the side of the house. 'I feel like I'm an intruder in my own garden,' Julie said testily as they got to the gate. They stopped and looked at each other. No words were needed: they knew it was going to squeak.

'I'll do it really fast,' Hazel whispered. She took a grip on it and yanked hard. It opened without making a sound. 'What was that you said about having your own guard dog?'

It was all they could do not to burst out laughing.

The 4x4 truck was still parked out in the road, but fortunately there was no sign of any of the army personnel.

'Be quick,' Hazel whispered to Julie. 'I'll keep watch for Action Man.'

Julie hurried across the front of the house, passed the camper and stepped nimbly over the low brick wall. Glancing furtively over her shoulder, she bent and pushed the box of supplies on the doorstep to one side and rang the doorbell.

Bing-bong.

There immediately came the sound of scampering feet inside and the little pads on Pip's front paws

85

appeared, pressed up against the glass panel at the bottom of the door.

But nobody came.

Squatting down on her haunches, Julie lifted the flap on the letterbox, put her mouth close to the slot and as loudly as she dared, called out. 'Mrs Parkinson? Lily? It's me, Julie, from next door. Is everything okay?'

At the sound of her voice, Pip started barking again excitedly.

'Lily, are you in there?'

'Jules!' The shout came from her left.

Julie turned her head to see Hazel gesturing frantically towards the road, before swiftly stepping out of sight round the side of the house.

Julie looked back over her shoulder and her face fell as she saw the female soldier step away from the truck and begin to walk briskly towards her.

'Ma'am, what are you doing there?' the woman called out. 'I'm afraid you can't be out here.'

Ignoring her, Julie turned back, pushed open the letterbox flap again and looked through. There wasn't much light, but she could just about make out a half-open door on the far said of the hall.

'Lily! It's Julie. Are you okay?' she shouted urgently.

'Ma'am, please will you stand up and step away from the door.' The voice came from right behind her.

Julie continued to ignore the woman. Her eyes darted desperately to the left – Pip was going crazy now, yelping loudly and scrabbling vigorously against the glass – and then to the right.

And that's when Julie saw it.

Her eyes widened. 'Oh, my God!'

Splayed out on the floor at the foot of the stairs was the body of an elderly woman. One of the arms was twisted awkwardly above her head. Although Julie couldn't see the face she knew straight away it was Lily Parkinson and that she was very possibly dead... or perhaps not.

'Mrs Parkinson!' Julie called. 'Mrs Parkinson, can you hear me? Lily...'

There was no response. As Julie's eyes became more accustomed to the weak light, they fell upon the treacly black mess pooling out across the floor from behind the curls of wispy white hair on Mrs Parkinson's neck.

The female soldier placed her hand on her shoulder. Julie had known the woman was there, but it still made made her jump.

'Ma'am you must return to your house.'

Julie turned to face her. 'Lily is laying on the floor, I think she's had a fall,' she implored.

'Ma'am will you please just return to your house. We'll see to your neighbour.'

'But...'

'You need to go back inside.'

Hazel reappeared from around the side of the house. 'What's going on?' she asked.

'Ma'am!' the female soldier bellowed. 'I'm going to tell you one last time, you and your friend get back in the house *now*!'.

Julie stood up. 'For God's sake!' she screamed. 'Mrs Parkinson's dead!' She walked briskly over to

Hazel, her face etched with a mixture of anger and sadness.

Hazel looked shocked. 'What did you say?'

'I said Mrs Parkinson's dead. Or at least I think she is. I saw her through the letterbox. She's laying on the floor at the bottom of the stairs in a pool of blood.'

The soldier went over to the door and peered through the letterbox. She looked back at Julie. 'You might be right.' She looked slightly flustered. 'I'll radio through to someone.'

'Radio someone?' Hazel said incredulously. 'Why can't *you* deal with it? You're the army.'

'This has nothing to do with you,' the woman said, stepping away from the door. 'It will be dealt with by the relevant authorities. Now get back inside or I'll have you arrested for obstruction.'

Hazel was incensed. 'So you can lord it around threatening innocent people – oh yes, that's absolutely fine – but when there's a real emergency you don't want to know!'

'Right!' the woman snapped. 'I don't want to hear another word out of you. Get back inside immediately.'

'Please, Hazel. It's not worth getting into trouble over,' Julie said.

Hazel scowled at the soldier. 'And you'll get someone to come and deal with Mrs Parkinson?'

'I will.' She was already walking away.

Hazel cast the woman a last look of disdain and then linked her arm through Julie's. 'Come on then.'

When they got inside they made their way through to the living room.

Julie's face was completely drained of colour. 'I don't feel very well,' she said.

'You sit here,' Hazel said, helping her onto the sofa. 'You've had a nasty shock. I'll make you a nice hot cup of tea. Where do you keep the teabags?

'Cupboard on the left-hand side of the sink, top shelf.' She gently rested her head down on a cushion. 'Can you make me a chamomile? I really feel quite dizzy.'

Hazel made the tea, then came and perched herself on the edge of the sofa. 'Drink this, it'll help to settle you.'

Julie sat up and took a sip. 'That's lovely. Thanks.'

Making sure her friend was with it enough not to spill the tea, Hazel got up and walked to the window. Pulling aside the net curtain, she looked out. She could still see the truck and the soldiers moving around delivering boxes of food. But much to her annoyance the woman she'd had the argument with was simply standing at the end of the drive just beyond her camper van.

Hazel dropped the net curtain back into place and turned to face Julie. 'I really don't trust that woman. I'm calling an ambulance.' She pulled her mobile phone out of her pocket and tapped in the emergency number. A moment passed and she said, 'It's dead.'

'What is?'

'999.'

Julie frowned. 'It can't be!'

'Well it *is*.' Hazel held out the phone and Julie could hear the faint continuous tone of a dead line.

She looked confused. 'What the heck's going on, Hazel?'

*

Scowling, Isaac gingerly lifted the tin of Spam from his box of supplies and waved it at the camera lens.

'And then there's *this*. Barely fit for human consumption. That Monty Python lot can sing about it all they like, but is this really the sort of cheap and cheerful sustenance that our Government think their people deserve to get them through the next fortnight? Sitting comfortably in their ivory tower they haven't a clue about the real world.'

He dropped the tin back into the box. 'What else have we got here? Ah yes.' He pulled out a tin of butter beans. 'Any of you ever had butter beans?' He paused and cocked an ear theatrically at the camera. 'No? Can't say I blame you. Takes bland to a whole new level. Eating these is like eating cardboard. In fact I'd go as far as to say they do cardboard a disservice. You really have to wonder who actually made the decisions about what we were going to get.'

Dropping the beans back into the box, he glanced down at the rest of the contents. 'Now, there's no question that this is an act of benevolence – they could have just left us locked up for two weeks reliant on whatever we already had in our cupboards. But most of this stuff probably isn't that far removed from the things folks had in their larders during the war. Although, looking at the state of some of it, it's possible that's where the Government got it from! Oh,

90

and as for bathroom visits…' – he bent and picked up the solitary toilet roll and showed it to the camera – '…One, people. Just the one. Take a look at it. We'd all better get used to crossing our legs, or things are going to start getting real messy.'

Grinning, he tossed the roll to one side. It hit the floor, bounced and then rolled across towards the door of his office, unspooling a trail of tissue in its wake.

Keisha was standing in the open doorway, quietly watching Isaac record his blog. She put her foot on the toilet roll to stop it going any further, then bent down, picked it up and rewound it.

Isaac sighed. 'Being serious for a moment, assuming this is pretty much what *everybody* got – and I can't believe we're the only ones to receive such a box of delights – the first thing that strikes me is there's been no consideration whatsoever for dietary needs. I actually *can't* eat half this stuff. And the meagre offerings that I can eat certainly won't stretch to a week.' He leant in close to the camera. His expression was serious. 'Rationing 2025 style. And mark my words: this is just the beginning, people. We'd all better prepare ourselves for a taster of the dystopian experience.'

He sat back in his chair. 'Until next time, this is Isaac Owusu signing off.'

He nodded, then tapped a key on the laptop keyboard. The little light that had been blinking away on the camera ceased.

'Well, baby?' He turned in his chair to face Keisha. 'What's the verdict then?'

'Overall pretty good.'

91

'Overall?'

'Yeah.' She squinted at him. 'I particularly liked the joke about the manky carrot.'

Isaac grinned. 'Yeah?'

'*No*, of course not! I thought it was disgusting.'

Isaac bellowed with laughter. 'I suppose it was a bit facetious.' He stretched in the chair and yawned. 'Don't worry, baby. I'll edit it out before I send it to Rory.'

'You do that. There's humour and then there's filth.' She sighed. 'Fancy a coffee?'

'You having one?'

'I think I will, yeah.'

'Yes please then.'

Without even looking, as she turned away, Keisha nonchalantly tossed the toilet roll back into the room. It hit the edge of the box and dropped neatly in amongst the other goods.

CHAPTER 8

'Considering how pale you looked earlier, you've certainly got a bit more colour in your cheeks now,' Hazel said.

Julie smiled as she took another sip from the warming cup of chamomile tea Hazel had made for her. 'I feel so much better now. Thank you.'

They were standing in the bay window of the living room, peering through the net curtains at the flurry of activity next door.

Ten minutes earlier a black transit van had arrived and reversed onto Mrs Parkinson's driveway. From where they were standing, Julie and Hazel could only just see the back end poking out from behind the camper van, but they had a pretty good idea what was happening.

Two burly men had appeared and with some effort had forced the door to gain entrance to Mrs Parkinson's house. They were dressed in hazmat suits, which was slightly alarming to see. A minute or two passed and then one of them had reappeared and opened up the back doors of the van. He had proceeded to pull out a wheeled stretcher and gone back into the house. A couple more minutes had passed and then the two men had re-emerged, carefully manoeuvring the stretcher – now bearing Mrs Parkinson's shrouded body – through the door.

Pip was jumping around their legs, yapping frantically, clearly extremely agitated.

'Oh look,' Julie said sorrowfully. 'Poor little Pip. She doesn't understand what's happening.'

Hazel raised her eyebrows. '*That's* Pip? How does a little sausage dog like that manage to make such a racket?'

The men deftly loaded the stretcher into the back of the van and closed up the doors. Leaving Pip scampering in frustrated circles behind the van, they walked out to the road where they stopped and spoke to the female soldier. She gestured towards Mrs Parkinson's house and then to Julie's.

'I wish I could hear what they were saying,' Hazel said.

'That makes two of us.'

The conversation was short and as the two men returned to the van the soldier made her way towards Julie's house. Spotting her standing in the window with Hazel, she mouthed something and pointed towards the front door.

'Oh, lord,' Julie said, setting down her cup. 'She wants to speak to us.'

They walked out into the hall and as Julie opened the front door the soldier stopped short and held up a hand. 'No need to come out. I just have to ask you a couple of questions.' She unclipped the popper on her breast pocket and pulled out a notepad and pen.

As the transit van started up and pulled off the drive, Pip spotted Julie, leapt over the wall and came bounding over. Julie squatted down to greet her and the little dog skidded to a halt, put her paws up on her chest and began licking her face enthusiastically.

'You're Julie Morrison, correct?' the soldier asked.

'That's correct,' Julie replied, tickling Pip's head to try to calm her down. She stood up and the dog scooted straight past her, between Hazel's legs and disappeared inside the house.

'And when did you last see your neighbour?'

Hazel frowned. 'Aren't these questions for the police? Five minutes ago you didn't want to know, you said dead bodies had nothing to do with you.'

The soldier ignored her. 'Last time you saw her, please' she repeated, looking at Julie.

'A couple of days ago I guess. I'm not absolutely sure. Lily, er... Mrs Parkinson I mean, she kept herself to herself.'

The soldier made a note. 'And what about next of kin?'

'What's going on with the 999 number?' Hazel asked. 'We tried calling and the line was dead.'

The soldier continued to ignore her. She was looking directly at Julie, waiting for an answer.

'Her husband died a few years ago,' Julie said. 'She has a daughter, but she lives in Australia. Oh... what's her name?' She scratched her head and thought hard. 'I *think* it's Linda. I don't know her surname though, I'm pretty sure she got married.'

'We'll find her,' the soldier muttered, making another note.

'It's a close-knit community round here,' Julie said. 'People are going to want to know what happened.'

'The body will be dealt with and the daughter will be duly contacted.'

'What exactly *did* happen?' Julie pressed.

'That's classified information,' the soldier replied.

'*Seriously*?!' Hazel scoffed.

At that moment Pip reappeared and sat down at Julie's feet. Baring her teeth, she growled at the soldier, who glanced down at her. 'The dog can go to the pound.'

'She most certainly can *not*!' Julie exclaimed. 'I'll take her.' She bent down and scooped up Pip into her arms, holding her protectively close.

Hazel was frowning. 'You said just now you'll deal with everything. Can you give us your assurance Mrs Parkinson's daughter will be informed?'

Looking suitably needled, the woman finally looked at Hazel, acknowledging her presence. 'And who exactly are *you*?'

Hazel was about to reply, but Julie intervened. 'She's my friend. She arrived just before they announced the lockdown rules, so she's staying here with me.'

The woman studied Julie's face, as if looking for any hint that she was being lied to. Then she nodded. 'Okay. Just make sure you follow the rules and stay indoors.'

'But...' Julie started.

'I think we're done here,' the woman said curtly. Tucking the notebook and pen back into her breast pocket, she turned her back on them and walked briskly away.

'Well!' Julie exclaimed indignantly. 'What a rude woman.'

Closing the door, they went through to the kitchen where Julie put Pip down on the floor and filled the kettle.

Hazel sat down at the table.

'I'm really not happy about this,' Julie said as she put the kettle on the hob and ignited the gas. 'I don't trust that woman as far as I could throw her. I know she was probably just following orders, but I have a horrible feeling she'll make no effort whatsoever to contact Linda.'

Pip was wandering around the room sniffing at the floor.

'I'm inclined to agree,' Hazel replied, taking a swig of water from her bottle. 'She was unnecessarily rude too.'

'A little politeness goes a long way,' Julie agreed. 'I feel I ought to try to contact Linda myself.'

'No chance you have a phone number for her I suppose?' Hazel asked, screwing the top back on her bottle.

Julie nodded. 'Actually I have. We weren't close, but Mrs P gave me some contact details a while ago, just in case of an emergency.'

'I'd say this ranks as an emergency,' Hazel said.

'The trouble is, I couldn't tell you for the life of me where I put it. Stupid.' Julie sighed.

Hazel pulled her phone from her pocket. 'We can try looking her up on Facebook. Just about everyone's on there these days.'

'Thing is,' Julie said, 'she wouldn't be Linda Parkinson any more. Like I said to that soldier, she married an Australian guy, er... Gavin? Graham? Something like that. I can't remember.'

Hazel tapped an app icon on her phone and the Facebook site opened. 'A lot of women put their maiden names on here too. Mainly so old acquaintances and schoolfriends can find them I suppose. God knows why, if I *ever* see any of the people I went to school with again it'll be a lifetime too soon. There can't be that many Linda Parkinsons on here and if she has a profile picture I assume you'll recognise her?'

Julie looked a bit awkward and shook her head.

Hazel rolled her eyes. 'Okay, well it's worth a shot.' She tapped the name into a search field at the top of the page and her face fell. 'There's masses of them!'

Julie finished making her cup of tea and sat down. 'I guess Linda Parkinson is a pretty common name after all.'

Hazel smiled. 'Shame it's not Ophelia or Seraphima or something there's only likely to be one of.' She put a consoling hand on Julie's arm. 'Never mind. It was worth a look.'

Pip finished her fervent investigation of her new surroundings and came over and sat down at Julie's feet, looking up at her hopefully.

'Then there's nothing we can do,' Julie said forlornly.

'Not unless you can remember where you put that number, no.' Hazel glanced down at Pip. 'Do you think she's hungry?'

'Oh!' Julie looked embarrassed. 'How awful of me, I hadn't even thought about that. Poor little thing.' She bent and patted Pip's head. 'Come on, let's see what I've got in the fridge, shall we? There just might be some leftover chicken. Do you like chicken?'

Pip wagged her tail excitedly.

CHAPTER 9

Sarah mostly preferred it when her husband had been drinking. Paul could be a violent drunk and she had suffered the consequences of that first hand – and on more occasions than she cared to remember. The thing was, regardless of whether he was drunk or sober, there was always the risk of altercation. A misspoken word, an expression on her face that he deemed derogatory, something entirely beyond her control that had upset him; the simplest little thing could trigger his wrath and Sarah always got the brunt of it. Yet he was generally happier when he was inebriated and largely – but not always – tended to leave her alone. Provided, of course, she was smart, let him do his thing, kept her head down and didn't do anything to precipitate conflict.

It was under these circumstances that their first morning under the Government's current lockdown rules had passed relatively without incident. Well, almost. The remark she'd made about his tracksuit bottoms when they got up had earned her a smack round her face. But it was minor and she was pretty much used to that happening anyway.

Bleary-eyed, Paul was slumped in his favourite armchair playing a video game on his PlayStation, and although it wasn't quite 11:30 in the morning he was already several sheets to the wind. As was customary these days, he had hardly bothered to get dressed properly. He was wearing grubby underpants and socks rucked around his ankles. One of them had a hole in it. He also had on a faded T-shirt bearing the words

I'VE GOT A DIG BICK
(YOU THAT READ WRONG)
(YOU READ THAT WRONG TOO)

Paul thought the shirt was hilarious. The day he'd arrived home wearing it – yes, he was drunk again – Sarah had managed to conjure up the requisite smile to ensure she dodged an argument and, potentially, a beating. The only thing that marginally amused her about it was the irony in the claim, and that was completely lost on Paul; the fact was he took being poorly endowed to a whole new level. Regardless, she didn't like the shirt and every time it went in the wash she gave it an extra rinse in the hope of accelerating the fading process so she'd have an excuse to consign it to the dustbin sooner rather than later.

Paul's current video game of choice was a first-person shooter, essentially pitting him against hordes of rampaging slaughtering zombies in a plague-ravaged wasteland. And he spent hours playing it every day.

He angrily pumped his thumb on the joystick "fire" button and let out a slurred snarl. 'Come onnn, come onnnnn…' On the TV screen a zombie's head exploded in a shower of bright red digital gloop. 'Yes!' he shouted jubilantly. 'Gotcha, you maggoty fuck!' He lurched forward, almost jumping out of his chair with excitement. As he flopped back, he knocked the glass ashtray off the arm of the chair. A cloud of ash and roll-up remnants flew into the air and settled among the half a dozen empty beer cans that littered the floor beside his chair. He glanced down at the mess – 'Shit!'

he muttered, without much evidence of real concern – then returned his attention to the game as the words END OF LEVEL 4 appeared on the screen. He grinned, feeling decidedly pleased with himself; a good day's work.

Reaching across to the table beside the chair, he picked up his can of beer. He pressed it to his lips and threw back his head to finish it off, but it was already empty. He frowned and made a tutting noise. He shook it in the air a couple of times, as if doing so would magically refill it, and put one eye to the hole on the top and tried to peer inside. 'Oi, Sar!' he shouted. 'Make yourself useful. There's a loada crap all over the floor in here that needs cleanin' up. And while you're at it bring me another beer.'

Sarah was sitting at the kitchen table sewing up a tear in Paul's tracksuit bottoms. Much like the T-shirt she loathed, they were reaching the end of their sustainable usefulness and would soon be relocated to the bin. Although, when she'd been foolish enough to lightheartedly remark upon it… well, for the time being here she was repairing them again.

She picked up a glass of orange juice from the table and took a sip, immediately wincing as the split on her top lip screamed in protest at the sudden dousing in citric acid. She dabbed at it with her finger. Yes, in future she'd think twice before making an innocent quip about the state of Paul's attire again.

At the sound of him calling, she got wearily to her feet and went to the fridge. As her eyes scanned the shelves her stomach turned. 'Oh, God…'

'Come on,' Paul shouted, his voice slurred and impatient. 'Make it fuckin' snappy.'

Sarah closed the fridge door. What was she going to tell him? Nervously biting her bottom lip, she crossed the kitchen and stopped in the doorway to the living room. 'I'm sorry, baby' she said, almost in a whisper. 'We haven't got any left.'

Paul had just activated the next level of his game. He didn't look at her, but he hit the pause button on the joystick.

Sarah stood in the doorway, her mind racing. Why wasn't he saying anything? I know, she thought, maybe he didn't hear what I said and he's waiting for me to repeat it.

She spoke a little louder. 'I said we haven't...'

'I heard you.' The slur in his voice was suddenly gone. 'You think I'm deaf?'

'No, of course not.'

Still he didn't look at her; he was staring fixedly at the frozen image of a choice of Level 5 weapons on the screen. He rested the controller on the arm of the chair. 'So what you gonna do about it?'

'What am I going to do about it?' she stuttered.

Finally Paul turned his head. He spoke slowly and quietly. 'You a fuckin' parrot now? I asked for a beer. Are you gonna get me one or not?'

Sarah didn't know what to say. 'I don't... We... I mean there's none left. I can't.'

'You *can't?*' To the casual observer Paul's voice might have sounded the epitome of calm, but Sarah knew her husband well enough to detect the tiny note of rage that was simmering beneath the surface.

'No, I can't.' Realising her choice of words sounded like a refusal as opposed to a reasonable response to the fact they had no beer for her to fetch, she forced a smile. 'It's silly, I can't get you what we don't have.'

He moved in the chair, turning to face her properly. 'What did you just say? Are you backchattin'?'

Sarah stared at him, struggling to think of a response that wouldn't exacerbate the situation. 'I... I don't know what to do.'

'You're gonna go out and get some, that's what you're gonna do.'

'I can't. I...'

Paul raised a finger to silence her. The dark eyes penetrated her. 'Now, y'see, there's that word again. I don't think you're listenin' to me.' The anger was beginning to seep through now. 'I'm fuckin' thirsty, okay? So you're gonna put your coat on and you're gonna go out and buy me some beer.'

Sarah's heart was banging twenty to the dozen. 'But we're not allowed to leave the flat. Even if we could there aren't any shops open.'

Paul laughed. But it wasn't a real laugh. There was no humour in it. Sarah was all too familiar with the theatricality of that laugh and it usually led to her nursing another bruise. 'You *really* aren't listenin' are you? I'm not askin' you, you stupid fuckin' bitch. I'm *tellin'* you.' The anger was unleashed now. 'The offy's open 24-7, and don't you pretend for one second you don't know it. So don't give me no more fuckin' excuses and take your bony arse down there and get me a beer right fuckin' now.'

103

Sarah was dumbfounded. Her eyes started to well up. There was a beating coming and she knew it. All sorts of things were spinning tumultuously through her mind, but the most appealing idea right now was to simply agree to do as he asked, put her coat on, go out and never come back. Suddenly a thought occurred to her. 'Wait! There might be some sherry left over from last Christmas.'

Paul squinted at her, considering her words. It was probably only for a few moments, but to Sarah it felt like an eternity. Her heart was pounding out of her chest. Then his anger seemed to subside. 'Well don't just stand there snivellin' like a little girl who just pissed her knickers. Go and fuckin' get it.'

Thank God, Sarah thought through a wave of overwhelming euphoria. Why hadn't she thought of that straight away? But the moment of exhilaration was fleeting as it transpired that a few glasses of sherry would only provide her with a stay of execution, for as she turned to go back out to the kitchen, Paul added, 'And *then* you can go out and get the beers.'

Her face etched with fear at the prospect of how this was going to pan out – it wasn't going to be a happy resolve, that was for sure – she hurried over to the cupboard above the sink and wrenched open the door. Right at the back, behind several assorted bottles of fizzy drinks, she spotted the sherry. She had to stand on tiptoe to reach it, but she smiled with relief as her fingers closed round the neck of the bottle. She pulled it out and her face immediately fell.

What remained, swilling around in the bottom of the bottle was barely enough to fill a single glass.

Unscrewing the top, Sarah went to the shelf and grabbed a tumbler. She drained the contents of the bottle into it and her fears were confirmed; there was precious more than a couple of centimetres of alcohol in the glass.

'What the fuck you doin' out there?' The angry tone had returned. 'If I have to come out there to get it…'

'It's okay, baby,' Sarah called, trying her hardest to sound buoyant. 'I found it. I'm just getting a glass.'

She heard the sound of shooting start on the television as Paul resumed his game, and she felt a surge of panic. What the hell was she going to do? She stared at the tumbler as if she were willing the alcohol to miraculously grow in quantity.

Then she had an idea.

She turned to the sink, spun the tap and topped up the glass to the brim. Then she held it up to the light. The content looked as weak as it obviously was.

But he's already drunk, Sarah thought, maybe he just won't notice.

It was a thin hope and she knew it, but it was all she had. Fixing a smile on her face, she went back through to the living room.

'Sorry, baby, we didn't have a clean glass, I just had to wash one out.' She held out the tumbler.

Paul put down the controller and snatched it from her. Without even examining the contents, he downed it in three large gulps. He scowled and spluttered. 'That was absolutely fuckin' vile.' Then with sudden ferocity he hurled the glass across the room. It hit the skirting board and smashed. 'Clean that up and then you can go get my fuckin' beer.' Picking up the controller, he returned his attention to the game.

'Sorry.' Sarah went out to the kitchen and collected the dustpan and brush. She came back into the living room, knelt down and began to sweep up the pieces of shattered glass.

Paul cleared his throat and glanced over at her, his eyes filled with contempt. 'Christ, you really have got a *nasty*, bony fuckin' arse.' He coughed. 'I dunno what the fuck I ever saw in you.' He coughed again.

Standing up, Sarah returned to the kitchen. As she did so, Paul tried to clear his throat, but something caught and the cough became persistent.

'Serves you right,' Sarah muttered under her breath. 'I hope you choke.' She went over to the pedal bin and emptied the contents of the dustpan. As she put it away in the cupboard under the sink, she could hear Paul coughing away in the living room. She frowned and went back to the doorway. Her eyes widened.

Paul was on his knees in front of the armchair, clutching at his chest. He was hacking violently and from where she stood, Sarah could see traces of blood on his mouth.

He looked up and reached out his arm to her for help.

Sarah remained in the doorway, rooted to the spot. Her mind was in turmoil, a dozen thoughts cascading through her head, all colliding and jostling for attention. An ambulance! Why in God's name was she standing here trying to figure out what was going on? She *had* to call for an ambulance. She hastened to her chair where her mobile phone was sitting on the arm, but as she picked it up the feelings of panic and horror suddenly and inexplicably dissolved away to nothing and an all-consuming sense of calm and satisfaction washed over her. Her husband was choking in front of her but she realised she didn't actually care.

Still reaching out, his eyes pleading and filled with terror, Paul tried to speak, but all that came out was a gurgle and a little spray of blood.

Now unperturbed by the drama playing out in front of her, Sarah walked casually over to his armchair and bent down. 'Look at all the mess you made,' she said quietly, gathering up the half dozen empty, ash-covered beer cans from beside the chair. She turned her head and her eyes met Paul's. She stared at him admonishingly for a moment and tutted. 'It's really not good enough, baby' she said, turning her head away again.

As Sarah picked up the last can, Paul keeled face-first onto the carpet. Without a trace of concern, she went out to the kitchen and dropped the cans in the bin. When she returned, he was laying on his back on the floor, convulsing violently, his head thrashing from side to side in a pool of thick vomit.

She bent again and carefully retrieved all the chewed ends of his roll-ups from the floor and emptied them into the ashtray. She frowned at the ash on the carpet and tutted again. 'I'm going to have to hoover that later.' Then she went back out to the kitchen, leaving Paul curled up in the fetal position, with vomit leaking from the corner of his mouth.

As the sound of her husband choking intensified, she emptied the contents of the ashtray into the bin, switched on the radio on the worktop and pumped the volume up high. Then she sat down at the table and, taking another sip of her orange juice – this time reveling in the sharp tingle as it assailed her split lip – she resumed sewing up the split in Paul's tracksuit bottoms.

When she'd finished the repair, she got up, turned the volume low on the radio and cocked an ear. There was no sound coming from the living room. She walked back to the door and stood for a moment looking down at Paul's body.

He was laid on the floor, dead.

No, wait, not *quite* dead. He was still twitching ever so slightly.

'I fixed your trackies,' Sarah said, holding the disheveled garment aloft. As she watched, a dark patch appeared on the front of his underpants and spread out, and then a trickle of urine ran down the side of his leg and soaked into the carpet.

Sarah gave the T-shirt she despised one final look of disdain – 'Dig Bick,' she mouthed silently – and looked at the tracksuit bottoms in her hand. Paul certainly wouldn't be needing those again. Bundling them up, she went back out to the kitchen, opened the pedal bin and forced them brusquely in among the beer cans and dog-ends.

Hastening to the coat stand just inside the front door, she took down her coat from the hook, then rummaged around in Paul's jacket pockets. Her heart was racing as her fingers found the car keys.

She quickly went through to the bedroom and opened the wardrobe door. Moving aside some boxes of books, she pulled out the small suitcase that she'd packed two years earlier – or was it three? She couldn't even remember now – in readiness for the day she knew would inevitably come when she'd leave Paul for good. How many times had she almost done that since?

Returning to the front door, she took a breath, curled her fingers around the handle, opened it... and stopped. She faltered and let out a huge sigh. No, she thought, I can't just leave him here like that.

Slowly closing the front door, she removed her coat, returned her case to the wardrobe, then sat down and dialed 999.

Even in death Paul had a cruel hold on her.

CHAPTER 10

'Can you believe it?' Julie grumbled, peering out through the darkness. 'Those flippin' teenagers are in the park again.'

She was standing at the rear of the living room engaged in a spot of curtain-twitching, unquestionably one of her most favourite pastimes. On this occasion she was observing the activity in the small recreation ground that backed the properties at her end of the Crescent. It wasn't particularly large; a stretch of grass, a couple of benches and a few randomly placed bits and pieces of play equipment – a set of swings, a small climbing frame, a roundabout and a slide. During the day it was often frequented by Mums and their toddlers, but the evenings were a different matter.

Hazel, dressed in her pyjamas, was sitting in the armchair, her legs curled up beneath her. As soon as darkness had fallen, she'd slipped out to the van to retrieve her tablet, and she was watching the latest episode of "Owusu's Eye". She looked up at Julie. 'What are they doing?'

Julie had her back to her. 'Not a lot really. I can't see very much. Sitting on the benches smoking. Chasing each other round, shouting. One of the girls was hanging upside-down off the climbing frame just now. A couple of them are necking… actually, I think it's two lads.' She made a noise of disapprobation.

Hazel smiled. 'Sounds to me like you can see quite a lot actually.'

Julie shot her an indignant glance over her shoulder. 'Well, it's dark. But I'm sure they're up to no good.'

'Why?'

'They always are.' Julie sighed. 'I don't know where the older ones come from to be honest. They certainly don't live round here. But they seem to gravitate to the playground most nights. Everyone this end of the Crescent has petitioned the council to have the play equipment and benches removed, but they say it's the only recreation area in the neighbourhood, which to be fair is true, and that removing it would deprive local parents of somewhere to take their children. The decision-makers wouldn't be so happy if the older kids congregated on *their* doorstep.'

'So what *are* they doing that's so awful?'

'Well...' Julie turned back to the window. 'Nothing I suppose. There's at least a dozen of them though.'

'They're just kids being kids. It's the same all over. When I was young my Mum and Dad wanted to know where I was day and night. I certainly wouldn't have been out hanging around on the streets like they do today. A lot of the parents nowadays don't give a toss. But if they're not actually causing any trouble, what does it matter?'

Julie dropped the curtain and turned to face her friend. She had a look of dismay on her face. 'Hazel, everyone's supposed to be confined to their homes. Or had you forgotten that?'

Hazel shook her head. 'Of course I haven't. But come on, Jules, this whole lockdown rule is a joke. It's bad enough they're dictating what we can eat, but trying to cage us up like animals...'

111

'But how can we hope to stop the virus spreading if people don't do what they're told? The Government…'

'The *Government* don't give two hoots about the likes of you and me. They're not trying to stop a virus – if there even is one – they're none too subtly trying to implement totalitarian rule.' She smiled. 'And the people aren't having it.'

Julie frowned. 'How can you say that?'

'If you want to know what's really going on, you should have a listen to this guy, Isaac Owusu.' She held up her tablet.

'I've never heard of him.'

'He's a vlogger, he has his own channel on NuTube,' Hazel said. 'He's been doing it for years. He covers all sorts of stuff, but it's mostly political. I don't always agree with what he has to say, but more often than not he hits the nail on the head. He's pretty switched on to what's happening at the moment, that's for sure.' She grinned. 'The Government must absolutely hate him.'

'If you ask me, if people listened to what the Government had to say and paid less attention to the armchair warriors, we'd all be a lot better off,' Julie scoffed. 'The Government knows what's best.'

'You think so?' Hazel retorted. 'You've just seen first hand what people think of their solution to eradicating the virus.' She gestured to the curtains. 'Locking people up just isn't going to work.'

'That's just a few unruly kids. That doesn't mean to say it's not working as a whole.'

'No?'; Hazel said, raising her tablet. 'I was on Facebook earlier and it looks as if there are a heck of a lot of people pretty much carrying on as normal. They might be able to close up all the shops and workplaces, but they're going to have a much harder time preventing people meeting up with their friends and families.' She tapped an icon on her tablet and opened up her Facebook page. She held it out so Julie could see. 'There are loads like this.'

Julie came over and squinted at the picture on the screen. It showed a group of teenagers laughing and holding aloft beer cans. 'Maybe they're old photos,' she said.

'I assure you they aren't. People have been through all this before with coronavirus and they're not prepared to do it again. I tell you, lovey, no-one's paying any heed.'

Julie harrumphed. 'What on Earth's the matter with everyone? It's not enough they're breaking the rules then, they're so flippin' blasé about it they're actually bragging about it on social media. It's utterly irresponsible!' There were tears in her eyes as she slumped down on the sofa.

Pip puttered out of the kitchen and, almost as if she knew Julie was upset, rubbed her head affectionately against her leg. If nothing else, her appearance diffused the tension that was building in the room.

Hazel put down her tablet, got up and went over to sit next to Julie on the sofa. She put her arms around her. 'It'll be fine, Jules. Honestly it will. A couple of weeks and there will be some other big news story and this whole ridiculous ORACULTE thing will be forgotten.'

Julie sniffed and leant her head on her friend's shoulder. 'Do you really think so?'

'I *know* so.'

If Julie had been able to see Hazel's face, she'd have seen from her expression that she knew no such thing.

*

'You coming in, baby? The midnight movie starts in five minutes,' Keisha called out from the lounge.

Isaac rubbed his eyes and yawned. He glanced at his watch: 11:53.

He loved his work, but that often proved to be a problem. He could lose hours absorbed in prepping a new blog for upload and by the time he was finished he'd be fit for nothing. At least with Keisha around for the next couple of weeks there would be impetus to stop before fatigue took a hold of him.

'Yeah, almost done,' he shouted back from the office, where he had in fact been about to call it a night anyway. He clicked the save option on the video file he'd been finessing. As he did so, his mobile phone rang. He picked it up and looked at the words on the screen: **No Caller ID**. He hesitated. His golden rule, seldom broken, was not to answer unknown numbers, and especially not this late at night. Just as curiosity got the better of him and he was about to bend his own rule, the ringing stopped.

He set the phone back down on the desk, plugged the charger into it and closed the lid on his laptop. Stretching, he stood up, and was about to flick off the light and go out to join Keisha when the phone rang again. He picked it up. **No Caller ID** taunted him on the screen.

He clicked the green accept option. 'Hello?'

The voice on the other end was muffled. It said something undecipherable.

'Sorry, mate, I can hardly hear you,' Isaac said, already wishing he hadn't answered. 'The signal here is crap. Can you repeat that?'

The young man in a white laboratory coat was standing with his back to the window. The only light in the room emanated from a small desk lamp, and it cast a dim glow across his unshaven face. He glanced warily towards the office door. The telephone receiver in his hand was attached to its base unit on the desk by a cord that was stretched to its maximum, positioning him as far away from the door as possible.

He scratched nervously at the stubble on his chin and spoke into the phone again, barely more than a whisper. 'I'm sorry, I can't talk any louder. I said my name is Damian.'

Damian Gardner was taking a huge risk. He'd been sweating on it all day and now the moment had come his stomach was so knotted that he felt as if he was going to throw up. Worse yet, his asthma was as bad as it had been in years. He took a puff on his inhaler and stuffed it back in his coat pocket.

Although it had struck him as an unorthodox prerequisite, Damian had willingly signed the nondisclosure paperwork presented to him when he had been offered the position at S&P Research. After all, maybe it wasn't so unusual. What did he know? He was 22 years-old, fresh out of university and he needed the employment. And the money. And if he hadn't signed they would simply have offered the job to someone else.

He'd worked hard as a junior laboratory technician, put in all the hours asked of him and more besides. He had only been there a couple of months before David Walsh, pre-eminent Professor and the man responsible for overseeing all the work carried out at S&P, revealed that he'd had a keen eye on Damian, was delighted with what he'd seen and there was no question in his mind that the young man was promotion material.

That was seven weeks ago now and despite having signed the non-disclosure order, Damian could no longer keep to himself what he had seen. Mobile phones weren't permitted in the building, so he'd had no option but to make his call using an outside line from one of the upstairs offices.

'I work for a privately funded virology research institute in Cambridge,' he said into the phone, as loudly as he dared.

'Okay, I can hear you a bit clearer now,' Isaac replied cautiously. 'How did you get my number?'

Damian pulled out his inhaler and took another quick puff. 'Never mind that. I haven't got long and I have some information you should hear.'

Isaac frowned. 'Okay, go on…' He put the light back on and sat down.

'ORACULTE isn't what people have been led to believe. It's man-made. It's been purposely engineered.' The line fell silent. 'Hello? Are you still there?'

Isaac grabbed up a sheet of paper and a pen. 'Yeah, I'm still here, mate. I'm just trying to process what you've just said.'

Damian continued. 'They've invested millions into the development of a unique pathogen that targets the unhealthy, those that they consider to be the dregs of society. If you're in good health you'll probably be okay, the symptoms would range from a bit of a cold to none at all. But if you've got a pre-existing health condition and you contract ORACULTE... well, you're as good as dead. I was led to believe that we're developing a vaccine for them, but we're not. They're orchestrating genocide.'

'You keep saying *they*,' Isaac interjected.

'The Government, of course. Stirling and his mob.'

Isaac's eyes widened. 'I knew it,' he exclaimed. 'I knew there was something screwy about this whole damned thing. It all happened so fast. But purposely manufactured? Man, this is *huge*! I assume you have proof to back up what you're saying?'

Keisha appeared in the doorway and raised her eyebrows. 'Film,' she whispered.

He held up a finger and mouthed at her: 'Two minutes.'

Keisha rolled her eyes and disappeared back into the lounge.

'It's already on its way to you,' Gardner was saying. 'Look out for a small padded envelope. There's a USB flash drive in there that looks like a packet of chewing gum.'

117

'A USB?' Isaac said. 'Containing what?'

'A shitload of emails. Trust me, you're gonna want to read them.'

'Emails?'

'From Downing Street. Downloaded from my employer's computer. You'll see. But listen, I can't talk any more tonight. I'm taking a huge risk ringing you as it is, but I had to let you know what's going on and that I've sent you the documents.'

'Okay,' Isaac said. He was still unsure whether this was some kind of a wind-up, or even a disgruntled employee kicking off. 'One thing though. Why me?'

'I've been watching your vlogs for a while now,' Damian said. 'You tell it how it is and people listen. I trust you.'

'Yeah, that's all very well, man,' Isaac said. 'But these emails you're talking about had better contain some pretty hard evidence before I can broadcast any of it. What did you say your name was?'

'Damian. Damian Gardner. Don't worry, you'll get your proof. Security round here is mega-tight, but I'll try to call you again tomorrow to make sure you've got it.'

Isaac scribbled down the name. 'Okay, Damian. I…'

There was a click and the line went dead.

Damian switched off the desk lamp, but the instant he did so the room was flooded with light. He spun round to see David Walsh standing in the open

118

doorway with his hand on the light switch. His stomach churned. 'Oh! You startled me, Professor.'

'Working late tonight, Damian?' Walsh said amiably.

'I'll be away shortly. Just wanted to call my Mum. Promised her I'd let her know when I'm on my way. I...'

'Your mother?' Two simple words, but they were laced with venom. Walsh's steely eyes studied Damian from behind the rimless lenses.

'Yes, I er...' Suddenly the lie seemed futile. 'How long have you been standing there, Professor?'

'Long enough.'

They stared at each other in silence for a moment.

'Yes, well, I suppose I'd better go finish up and get myself off home,' Damian said, the slight tremor in his voice all too obvious. He withdrew his inhaler from his pocket and tried to take a puff on it, but it was empty.

Walsh spoke quietly. 'Are you alright, Damian? You don't look at all well.' The words might have suggested a modicum of concern, but the tone was bluntly devoid of any.

'I'm... I'm fine, thank you. Just... just a little short of breath,' Damian stammered.

'Are you quite sure? You look hot. And you're sweating.' Walsh's eyes narrowed. 'Would you like me to get you a glass of water?'

'No, really, I'm absolutely fine.'

Damian started to walk towards the door, but Walsh took a swift step to one side and blocked his exit.

'I insist.' Walsh's face darkened and two security guards appeared in the doorway behind him.

119

CHAPTER 11

Julie was just finishing off a slice of toast when Hazel, looking sleepy-eyed, came into the kitchen.

Julie washed down the last morsel of crust with a mouthful of tea and stood up. 'I got on and had my breakfast. I hope you don't mind. I did look in on you, but you were soundo and I didn't like to wake you.'

Hazel yawned and shook her head. 'No, it's fine. I slept like a log.'

Julie stood up. 'Tea?'

'Please.'

'Toast?'

'No thanks. I'll have some cereal if you have any though.'

Julie nodded. 'Take a pew.' She opened the cupboard and took out a box of Bran Flakes. 'This is all I've got, I'm afraid. I don't eat cereal much, I only eat these when... well, you know.' She glanced at the best before stamp. 'They're still in date.'

'Thanks,' Hazel said, planting herself on a chair at the table. 'I had a really lovely dream last night.'

'Lucky you!' Julie laughed. 'I can't remember the last time I had a pleasant dream. Mine are always about horrible things, usually a sort of manifestation of things that have been worrying me and have been playing on my mind. And then I wake up feeling all discombobulated and it takes me ages to settle.'

'Oh, I get dreams like that too,' Hazel said. 'But this one was different.'

'What was it about?'

'Well, you guest-starred in it.'

Julie laughed. 'I hope I'll be getting royalties.'

Hazel thought for a moment. 'It's already a bit hazy. But we were parked up in the camper beside the most beautiful lake. In the dream I knew exactly where I was, but I don't think it's anywhere real, or not somewhere that I've ever been to anyway. The sun was coming up, shimmering through the trees and there was nobody around, so I decided to go for a swim. You wouldn't come with me and went back to the van. I took off all my clothes and as the cool breeze caressed me, the feeling of contentment and freedom and serene oneness with nature was overpowering. I knew that it was exactly where I was meant to be.'

Julie rubbed her arms briskly. 'That's made me go all goose-bumpy.'

'It was pretty idyllic. Anyway, the water was icy cold, but crystal clear, and as I was swimming I could see all these vast shoals of brightly coloured fish on the lakebed underneath me. It's weird, they were like those ones you see in tropical aquarium – Neon Tetras and Rainbowfish and Zebra Danios, you know, all those types you see in those illuminated pet shop tanks swimming around miniature castles and pieces of plastic coral. Anyway, they were darting about all around me, and when I reached out and touched them they didn't seem frightened, they gathered around my hands and seemed to accept me as one of them. You called out to me that it was time to go, but when I looked I couldn't see you or the van. I swam back to the shore and everything was gone – you, the van, my clothes, *everything*. But the weird thing is I wasn't worried about it, not even slightly. I lay down on the grass and even though I knew I should be trying to find you, there was no sense of urgency. So I lay there, basking in the warmth of the sun, feeling it drying me, and listening to the distant chirruping of the birds. Then I woke up and, I tell you, I haven't felt as relaxed and refreshed after a night's sleep for years.'

'Wow,' Julie said, crossing to the fridge. 'I wish I could have a dream like that.' She laughed. 'Except for the bit about taking off all my clothes.'

Hazel smiled. 'I'm not sure I'd ever do that either. But in the dream it felt incredibly liberating.'

Julie passed Hazel a bottle of milk. 'Changing the subject, they said on the radio first thing that the Prime Minister is going to be making a live announcement at 8 o'clock.'

'8 o'clock?' Hazel echoed, pouring the milk on her cereal. 'Do you think he'll actually be able to drag his sorry carcass out of bed that early?'

'It must be something pretty important to be making an announcement so early. I have to say, I fear it's going to be more bad news.' Julie glanced at the clock on the wall: it was just coming up to 7:54. Walking over to the worktop, she switched on the portable television and dipped the volume low. She noticed Hazel was frowning at her. 'Don't want to miss it, do we?'

Hazel rolled her eyes. 'I told you, if you want to hear the unvarnished truth, you should forget about Stirling and his mob of monkeys and listen to what Isaac Owusu has to say.'

'So you said last night. But that's just one man's opinion.'

'Based on fact though. He can see what's happening.'

'Well I'd rather listen to the facts from our elected officials. People may or may not be listening to them, but they're the ones who are looking out for our best interests, not some vogger, or whatever they call themselves.'

Hazel shook her head and smiled. 'Vlogger. And honestly, Jules, he's really worth listening to.' She scooped up a spoonful of cereal. 'Listen, that dream has got me thinking,' she said between mouthfuls. 'It's been really good of you to put me up for a few days. I appreciate it a lot.'

Julie smiled. 'You don't have to thank me. It's nice to have some company.' She bent and retrieved the empty dish from which Pip had eagerly wolfed down a few scraps. The little dachshund was now curled up in the makeshift bed that Julie had prepared for her the previous evening; the cardboard box in which her supplies had arrived, lined with an old coat she'd been meaning to drop off at the charity shop for weeks. 'You're welcome here any time,' Julie added. 'You know that.'

'Yeah, about that,' Hazel said, looking slightly awkward.

Julie's smile faded.

'I've come to a decision.' Hazel was avoiding making eye contact. 'I can't stay here like a caged animal. I just can't. I need to be free, out in the open air, like in the dream.'

123

'I'm not sure I like the sound of where this is going,' Julie said.

'And besides,' Hazel continued, 'that parcel of groceries they gave you was barely enough for one, let alone two.'

'I'm not a big eater anyway, I'm sure there's more than enough for both of us,' Julie said. 'It's not as if I haven't got anything else in the house.'

'You haven't got much,' Hazel argued. 'You said yourself the other night that you'd been intending to go shopping.'

'That was just for a few fresh bits and pieces. Even without the delivery yesterday, it's not like we'd starve. I've more than enough for two.'

'Thanks, but no.' Hazel finished her cereal and put down the spoon.

Julie had known Hazel for years and she was all too aware that if she made up her mind to do something there was nothing anyone could say or do that would sway her. She looked at her friend sorrowfully. 'What are you going to do then?'

'I was thinking I might go and stay with my brother for a bit.'

'Ashley? I didn't know you were still in touch.'

'Ash, yeah. I've not seen him for a while, but he's got a boat just outside of Yorkshire at Ripon Marina.'

'Ripon!' Hazel exclaimed with dismay. 'That's miles away. How are you going to get there?'

Hazel laughed. 'Drive of course.'

Julie frowned. 'Oh, ha ha, very funny. I meant how are you going to avoid getting caught breaching lockdown?'

'I'll take the back roads. It'll take a lot longer, but it should be safer. They should be pretty much deserted anyway.' Hazel stood up and went to the sink to wash out her bowl. 'And once I get there I'll be all but off the grid. Ash has pretty much lived his whole life like that. He won't have much time for draconian lockdowns and dodgy viruses, that's for sure.'

Julie looked a little forlorn. 'I don't know what to say. It sounds like you've made up your mind.'

'Yeah,' Hazel said. 'Sorry.'

Julie forced a smile. 'No need to apologise. I won't pretend I'll not miss you though. It's been lovely having you here the past couple of days.'

'It's been nice,' Hazel said. 'And hey…' – she pointed to Pip, who was sound asleep – '…at least you have a little friend to keep you company now. She's clearly very fond of you.'

'True enough.' Julie sighed and sat down at the table. She looked as if she was going to burst into tears. 'Poor Mrs Parkinson.'

A silence fell in the room. Hazel picked up the drying up cloth and wiped her bowl. As she put it away in the cupboard, she suddenly cried out, 'Hey!' She spun round. 'I've had a great idea. Why don't you come with me?'

'Oh, I don't know about that,' Julie said.

'Come on, why not? There's nothing keeping you here is there? The trip would do you good, out in the fresh air and away from all this madness. And there's more than enough room in the van for two.'

Pip raised her head and barked.

Hazel laughed. 'Alright, three then.'

125

Julie looked pensive. Her attention turned to the TV screen. 'Oh, he's coming on now.' She leant forward and turned up the volume.

Hazel glanced at the screen with disinterest. 'Don't let that distract you. What do you say?'

'Maybe.'

'*Maybe*? Come on. Road trip! It'll be fun!'

'I'll think about it. Now shoosh, I want to hear what he's got to say.'

Cameron Stirling was standing at his now familiar lectern, fronted by the **Keep Hydrated :: Stay Healthy** banner. The expression on his face was grim.

'I must begin this morning by making it clear, beyond a shadow of a doubt, what the country is dealing with right now. ORACULTE is a mutation unlike any virus mankind has ever encountered before. It preys on the respiratory system and, if contracted by anyone with a pre-existing health condition, the likelihood of dying from asphyxiation or cardiac arrest is far greater than the likelihood of survival. The death toll – which has trebled in five days – bears testament to this. If ever there was any doubt in anyone's mind, it is becoming increasingly obvious just how deadly ORACULTE is, and the situation we have fought to avoid is now a reality: our hospitals are filled to untenable capacity. As such the tough decision has been made to suspend admissions, effective immediately. This is the dreadful state of affairs in which England is now mired. You don't need me to tell you how serious this is. And yet I stand here now, immeasurably disheartened by the fact that the directives laid out to you all so clearly in yesterday's address have, at least in part, fallen on deaf ears. Although the majority of you are behaving responsibly, far too many households are continuing to mix, and children have been gathering in large numbers on the streets. We have seen a dramatic increase in incidents of looting, not only in the major cities but in smaller environs too. This will *not*...' – his voice cracked and he raised a clenched fist – '...be tolerated.'

He paused and, lowering his fist slowly, glanced down at his notes. 'As a result of the flouting of lockdown protocols, a more authoritarian stance has regrettably been decided upon and will be implemented immediately. I cannot stress strongly enough that ORACULTE will continue to spread and the numbers will multiply exponentially if people do not remain in their homes and desist from breaking the rules.'

Taking a sip of water, he stared hard into the camera. 'The only way that we will get this epidemic under control is if everyone complies. We *must* bring down infection rates. The consequences of a failure to do so are unthinkable. Lockdown will therefore now be extended for an additional two weeks beyond the end date that was originally mooted. Furthermore, anyone found outside their home without a legitimate reason for being so will receive an on-the-spot fine of £1000. There will be a dramatically increased and armed military presence right across the nation to enforce this. Of course, those of you who follow the rules and remain inside have no reason to be concerned by these measures. Those who don't, however...' He paused to let the unspoken but clear threat sink in. 'Now, although it may seem an unethical approach to the situation, using a sledgehammer to crack a nut so to speak, in order to further discourage those who feel the rules don't apply to them, I am asking anyone with information pertaining to dissension to come forward. Those who assist us in this way will be duly rewarded with a substantial cash sum.'

Suddenly and unexpectedly he smiled. 'Now, while it is regrettable we have been forced to implement these harsh measures, rest assured that the decision to do so has been made for the greater good. Already, just a day after taking people off the streets, there has been evidence of environmental improvement. I looked out of my window when I got up this morning and I can see right across the city. In just 24 hours the smog has all but disappeared. And there is a glimmer of light at the end of the tunnel. Our researchers have been working tirelessly in order to find a solution to this epidemic and although we have yet to find a proven cure, I can confidently repeat my message of yesterday. That being: We know with certainty that those who *do* become infected with ORACULTE stand a better chance of minimising the severity of the symptoms by drinking plenty of water. So keep healthy, stay hydrated and *please* adhere to the rules.'

Isaac scowled. 'As if you're worried about finding a cure, you dirty, lying fucker!' He switched off the television and walked to the window. He could hear a motor running somewhere in the distance, but there wasn't a soul about. And except for a black transit van parked outside the house opposite, the street was devoid of traffic too. Usually at this time of the morning it would be a hive of activity as residents set off for work.

Isaac had seen the van arrive about 15-minutes earlier and had felt a horrible sinking feeling as he observed two men climb out and go into number 14, Mr Cryzinski's house.

Whereas Isaac would never have referred to Aleksy Cryzinski as a friend, he used to exchange morning pleasantries with him often. But Cryzinski had been devastated when he lost his wife of 47 years, Zuzanna, to sepsis five weeks earlier and Isaac hadn't seen hide nor hair of the grief-stricken man since the day of the funeral. That had been three weeks ago.

Having been distracted for a few minutes by Stirling's petulant little strop, now back at the window Isaac watched as the two men emerged from the house wheeling a gurney with a shrouded body on it. He watched with growing sadness as they loaded it into the rear of the van, climbed in and drove away.

He suddenly felt a wave of intense regret that he'd never taken the time to get to know the man who'd lived opposite him for more than two years, and guilt that not once in the past three weeks had it even occurred to him to go and knock on the door to check that he was okay.

'Do not go gentle into that good night,' he whispered under his breath. 'You go give 'em hell, Aleksy.'

He was about to turn away from the window when his eye caught a movement to the right.

A metallic silver Audi with the windows blacked out was coming along the street. It cruised to a halt directly below Isaac's window, and then slowly accelerated away. Isaac watched as it paused briefly at the T-junction before taking a left and disappearing from sight.

The rattle of the postbox gave Isaac a start.

He went out to the hall and saw a small pile of envelopes scattered on the doormat. Gathering them up, he sifted quickly through the assortment of bills and circulars. Second to last in the not inconsiderable heap was a small, yellow padded envelope.

Dropping the rest of the mail on the hall table, he walked through to the lounge and tore open the jiffy bag. Inside was what looked like a packet of Wrigley's Juicy Fruit chewing gum. He took it out and looked at it. Had he not known exactly what it was, he honestly would have believed someone had sent him a packet of gum. He took hold of the end between his thumb and forefinger and pulled hard. It separated along the line of the red rip tag to reveal the silver hub of a USB flash drive. 'That's *so* cool,' he muttered. He checked the padded envelope to ensure there was nothing else inside – there wasn't – and dropped it into the waste basket.

He went to the bedroom door and pushed it open a few inches. From where he was standing he couldn't even see Keisha, but from beneath the mound of the duvet he could hear the sound of soft snoring. He smiled.

Pulling the door shut, he walked through to the office and sat down. He opened his laptop, plugged in the USB stick and spent the next few minutes looking through the content. By the time he'd finished his heart was racing – in part due to the disbelief at what Damian Gardner had sent him, but also because the familiar rush of adrenalin had kicked in, that sensation of excitement he got whenever he was working on a story he knew was going to be big. Except this one wasn't just big; it was going to be globally significant.

He copied the files to a folder on his desktop and then, with a shaking hand, disconnected the USB. Replacing the cap and again marveling at how convincingly it replicated a packet of gum, he put it on the desk beside the laptop.

Picking up his mobile phone, he scrolled through his contacts and made a call.

'Rory, it's Isaac. Gardner's USB just turned up in the post. I tell you, man, this is real James Bond stuff. The thing looks like a packet of chewing gum.' He chuckled. 'It's bananas.'

On the other end of the line Rory laughed. 'I've gotta say, when you told me about it last night, it sounded too crazy to be true. Do you think it's kosher?'

'Yeah, for what it's worth I'm convinced it's the real deal,' Isaac replied.

'How can you be sure?'

'Gut feeling,' Isaac said. 'If you'd read what I just read you'd feel the same.'

'So you don't reckon it's some disgruntled bod out to shaft his employers?' Rory said cautiously. 'You kind of intimated last night that might be the case.'

131

'No. I don't think so. This is corruption, man, on a *vast* scale. I should probably take it to the cops, but it wouldn't surprise me if Stirling had them in his back pocket too. How can we be sure they wouldn't just bury it?'

Rory still sounded unsure. 'Is there no way you can speak to this guy at the lab again and get some more out of him?'

'Yeah, I'd have liked to have had a chance to talk to him again first, but I don't want to wait on a call that might not come. I tell you, man, it's insane. This is gonna be fucking *huge*. But listen, I'll WeTransfer you the files later, but first I'm going to go ahead and record a piece. If by some chance Gardner does call before I send it to you, I can add in anything relevant. But soon as you have it, can you get it online straight away?'

'Sure. And make sure you don't lose that stick!'

'I won't! Thanks *so* much, mate. I'll catch you shortly.'

Tapping the screen to end the call, Isaac settled himself in his chair and hit the key on the laptop that activated his camera.

'Hello, people. Isaac Owusu back again with a scoop like nothing you've ever heard before. Never in my whole career as a vlogger have I ever encountered anything as devastating as what I am about to tell you now. So listen up. I have been provided with information from an inside source that serves to prove indefensibly that a corrupt Government and a charlatan Prime Minister are lying to us. What you're going to hear in the next few minutes will show you just what lengths the people in the corridors of power will go to in order to implement and enforce their self-serving, totalitarian agenda.'

'Baby…'

Dammit! Couldn't she see he was recording? Isaac hit the pause button and angrily spun round in his chair, ready to give Keisha a mouthful.

His face froze.

Keisha was standing naked in the open doorway, her eyes filled with fear. Right behind her, Isaac could see a man with a mop of blonde hair, dressed entirely in black. The man's eyes glistened in the light. One of his huge gloved hands had hold of Keisha by her long dark hair, forcing her head back at a skewed angle, the other was pressing something against her head; it took Isaac a moment to comprehend that it was a gun with a silencer fitted to the barrel.

'You have something we want,' the man said.

'Please, don't hurt her,' Isaac said. He started to get up.

'Stay sitting and shut up,' the man said. He spoke quietly, but without any room for doubt that there would be consequences if Isaac didn't do as he was told. 'Where is it?'

'I don't know what you're talking about, man. I…'

'You don't seem to understand your predicament, Mr Owusu. We know Damian Gardner contacted you and we know he mailed you a flash drive. Give it to me.' He forced the tip of the silencer hard against Keisha's temple.

Isaac's mind was racing. 'Honestly, I don't know what you're talking about,' he said. 'Yes, Gardner called me, but I get calls all the time from all sorts of whackos. I just told him to piss off.' Had that sounded as unconvincing as he thought it did?

Keisha's eyes were wide and pleading with him silently.

'I'll ask you one more time. Where's the USB?'

'I tell you, I don't have it.' Isaac's voice was trembling now. 'Look, man, this has nothing to do with her. Please just let her go and I'll do whatever you want.'

'Where's the fucking...?'

There was a soft phutt sound and Keisha's legs seemed to give way beneath her. She dropped like a stone to the floor.

Isaac let out an anguished howl.

A second man with a bald head, who Isaac hadn't even been aware was there, stepped into view behind the first. He too was dressed in black and his gloved hand was also gripping a gun with a silencer fitted to it. 'Too much talk,' he said gruffly. He raised the gun and pointed it directly at Isaac. 'We don't negotiate with rats.'

They were the last words Isaac ever heard.

The soft phutt sounded again and Isaac jerked back in the chair.

'For Christ's sake, Chris!' the first man exclaimed, wincing at the sight of the small red hole in Isaac's forehead. It pulsed once and leaked a single tear of blood.

The bald-headed man pushed past him and stepped over Keisha's body. Leaning across Isaac, he violently wrenched all the connection cables out of the laptop.

134

Then he pulled the camera off the top of the screen, laid it on the desk and shattered it with the butt of the gun. Just to be sure, he hit it again.

The vibration caused the USB to drop off the end of the desk onto the carpet.

Closing the lid on the laptop, he picked it up, tucked it under his arm and turned to face his accomplice. 'Sorted,' he said. He stepped back over Keisha's body. 'Check the desk drawers and be quick about it. I'm going to drop this in the car. I'll be back in a sec.'

The bald-headed man who had murdered Keisha and Isaac in cold blood crossed the lounge and disappeared into the hall.

The first man quickly rifled through the drawers. There were a lot of cables and a Seagate external hard drive; he took the latter and stashed it in his jacket pocket. In the bottom drawer he found a small Tupperware box. Opening it, he saw that it was full of an assortment of USB sticks. We've got fuck all to check them on now, he thought irritably – better just take the lot.

As he sealed the lid on the box, the bald-headed man reappeared in the doorway.

'Well?'

'A drive and a fuckload of USBs. Must be thirty or more.' He rattled the box and the lid popped open, depositing one of sticks on the floor.

The bald-headed man scowled. 'Fuckwit!'

As the first man bent to retrieve it, his eyes fell upon something laid just beside the leg of the desk. He popped the errant USB back into the box and resealed the lid. Then he reached for the packet of chewing gum on the carpet and stood up.

'What you found?' the bald-headed one asked.

The other man turned the packet in his gloved fingers, squinting at it. 'It's gum,' he said after a moment. Grinning, he held it out to his partner. 'Want a bit?'

The bald-headed man looked at it and grimaced. 'Juicy Fruit? You fucking pansy! Now stop pissing around and come on.'

The blonde haired man laughed. Tossing the packet of gum back onto the desk, he followed the bald-headed man out and across the lounge. They paused for a moment and surveyed the room to be sure they'd left nothing behind, then they went down the hall to the front door and left as silently as they had arrived.

CHAPTER 12

Hazel had to admit she hadn't really expected Julie to take her up on her suggestion of a road trip. She'd only voiced the idea in the first place to soften the blow that she was leaving. As much as she loved Julie, she was all too aware what a stickler for conformity she was and that the chances of her agreeing to break the rules to accompany her on a drive to God knows where were as likely as Cameron Stirling coming along too. And yet it had turned out to be Stirling that convinced Julie to say yes. Or rather the man's speech. The announcement that what was to be a two-week lockdown – bad enough in itself – was being extended to a month was the straw that broke the obedient camel's back. 'You're punishing us for the misdemeanours of other people who won't do what they're told!' Julie had shouted angrily at the television before turning it off in disgust. Then, turning to Hazel, she'd said simply, 'I'm coming with you.'

It had taken Julie an hour to pack up everything she felt she would need for the trip and pile it all up just inside the front door. Hazel couldn't quite believe how much of it there was: two suitcases, one large and one slightly smaller, a chunky holdall and three carrier bags. 'I think you forgot the kitchen sink,' Hazel had joked. 'I hope the Green Machine doesn't collapse under the weight!' she'd added, sticking her head outside the front door to ensure there was nobody about.

Although the road was completely deserted, Julie had voiced her concerns that one of her neighbours would see them and be tempted to cash in on Stirling's awful bribe: 'Mr and Mrs Franklyn three doors down wouldn't hesitate to blab. We've never got along.'

For the past few minutes they had been moving stealthily back and forth, loading up the luggage box on the back of the van as swiftly as they could.

'Crikey, this is heavy!' Hazel said, as her shoulder muscles twisted under the strain. 'What the heck have you got in here?'

They were carrying the Government's box of rations over to the camper van.

'I thought it was best to top up what they gave us with a few more palatable odds and ends.' Julie rolled her eyes. 'I think I've pretty much emptied the cupboards.'

Pip was scampering around in excited circles.

'Hush, Pip, and keep out of the way or you'll get trodden on!' Julie exclaimed.

They set the groceries down beside the van and Hazel opened the side door. 'Why don't you pop Pip in the front seat while I finish loading up?' she said, massaging her shoulder.

'Good idea.' Julie looked down at Pip and smiled. 'Come on then, pest,' she said playfully. Opening the passenger side door, she picked up the little dog and put her on the front seat. She kissed the top of Pip's head. 'Now you be a good girl and stay there. We're nearly finished.'

Shutting the door, she walked back along the side of the van. Hazel was inside shifting around Julie's luggage, trying to create a bit of space.

She climbed back out and together they lifted the box of groceries inside.

'We can sort it all out later. I think we need to get moving as quickly as possible now. While you were dealing with Pip, there was a man in the upstairs window over the road watching us.'

Julie leaned out of the door. 'The one directly opposite?'

'Yes.'

'Mr Knight,' Julie said. 'He's not watching now. But he's a nice man, he wouldn't turn us in. Well, I don't think he would anyway.'

'Money is a great persuader,' Hazel said. 'Even for those who already have it. Everyone can be bought. I don't think we should hang about to find out.'

'Okay. I think I've got everything. Let me go and lock up.' Julie stepped out of the van.

'Hang on a sec,' Hazel called. She appeared in the doorway. 'Are you sure you want to do this?'

Julie gave her a broad smile. 'Absolutely. You're always telling me I need to live a little. It's going to be fun. We'll be just like Thelma and Louise.'

'We will.' Hazel smiled. 'Except hopefully without the cops on our tail.'

'I don't even want to *think* about that!' Julie exclaimed.

'Or driving off a cliff in a blaze of glory,' Hazel added with a chuckle

139

Julie grimaced, hurried quickly to the front door and disappeared inside.

Hazel closed up the side door on the van and went round and climbed into the driver's seat. Pip immediately hopped over and started licking her hands. She laughed. 'Do I taste good?'

A few moments later Julie reappeared carrying her handbag. She locked the front door. Then, taking a step back, she stood for a moment looking at the house with its bay window fronted by a beautifully kept shrubbery. There was a hint of melancholy on her face. She was a home bird by nature, and although there was no doubt in her mind that she would be returning soon, she was suddenly engulfed by a feeling of sadness and doubt. She couldn't help wondering whether she was doing the right thing.

'What you doing?'

Julie turned to see Hazel leaning out of the window.

'Just coming,' she replied. With one last look around her – 'Goodbye, little house,' she whispered, 'I'll see you soon.' – she took a deep breath, walked to the van and climbed into the passenger seat. Pip hopped straight back over onto her lap.

Hazel winked at her. 'Ready then?'

'Ready. I *think*.' She frowned. 'I hope I haven't forgotten anything.'

'Looking at all that stuff we've loaded up in the last few minutes I think it's a pretty safe bet that we've got everything we need. I've even brought a little friend along in case we encounter any trouble on the way.' She reached under the seat and pulled out a baseball bat. 'Meet Donald.'

Julie's face dropped. 'You don't really think there'll be any trouble do you?'

'No. But it doesn't hurt to be prepared. Just in case.' She pushed the bat back under the seat, and turned the key in the ignition. The engine coughed once and then rumbled into life.

*

Malcolm Stone glanced at his watch. He was sweating slightly and despite the dressing down that Stirling had given him a couple of days earlier, his general appearance was as disheveled as it ever was.

Beside him, Health Secretary Michael Simpson was staring into space and idly picking at a broken fingernail. Also present among the smaller than usual assembly of ministers were General Mathers and Professor Walsh.

The door at the end of the room opened and two men walked into the room; the two men who, just hours earlier, had mercilessly taken the lives of Isaac and Keisha. They stopped inside the door and waited.

Mathers looked up from the paperwork in the folder laid open on the table in front of him. He raised a hand and beckoned the two men over. They marched across the carpet and came to a halt in front of him.

'Well?' Mathers said.

The bald-headed one smiled thinly. 'You'll not be hearing anything more out of him, sir.'

'And the USB?'

'Not yet identified specifically, sir,' the blonde-haired man said. 'But we cleared the place of every storage device Owusu had.'

'His laptop too,' the bald one added.

The General's eyes filled with satisfaction. 'Good job.'

'Yes, very well done, gentlemen.' The voice came from behind them.

The two men turned their heads in unison to see Stirling striding purposefully across the room, a folder tucked beneath his arm. 'Very well done indeed.' He took a seat and set down the folder on the table.

The bald-headed soldier glanced at Mathers.

'Dismissed,' Mathers said curtly.

The two men stood smartly to attention, gave a sharp nod of their heads at Mathers, then spun on their heels and marched back across the room.

Stirling opened the folder. He watched and waited for the departing men to close the door behind them and then he spoke.

'Providing the general public stay at home as they've been instructed, the situation will be under control as planned. I'm pleased to be able to report that all the effort we've put into this is paying off beyond our wildest dreams. The diligent and extensive studies carried out by Professor Walsh and his team...' – he glanced at Walsh, who nodded appreciatively – '...have enabled us to perfectly engineer the ORACULTE nerve agent to target the feckless populace swiftly and effectively. The diabetic, the morbidly obese, the terminally ill... *anyone* with long-term health issues will be eradicated. With all the shops closed and access to bottled water effectively cut off, people will have no other option but to drink water from the tap. Before long our great nation will be cleansed of those who are, quite frankly, a drain on our welfare system and our health service. The death toll is continuing on an upwards curve and it won't be…'

Simpson raised his hand.

Stirling looked at him, slightly annoyed at having been interrupted. 'Yes, Michael?'

'You mentioned the health service, Prime Minister. As you've made it abundantly clear to the public, hospitals across the country are full to capacity and beginning to buckle under the strain. You've announced that admissions have been terminated. But we're dealing with an entitlement mind-set. How exactly are we going to control the numbers that are inevitably still going to turn up demanding treatment?'

'A valid enough question, and all I can say at the moment is it has been discussed and they will be dealt with in the appropriate way.' His eyes darted towards Mathers, then back at Simpson. 'In the long term there are other measures under consideration.'

Stirling turned to Walsh. 'What would happen if we were to increase the dosage, Professor?'

Walsh pursed his lips and addressed the table. 'Well, GX-23, which as you are all aware is the lethal active ingredient in ORACULTE, is currently being infused into the water supply in carefully monitored concentrate form. But as was clear from the outset, by the time it reaches the reservoirs it has been significantly diluted and as a result is substantially less efficacious.'

143

Stirling frowned. 'I'm aware of all that. What I want to know is how can we overcome that issue.'

'In my estimation, if, as you suggest, we were to increase the dose being fed into the fresh water supply – double it perhaps? – that would greatly amplify its accomplishments.'

'Elucidate, Professor.'

'Well, put simply, a higher dose will kill the person who consumes it far more quickly. Faster deaths equals less people vying for medical attention.'

Stone raised his hand. His face was looking pasty and he was sweating freely now. 'I'm sorry if there's something I'm not seeing here, but it strikes me that doubling the dose would risk broadening the susceptible demographic.'

Walsh shook his head. 'I don't believe so. At least not in significant enough numbers anyway.'

Stirling sat watching Stone with interest.

Stone ran a hand across his brow and through his hair. The bags of skin beneath his eyes were dark, suggestive of a man deprived of sleep. 'May I ask what you mean when you say not in significant enough numbers?'

'GX-23 has been designed specifically to target those with health issues. The outcome of doubling the dosage cannot be one hundred percent predictable. It may result in a few hundred thousand additional deaths, but…'

Stone's eyes widened. 'A few hundred *thousand*?'

'All wars have collateral damage, Malcolm,' Stirling said dispassionately.

'I know,' Stone said, 'But…'

144

Stirling cut him short. 'Please continue, Professor.'
Stone sat back in his chair.

Walsh cleared his throat. 'As I was about to say, we're moving into unknown territory. Given time I would be able to answer your question with more certainty. But although what you're asking for might – and I stress, *might* – result in deaths we cannot account for, it would still primarily be the most vulnerable who would perish. To date it has been almost exclusively those with minor underlying health conditions that are being hospitalised. Those with more serious conditions who ingest GX-23 are pretty much dying where they stand. Ergo, increasing the dosage to create a faster acting agent would technically have the same affect on the mildly unhealthy as it's currently having on the more severely so. Thus the demand for medical treatment is negated. But I must reiterate, this is theoretical.'

Stirling nodded. 'Theoretical or otherwise, it's what needs to be done. You may begin immediately, Professor.'

He looked at Mathers. 'The military presence on the streets must be strengthened post-haste. And I want the implementation of a Stop-and-Search strategy in place and operating within twelve hours. There are still far too many vehicles on the roads. I want the tracking of mobile phones and navigation devices activated immediately.' He looked at one of the men at the table. 'Deal with that, Peter.'

The man nodded. 'Yes, Prime Minister.'

'Nobody,' Stirling continued, 'I repeat *nobody*, except for key workers and emergency service staff are permitted to leave their home and anybody failing to comply is to receive the maximum penalty. No exceptions.'

Mathers nodded. 'Are we talking about enforced fines?'

'No, General, we are not.' Stirling closed the folder and abruptly stood up. 'I mean the *maximum* penalty.'

Mathers smiled and his dark eyes sparkled. 'Understood, Prime Minister.'

*

It was a little past 8 o'clock in the evening and with the exception of a lightning stop to relieve their bladders, Hazel and Julie had been on the road since they left the house at lunchtime.

Hazel glanced at her friend, who had her head back against the headrest and appeared to be struggling to keep her eyes open. Pip was curled up asleep on her lap.

Hazel yawned.

'Don't start that,' Julie said. 'You'll set me off too. Would you like me to take the wheel for a while?'

Hazel chuckled. 'Er, correct me if I'm wrong, but I don't think you've ever driven anything bigger than your little Fiat 500, have you?'

'Well, that's true,' Julie said. 'But…'

'No offence,' Hazel said, patting the steering wheel, 'but Greeny can be a bit tricky to manoeuvre, especially round these twisty-turny lanes at night.'

'I'm sure I could manage. You look so tired.'

146

'Really, I think she'd be more than you could handle.' Hazel yawned again. 'I *could* do with a break though. Shall we find a suitable place to pull over and put the kettle on?'

'Ooh, a cuppa sounds great.'

'Just for half an hour, wake myself up a bit. Then we'll press on.'

Five minutes later their headlights fell upon a small lay-by. Hazel just managed to squeeze the van into the space and switched off the engine. 'Right,' she said, smiling. 'Tea. I'll have to get out on your side, there's not enough room for me to open the door this side.'

Julie gently woke Pip, who immediately became alert. She moved the little dog onto the seat between herself and Hazel. Then she got out and stretched – 'Lord, I ache all over.' – and leaned back inside to pick up Pip. After Hazel had scrambled across the seats and climbed out, they walked across the gravel to the side door and went inside.

As Julie shut the door behind them, Hazel switched on the light.

'I'll make the tea,' Julie said. 'Here, you take Pip.' She handed her to Hazel, who took her and sat down on the neat little two-seater couch below the window.

'Thanks.'

She watched her friend busying herself at the small gas hob and smiled. She genuinely hadn't expected for one moment that Julie would come along, but she felt really glad of the company.

Julie tipped half a bottle of water into the kettle.

'Bottled water not so bad after all, eh Jules?'

147

Julie laughed. 'Alright, alright, I concede it has its uses.'

Putting one hand on Pip to ensure she didn't fall off her lap, Hazel reached under the couch and pulled out a duffle bag. Withdrawing her tablet, she flicked the switch on the side and the screen lit up. 'Let's have a quick look at what's going on out there in the world, shall we?' She tapped the BBC News app icon.

Julie was muttering to herself. 'It's lucky I brought teabags. That's something the Government forgot to give us. I ask you, how can they overlook something as fundamental as a cup of tea? Or maybe you fancy a hot chocolate? If I...' She trailed off as she saw the look on Hazel's face. 'What's wrong?'

Hazel was staring at the tablet. 'Come and look at this.' She turned the screen so that Julie could see.

It was a live broadcast from the BBC newsroom.

'The headlines again. The riot which began in central London earlier this afternoon is still not under control,' news anchor John Mitchell was saying. 'What started as a peaceful protest against the extended lockdown restrictions announced by Cameron Stirling this morning, quickly deteriorated into violence when the military intervened.'

Julie's face was ashen. 'This is getting really frightening.'

'Don't worry,' Hazel said, trying to sound calm, although in truth she felt anything but. 'Where we're headed it's nice and quiet. Miles from anywhere. We can hunker down and wait for all this to blow over.'

She was just about to switch the tablet off when a photograph of a familiar face appeared on the screen.

'And finally tonight,' Mitchell said, 'Police are investigating the murder of popular Nu-Tube vlogger Isaac Owusu and his partner Keisha Lange, whose bodies were discovered in their London home first thing this morning.'

'Oh good Lord,' Julie said. 'Isn't that the man we were talking about at breakfast?'

'Yeah,' Hazel said, not quite able to grasp what she'd just heard. 'It is. Or rather *was*.'

'The world is going mad!'

The kettle on the hob began to whistle and Julie turned off the gas.

'Come on,' Hazel said. 'Let's have that hot drink.'

CHAPTER 13

By the time they had eaten, the weather had taken a turn for the worse.

The two friends were sitting drinking hot chocolate, curled up beside one another on the couch in the cosy sanctuary of the van.

Pip was asleep on the floor between Hazel's feet, apparently oblivious to the rain pounding on the roof.

'I haven't had hot chocolate in years.' Julie dabbed at the corner of her mouth with her index finger. 'I'd forgotten how nice it is.'

Hazel smiled. 'There's nothing like a mug of hot chocolate to make you feel better.'

'Tell me a bit about Ash,' Julie said, adjusting the blanket she had around her shoulders. 'You've mentioned him before, but you've never really told me anything much about him.'

'There's not a lot to tell,' Hazel said.

'Well it's not quite bedtime, so unless you don't feeling like telling me, I'd like to know a little bit about him, especially if I'm going to be meeting him.'

'Sure,' Hazel said, setting down her mug. 'I think you remember our Mum and Dad lived a very bohemian lifestyle?'

'I do, yes.'

'Well, it was pretty tough to be a kid in that environment, especially when you could see other kids leading a completely different sort of life. But it taught us core values, the sort of stuff you don't really appreciate until you get older. Anyway, when he was 18, Ash had a big falling out with Dad and he moved out. Mum was heartbroken.'

'I'm so sorry.' Julie looked as if she really meant it. 'May I ask what the falling out was about?'

'All sorts of things. The life he wanted to lead mainly. Being two years younger I didn't really understand what was going on at the time. But it worked out for the best and it gave Ash the impetus he needed to follow his dreams of living on a houseboat. I didn't see much of him for a long time after that. Dad never spoke of him again. It was weird, it was almost like Ash never existed.' Hazel looked a little misty-eyed. 'Mum and I would talk about him often though, and she used to write to him without Dad knowing. He'd have been livid if he'd ever found out. Still, he didn't. When Mum and Dad died I was kicked out of our council accommodation. I think you knew that?'

Julie nodded.

'There was no way I could afford a mortgage,' Hazel continued, 'so I bought the van and took up the traveling life. I reconnected with Ash and stayed with him a couple of times, but for some reason we just drifted apart again. I'm not even sure why now. There was certainly never any animosity between us. I suppose that's just the way it goes sometimes, siblings get scattered to the four winds by circumstance and then get too wrapped up in their own lives. Ash is a really good guy though.'

Julie had been listening attentively. 'I admire you so much. It must be so tough on your own sometimes, but you always seem to make the best of it. Even in the middle of a crisis like this bloody virus, you still manage to keep smiling.'

Hazel raised her eyebrows. 'Do you know, I think that's the first time I've ever heard you swear.'

'You should hear me when I get really worked up.' Julie laughed. 'I use the awful C word quite a lot.'

Hazel's mouth dropped open. 'Now *that* I can't believe! Even *I* avoid using that one.'

'That's not true! I've heard you say crap loads of times!'

Hazel cackled with laughter. 'You're absolutely hilarious, Jules, do you know that?'

Julie frowned. 'What have I said?'

'It doesn't matter. Please just never change.'

Julie looked for a moment as if she might press for an explanation, but then thought better of it. 'Go on with what you were telling me.'

Hazel wiped the tears of laughter from her eyes. 'I've forgotten where I was.'

'You were saying that you and Ash had drifted apart.'

'Oh, yeah. Well, that's it really, I never realised how trapped in conformity I was until I took up life on the road. I get to go anywhere I want, *whenever* I want. Just look at how the people in this country live now, being told all the time what they can and can't do. They think they're free to do what they want, but the fact of the matter is we're all slaves to conformity whether we realise it or not.'

'Things aren't really *that* bad,' Julie said. 'We've got it very easy compared to some countries.'

'Yeah, okay, that's true, but just think about it for a minute.' Hazel pointed to her mobile phone on the side. 'Take mobile phones: Every time you pick it up someone can trace it. The SatNav on the dash: They know exactly where you are and follow every single move you make.' She picked up her tablet. 'Websites and app stores. Subscribe to this, download that. So many things are being made mandatory. Your devices get updated without your consent, it happens automatically. How do we know what's being installed?'

'This all sounds very conspiratorial,' Julie said apprehensively.

'Not without reason! The freedom everyone once enjoyed is being chipped away bit by bit. Governments are constantly coming up with new ways to control us. In "1984" George Orwell wrote that the only thing people were allowed to go out on the streets for was to go to work, and everything else like singing and dancing and socialising – *anything* that made life fun – was forbidden. How prescient was that? You've only got to look at the extra two weeks' lockdown they've thrown at us. What's *that* all about, eh? It sure as hell hasn't got anything to do with containing a virus. If it was, why didn't they make it four weeks instead of two from the get go?'

'It does seem a little draconian.'

Hazel nodded. 'Exactly. A few people weren't doing what they were told to do, so it's slapped wrists all round for everyone. "You were only going to have to stay in for two weeks, but you've been naughty, so now it's four. If you don't want it to be six, do as you're told, toe the line, or things will get a whole lot worse." Isn't that sort of thing the implicit threat of every dictatorship? It's punishment, plain and simple. Before you know it they'll be conscripting us to undertake vaccine trials like guinea pigs in their sordid new world order.'

Julie was looking at Hazel in disbelief. 'You don't *really* think all that stuff, do you?'

'Quite frankly I wouldn't put anything past them. I certainly wouldn't trust that Stirling creature any further than I could throw him. And that's why I choose to live the way I do.' She noticed the shocked expression on Julie's face. 'Well, you did ask.' She laughed, diffusing the tension, and yawned.

'You look so tired. I know you said this would be a quick stop, but why don't we just stay here for the night? It's lashing down out there.'

Hazel pulled aside the little curtain on the window. She shivered. 'Yeah, that's not such a bad idea. I'm absolutely beat. We'll probably make an early start in the morning.' She stood up. 'Come on then, bed.'

Pip lazily opened her eyes and looked up at Hazel.

Julie suddenly realised they hadn't discussed sleeping arrangements. She looked up at Hazel. 'Er... where exactly do we sleep?'

'That couch you're sitting on folds out into a bed.'

'It's very small, surely there's not enough room for two.'

Hazel winked at her. 'Would you like to go on top or underneath?'

Julie flushed and her eyes widened with concern. 'I... I'm not sure what... Er, what I mean is...'

154

Hazel laughed. 'Panic ye not.' She reached up and pulled down a small ladder from a compartment backing the cab. 'You have the bed. I'll sleep up here.'

'For one moment I thought you were going to suggest...' Julie trailed off. 'Well, you know.'

'Come on,' Hazel said, resisting the urge to make a lewd remark. 'Stand up and I'll make up the bed for you.'

The storm had petered out in the early hours, but both women had a restless night.

There was barely enough room to roll over in the bunk behind the cab and Hazel spent the entire night in a state of half-sleep trying not to fall out.

Julie's dearth of slumber was more to do with her overactive mind; she lay awake for a long time thinking about the situation into which she'd allowed herself to be coaxed, and at least partially wishing she were back home in the comfort of her own bed.

It was just before six o'clock when Hazel awoke and when she looked out of the bunk she was surprised to see the bed had been folded back up to its couch incarnation and Julie was gone. So too was Pip.

She swung her legs over the side of the bunk, clambered down the ladder and peeped out through the curtain. The sky was blue and there wasn't a cloud in sight.

Briskly rubbing her arms to get warm, she quickly threw on some clothes. Just as she'd finished, the side door opened and Julie appeared carrying Pip.

'Morning. I hope I didn't wake you moving about,' she said, stepping inside and closing the door.

'No, it's fine,' Hazel replied. 'It felt like it took me half the night to get off. I just couldn't get comfortable. But the last couple of hours I was completely out for the count.'

'I tried to be quiet getting dressed.' Julie put Pip down on the couch, but she immediately hopped off onto the floor. 'Pip was desperate to go and I had to stretch my legs too.'

'Did you find a suitable bush?'

Julie laughed. 'I did.'

Hazel chuckled. 'And you've emptied the dog?'

'We did, didn't we?' Julie squatted down and ruffled Pip's head. 'We didn't want you making a mess on Hazel's lovely clean carpet, did we?'

The little dog looked up at her appreciatively, then rolled over onto her back, presenting her tummy, tacitly demanding more attention.

Hazel smiled. 'How come you never got a dog of your own?'

'To tell the truth I don't really like dogs all that much,' Julie said, tickling Pip's tummy. 'But you're an exception, aren't you? You're bootiful, you are.' Pip was squirming with delight. 'Yes you are. You're very bootiful.'

'You could have fooled me,' Hazel said, looking at her friend warmly. 'You two get on like old pals.'

'I guess by accident or design I *have* now got a dog of my own.' Julie stood up. 'She's a sweet little thing. Would you mind getting that last little bit of leftover

156

chicken out of the fridge? I'll sort Pip out and then we can have our own breakfast in peace.'

Hazel handed her the plate. 'Do you fancy scrambled eggs on toast?'

'Ooh, that sounds divine,' Julie said, putting the plate down for Pip, who eagerly pounced on it and began devouring her meal. 'I'll pop the kettle on.'

Hazel grinned. 'It wouldn't suit you, you know.'

Julie rolled her eyes. 'Oh hardy-ha-ha, very funny.'

Hazel pulled out a pan. 'Sit yourself down, I'll get breakfast. You're *my* houseguest now.'

Julie sat down at the small table. 'I could get used to this silver service.'

'I'm sorry about last night,' Hazel said, igniting the hob. 'I didn't mean things to get so heated.'

'Forget about it,' Julie said. 'It was certainly… well, eye-opening.'

When the food was ready they sat and ate in silence.

Half an hour later they were sitting up front and ready to move on.

Hazel turned the ignition. The engine spluttered once and stopped. She tried again with the same result. On the third attempt it shuddered into life, but a glance at the fuel gauge caused Hazel to grimace. 'Damn. I filled up a couple of days before I arrived at yours and I knew we were going to have to fuel up at some point, but it looks like it's going to be sooner rather than later.' She tapped the glass on the gauge. 'Less than a fifth full. We'll not get far on that. Certainly not to Ripon.'

Julie looked uncomfortable. 'How are we going to get fuel? We're not even supposed to be on the road.'

157

'Don't worry,' Hazel said. 'I actually know a little Gulf filling station in Berriton. It's not too far from here. I've gassed up there a few times when I was on the way to see Ash. It was a few pennies more than Tesco's, but a heck of a lot less than the services. It means a longer diversion than I'd have liked too, but we'll be safer if we continue to stick to the B roads.'

'You said you hadn't visited Ash for a while. What if it isn't there any more? What if it's closed up because of lockdown?'

Hazel shook her head. 'There are still people who need to get from A to B to go to work, you know. They can't shut filling stations.'

'I admire your confidence,' Julie said with a note of doubt. 'I wish I was so sure. I mean, what on earth are we going to do if we can't get any fuel?'

Hazel winked at her. 'It'll be fine. Have a little faith, Jules.' She pulled carefully out of the lay-by and they set off down the lane.

Three quarters of an hour later they passed a sign that said **WELCOME TO BERRITON**, and in smaller letters beneath, **PLEASE DRIVE CAREFULLY**. The road through the village was deserted and they passed by a few small shops; all of them were closed.

'It's like a ghost town,' Julie said. 'I suppose the whole country must be pretty much like this at the moment.'

Hazel nodded, and as she did so the filling station came into sight on the bend a few hundred yards ahead. 'Hmm, it looks like it's a Texaco now.'

'Is that likely to be a problem?' Julie said, slightly nervously. She had been feeling more and more apprehensive about the prospect of having to refuel.

'Not if the little old guy who's been on the counter every time I've stopped by still works here,' Hazel said. 'You get real old-fashioned service with a smile from him. Soon as he sees you coming he runs out and tells you to sit tight while he fills you up.'

'Let's hope he's there then,' Julie said, not feeling particularly appeased.

Hazel grinned. 'He's a devilish flirt too, so it shouldn't be too difficult.'

'Devilish flirt?!' Julie exclaimed. 'I'm not sure I like the sound of that.'

'He's harmless. Last time I saw him he must have been 75 if he was a day.'

Julie looked taken aback. '75? That's old enough to be your grandfather!'

Hazel laughed. 'Whenever I went in he chatted me up, but it wasn't anything pervy, just a bit of banter. He probably does it with all his customers. I expect most of them come from round here and he knows them all by their first names. It's that kind of place. I doubt there are many passers-through like us.

Julie shook her head. 'Well I think it's disgusting.'

'Relax.' Hazel smiled. 'If he's still there it'll be a doddle to fill up. I'll just flash my boobs at him.'

Julie looked aghast. 'You *can't* be serious!'

Hazel burst out laughing. 'Of course I'm not serious. Just stop worrying. If he *is* there I'll let him chat me up, give him my winning smile, and we'll be refuelled and on our way in a jiffy.'

'And what if he's *not* there?'

'We're about to find out.'

CHAPTER 14

Hazel swung the camper van up onto the forecourt and glanced to her right as they passed the small convenience store, but although she glimpsed someone on the other side of the glass at the counter, she wasn't able to see who it was.

They pulled to a stop beside the dispenser island. Before turning off the engine she looked at the fuel gauge. 'Another hour and we'd have been coasting on fumes.'

The island housed a line of four dispensers. Two of them had small handwritten signs attached to them declaring that they were empty. The one at the end was labeled up for diesel, but although there was no sign to indicate there wasn't any fuel available at all, both women immediately spotted that the handle had been fitted with a lock.

'You sit tight with Pip,' Hazel said. 'I'll nip inside and see if I can work my magic.'

'Can you see if they've got any spaghetti hoops? I've got a hankering for them.'

Hazel pulled a face and laughed. 'Okay, I'll have a look and see what they've got.'

As she crossed to the store, she heard laughter and looked to see four teenagers wearing hoodies, all huddled together and sharing a cigarette beside the wall at the far end of the forecourt.

Hazel smiled at the thought of a squadron of soldiers being deployed due to reports of four boys

161

hanging round the streets sharing a cigarette. Adopting a cod German accent, she muttered to herself, 'Ze breaking of ze rules vil be subjected to ze maximum penalties!'

As Hazel pushed open the swing door it made a little *bing-bong* sound, announcing her arrival.

The elderly man at the counter looked up from his newspaper. He grinned, revealing a mouth full of gravestone teeth. 'Good mornin' to you,' he said.

Hazel felt a wave of relief as she recognised the face of the man who had served her when she'd been here in the past. 'Hello there,' she replied cheerfully.

'I saw you pull in. That's a smashin' little bit of kit you've got yourself there. Always fancied one of them for m'self, but her indoors won't let me.' He chortled. 'She likes her home comforts too much.'

'She gets me around.' Hazel looked up at the shelf in front of her and spotted spaghetti hoops. She picked up a couple of tins and crossed to the counter. She noticed that the man was wearing a badge bearing the Texaco emblem, with his name printed neatly beneath. 'It's William, isn't it?' she said.

The man looked momentarily confused. 'I'm sorry, I don't quite ...'

Hazel smiled. 'It's okay, you won't remember me. I've not been in for quite a while.'

'Oh, okay.' He grinned again. 'I thought there was *somethin'* familiar about you. That van of yours too. But the name... it escapes me.'

'Hazel.'

'Of course, Hazel, I remember you now!' he exclaimed, although he evidently really didn't and nor

162

was there any real reason that he should. He tapped his temple with a finger arthritically twisted out of shape. 'It might take me a minute sometimes, but I never forget a face.' His eyes twinkled. 'Especially one as attractive as yours.' He leaned forward and beckoned Hazel to come closer. As she did so she caught the scent of peppermint on his breath. 'Berriton's not exactly renowned for good lookers,' he said quietly. 'There's not many lasses as pretty as you round here, I don't mid tellin' tell you.' He winked and his eyes unashamedly dropped down to admire her chest. 'It's quite made my mornin' you comin' in here.'

'Flatterer.' Hazel said, affording the old man a coy smile. She set the tins on the counter.

William looked down at them. 'I'm really sorry, but I can't sell you those. Government restrictions. And I should warn you before you ask, I'm afraid I can't let you have any fuel either.'

It was pretty much what Hazel had expected, but she adopted a doleful expression anyway. 'Oh no, really? I was hoping…'

William held up an apologetic hand. 'Sorry, nothin' I can do about it. Them's the current rules y'see. Pumps are locked and I'm not allowed to serve anyone who doesn't have the proper dispensation, you know, key workers and the like.' He thought for a moment. 'I do apologise, that was very presumin' of me. Are you a key worker?'

Hazel nodded. 'Er… I am actually, yes.'

'Oh!' He looked slightly surprised. 'Well that's alright then. What is it you do?'

163

Hazel hated lying, but she had no choice. Leaving without filling up wasn't an option; they probably wouldn't even make it out of Berriton on the little remained in the tank. 'I'm a nurse.'

'A nurse, you say? I should've guessed it. I can just imagine you in a nurse's uniform.'

I bet you can, Hazel thought. She smiled at him sweetly.

'Good for you,' William continued. 'A much under-valued profession in my humble opinion. I've never admired you medical folks more than I do at the moment. It must be an absolute nightmare.'

The note of genuine appreciation in his words compounded Hazel's guilt over the lie.

'Anyway,' William said, 'if you can just show me some ID please, then I'll come out and unlock the pump.' He reached behind him for a set of keys and started to move round from behind the counter.

'Ah…' Hazel said. 'There's a bit of a problem there.'

The man stopped. 'Oh?'

'Yes. You see, I came out in a bit of a hurry and, well, stupid me…' – she rolled her eyes – '…I left my ID at home.'

The man's expression turned to one of slight suspicion. He looked Hazel up and down, perhaps only now registering that her casual attire didn't suggest she was a nurse at all. 'So you've no identification?'

Hazel shook her head. 'As I said, I left it at home.'

'Well, I'm sorry then, I can't help.' He moved back behind the counter.

'Couldn't you make an exception? Just this once? I'll not tell anyone.'

William shook his head. 'I would if I could, but it'd be more than my job's worth.' He hung the keys back on the hook.

Hazel was about to make a feeble plea when the *bing-bong* chime of the swing door opening sounded and she glanced back to see one of the lads she'd noticed beside the wall at the end of the forecourt come slouching in, pulling his hoodie up over his head and carrying a holdall. He pushed the door hard and it wedged open, then barely bothering to pick up his feet he ambled over towards the racks of sweets.

'Mornin', William called out. 'Would you push the door to please?'

Either the lad didn't hear or he simply chose to ignore him.

William returned his attention to Hazel. 'Youngsters, eh?' he said, rolling his eyes. 'I blame the parents. Don't know, don't care. They shouldn't even be out of their homes at the moment, let alone coming in here for things I'm not permitted to sell them.'

There was a sudden clattering sound and Hazel looked round to see the boy scooping armfuls of sweets off the shelf into the holdall.

'Oi!' William shouted angrily, stepping out from behind the counter. 'What the hell d'ya think you're doin' there, son?'

The boy ignored him and carried on filling the holdall.

William walked over and put a hand on the boy's shoulder. 'I said…'

The boy spun round and batted his hand away. 'Get your hands off me, you dry fuck!' He pushed back the hoodie to reveal his face and fumbling in his pocket withdrew a small penknife. 'Now back the fuck off or I'll merk ya!'

William held up his hands and took a step back. 'Woah there, don't do anythin' rash!' He squinted at the boy's face. 'Hang on a minute, I know you. You're Neil Mortlake's boy. It's Leon, isn't it? You're not even fifteen, son, what are you doin' wavin' knives around?'

Hazel couldn't stand by any longer. She took a step forward. 'What the hell's the matter with you? He's an old man!'

The boy shot her a filthy look and waved the knife in the air. 'Stay out of this or you're both fuckin' dead.'

Hazel stopped in her tracks. Her heart was pounding.

Realising it was time to make a run for it, Leon edged towards the door, holding out the knife at arm's length. As he turned to make a run for it, Hazel darted forward and stuck out her foot. Leon was sent sprawling a few feet from the exit, and the knife flew out of his hand, skittered across the floor and hit the side of the swing door.

William was on him in a moment, pinning him to the floor. 'Gotcha, you little toerag!'

'Get the fuck offa me!' Leon was squirming around trying to get up, but the old man had his full weight on him.

As Hazel bent to pick up the holdall, there was a yell from the open doorway – 'Lee!' – and she looked up to see two of the other boys standing there.

Leon craned his head to try to see what was happening. He spotted his friend. 'Daz! Help me!' He was still trying to throw William off, but the old man's stature belied his weight and there was no way he was budging.

'Get the knife!' William shouted at Hazel.

Hazel shot a glance at the abandoned penknife beside the door near the boys' feet, but following her eyes they saw it too. There was a pregnant pause during which nobody seemed to be sure what was going to happen next. Then the stockier of the two with an acne-stippled face made a lunge for it.

But so too did Hazel.

She dropped the holdall and grabbed the knife a split second before the boy was able to; she snatched it up off the floor, but lost her balance, fell sideways and landed in a heap at the boy's feet.

Laughing triumphantly, the boy bent and grabbed Hazel by the scruff of her neck. 'Gimme the fuckin' knife, bitch!'

As the words left his mouth, there was an angry cry from behind them – 'Hey!' – and the boys spun round to see Julie advancing across the forecourt towards them brandishing a baseball bat. They looked at each other and it took them all of two seconds to weigh up their options and make a decision: they spun on their heels and scooted off across the forecourt, abandoning Leon to his fate.

167

As Julie reached the doorway, Hazel turned back to William. 'Are you okay?' she asked?

'A little shaken, I don't mind tellin' you,' William replied. 'But I'll be fine.' He chuckled. 'Nothin' a nip of brandy won't cure.'

Julie glanced back across the forecourt – there was no sign of the boys – then stepped into the store and pushed the door shut.

Leon had stopped struggling.

'You should pick your friends more carefully, son.' William grinned. 'They've left you to carry the can.'

Leon grunted.

'If I let you up, are you gonna behave yourself?'

'Just get offa me.' The boy had lost his fight. '*Please…*'

William climbed off him and stood up.

Hazel handed him the knife and he tucked it into his pocket. 'Come on then, up with you.' He extended his hand to Leon.

Looking suitably contrite, the boy took William's hand and allowed the old man to help him up off the floor. 'I'm sorry,' he mumbled. 'I didn't really want to do it. They bullied me into it.'

'No real harm done I s'pose. But I'd have thought you'd have known better than to mix with those lads,' William said admonishingly. 'They're bad news. Especially that Darren kid. You're better than that. Now you get yerself off home make sure you bloomin' well stay there.'

Leon nodded and held out his hand. 'Can I have my knife back?'

William shook his head. 'No, no, no, son. I think it's best it stays here.'

'But…'

'Be off with you now before I change my mind and report you.'

Leon walked petulantly to the door, where he stopped and looked back. 'I really am sorry.'

William winked at him and the young man turned away and left, pulling the swing door shut behind him.

'That was incredibly lenient of you,' Hazel said.

'And that was very brave of *you*,' William said. He took the penknife out of his pocket. 'The lad probably wouldn't have done too much damage with this little tinkertoy, but he might have made a bit of a mess of you tryin'. Shakes you up when someone pulls a knife on you, don't it?'

Hazel nodded. 'What do you want to do with this?' She raised the holdall.

William walked back round behind the counter and tucked the knife safely out of sight. 'If the lad had taken the stuff that would have opened up a whole big old can of worms and I'd have had to report him. I can well do without any of that nonsense. Just leave it here.' He tapped the counter. 'I'll re-shelve the booty later.'

Hazel set the holdall down, looked at Julie and raised her eyebrows. 'Well, that was a darned sight more excitement than I'd expected when I got up this morning.'

Julie laughed. 'Me too!'

'Come on,' Hazel said. 'We'd better get moving.' She looked back at William. 'I don't suppose there's anything I can say that will make you change your mind about fuel? I'm not sure we have enough to get us up the road, let alone to another filling station.'

William hesitated for a moment. He reached for the pump keys and handed them to her. 'Go fill her up. Far as I'm concerned you're a bona fide nurse.' His eyes dropped to Hazel's chest. 'I've seen your credentials.' He chortled and waggled his eyebrows.

Hazel smiled. 'You're a Godsend. Thank you *so* much. I'll bring the key back and settle up in a moment.'

William nodded. 'My pleasure. You ladies did me a huge favour. Besides, you sit in here all day on your own waitin' for one pretty lady to stop by…' – he winked at Julie – '…and then, lo and behold, you get two come in together.' He pushed the cans of spaghetti hoops across the counter. 'Here, take these too. On me.'

Julie smiled gratefully. 'Thank you.'

The two women walked to the door.

'Just one thing though,' William called out after them.

They stopped and turned.

'Next time you're passin' through, don't forget to wear that nurse's uniform, eh?' He chuckled and waggled his eyebrows again.

Hazel smiled and blew him a little kiss.

Outside, while Hazel filled the camper van's tank, Julie explained what had happened.

'You'd only just gone inside when those boys appeared. I don't know where they came from.'

'I saw them hanging around by the exit,' Hazel said.

170

'Okay. Well, they didn't notice me sitting in the van watching them, but I could tell straight away they were up to no good. The three older ones were pushing the little one towards the door like they were trying to bully him into doing something he clearly didn't really want to do. As soon as he went inside the others ducked out of sight around the corner. I guessed they were waiting for the little one to come back out and it was obvious there was going to be trouble. A minute went by and then I saw the scuffle in the doorway. One of the other boys took off like his feet were on fire, I've no idea where he went, but the other two ran over to the door. That's when I decided I had do something. My heart was pounding so hard I thought I was going to be sick, but I grabbed your baseball bat and ran across the forecourt. I think I looked threatening, but God knows what I'd have done if they'd stood up to me!'

Hazel smiled. 'You saved the day, Jules.' She finished filling the tank and relocked the pump. 'There you go,' she said, grinning. 'Told you coming here would be a cinch.'

'I wouldn't call this morning a cinch!' Julie exclaimed.

Hazel laughed. 'I'll just drop the keys back inside and pay William, then we'll be off. Let's hope the rest of the journey will be far less dramatic.'

CHAPTER 15

Relieved to put Berriton and the incident at the filling station behind them, as they drove out of the village and onto the lane that circled Blechnum Woods, Hazel switched on the radio and the sound of Ray Frost singing "Lucky To Be Me" boomed out.

'Ooh, I love this song,' Julie said enthusiastically.

Hazel cocked an ear. 'I don't think I've ever heard it before.'

'They've been playing it for weeks. It's really catchy.' Jigging Pip from side to side on her lap, she started to sing along. 'Spent some time in a foreign land, I even played in a foreign band...'

Hazel grinned. 'You've certainly cheered up.'

'I don't mind admitting I was a bit worried we weren't going to get any petrol.'

'I was never in any doubt.'

Julie frowned. '*Really*?'

'Well...'

They both burst out laughing.

The song came to an abrupt end and the presenter said, 'We must interrupt this broadcast to go to a live message from Downing Street.'

Julie looked at Hazel in dismay. 'Oh, God, what now?'

Cameron Stirling's voice cut in. 'Good morning. I am aggrieved to have to report that the riots which started yesterday in central London have not only continued overnight, but have spread to further towns

172

and cities across the country. The military are working hard to get this situation under control, but there are still scattered pockets of resistance that have yet to be contained.'

'They can't really be surprised, can they?' Hazel said.

'Shhhh.' Julie put a finger to her lips.

'It angers me beyond measure,' Stirling continued, 'that not only are our crystal clear instructions still being ignored, but this civil unrest is draining precious resources and further compromising our struggling health service. This will *not* be tolerated. Stricter enforcements are being drawn up. Furthermore…'

Hazel reached out and switched off the radio. 'That's quite enough of that.'

'It might have been important,' Julie said.

'I doubt it. Every time that man gets up on his podium he regurgitates the same old tripe, telling us what naughty children we've been and tightening the noose on our liberty more and more.'

'Things are getting worse though,' Julie said miserably.

'Don't start worrying again, Jules,' Hazel said. 'We're going to be fine, okay?'

'I know. It's just it's starting to feel like things will never go back to normal.' She wiped a small tear from the corner of her eye.

'We'll be at Ash's soon and we can shut the world out.'

'What if we don't make it? You said last night that the Government can track us through our mobile phones. What if they're tracking us right now?' Julie was beginning to sound panicky.

'They'd have to have a reason to specifically be tracking us in the first place. Besides, I'm not using the SatNav, my tablet has been turned off since we were parked up last night and aside from switching on my mobile to send Ash a quick text yesterday, I haven't had it on since I arrived at yours the other day.'

Julie's face dropped. 'Oh no!' She reached down between her legs and retrieved her handbag from the footwell. 'I think I've had mine on since we left the house yesterday.' She pulled out her phone and looked at it with concern. 'Yes, it's still on. How can I tell if I'm being tracked?'

Hazel glanced at the Nokia 105, barely larger than the palm of Julie's hand, and laughed. 'I don't think we need to worry about that. They can't track the prehistoric ones.'

They drove on in silence for a mile, then as they took a left into one of the lanes that bisected the woodland Julie said, 'What's this place like?'

'Blechnum Woods?'

'No, where Ash lives.'

'Oh.' Hazel smiled. 'Well I haven't been there for a long time now, but I doubt it's changed very much. It's like a little community of boat people. They're a lovely crowd. It's remote. It's beautiful. It's tranquil.'

Julie smiled. 'It sounds idyllic.'

'It is. I reckon you'll love it. And you can be sure Ash will make us both very welcome.'

As they took a bend in the lane, the smile dropped from Julie's face and she gasped and pointed ahead. 'Look!'

About twenty yards ahead there was a car lodged at a skewed angle on the right hand verge, its front staved in against a tree, its back end with the tail lights on jutting out several feet into the lane.

Even from this distance the white Volkswagen Polo looked as if it had seen better days before it had hit the tree – it certainly needed a wash – and, as they slowed down to a crawl and drew closer, Hazel could see the driver side door was slightly ajar and there didn't appear to be anyone inside.

The van came to a stop alongside the rear of the car and Hazel shut off the engine. 'Stay here,' she said, opening the door to get out. 'I'll just take a quick look.'

'Please be careful,' Julie said. She looked characteristically nervous. 'It might be a trap.'

Hazel laughed. 'C'mon, Jules, a trap? To what end? We're in the middle of nowhere! They might have had to wait days for someone to come past, especially as the country's in lockdown.'

Julie looked doubtful. 'It just doesn't do any harm to be alert. You hear about these people who fake an accident and then when someone pulls over to help them out they get mugged.'

'Don't worry,' Hazel said. 'We aren't going to get mugged, I assure you.' Despite her note of confidence, she paused to withdraw the baseball bat. She pulled an angry face. 'But if anyone *does* try anything, I'll bash 'em from here to kingdom come!'

'Well, I'm coming with you then. There's safety in numbers at least.' Julie lifted Pip off her lap and put her down on the seat. 'You stay here, Mummy will be back in a moment.'

Hazel rolled her eyes. 'Mummy?'

Climbing out of the van, she gripped the bat hard in her right hand, treaded softly over to the driver's side door and peered through the glass. She'd been right on first glance; there was nobody inside.

Julie came round to the front of the van and waited there while Hazel moved along the side of the car to inspect the damage.

The bonnet was buckled inwards where the vehicle had collided with the tree; evidently it must have been going at some considerable speed when it came off the road. A closer look revealed that the driver's side headlight and indicator were smashed – Hazel couldn't see the other one from where she was standing, but it was likely that it too was busted – the radiator grill was hanging off, the bumper was bent out of shape and one of the fenders was lying on the ground. It was a write-off if ever Hazel had seen one.

Miraculously, the broad trunk of the oak had sustained hardly any damage. The result of a *stoppable* force hitting an immovable object, Hazel mused.

As she returned to the driver's side door, she glanced at Julie, who was still watching fearfully from beside the van. Hazel shrugged. She tried the handle and the door opened. Putting a knee on the edge of the seat, she was just about to lean inside when she heard a soft moaning noise.

She jerked back and looked at Julie. 'Did you hear that?' she whispered.

Julie nodded. 'It came from over there,' she whispered back, pointing towards the far side of the car.

Tightening her grip on the bat even harder, Hazel crept around the back of the car. Then, crouching low, she raised the weapon above her head in readiness to strike, took a deep breath and leapt out.

Sitting on the grass with her back to the passenger side door was a young woman, discernibly shivering, her head hung low. Her long blonde hair was matted with blood and the fur collar on her pale blue Parka was stained with it.

Hazel lowered the bat, hurried forward and bent down. 'Oh my God, are you okay?'

With hindsight it was an absurd thing to say, for very clearly the woman wasn't okay. She slowly raised her head and Hazel saw that her whole face was caked in dried blood.

'What time is it?' The voice was slightly slurred.

'The time?' Hazel glanced at her watch. 'Almost ten.'

'Almost ten,' the woman repeated slowly and very precisely. She let out a little sigh. 'I must be a bit late.'

Hazel frowned and looked into the woman's eyes. The pupils in the pretty green eyes were dilated.

'Is she okay?' a voice said shakily from behind them.

Hazel looked back over her shoulder to see Julie standing at the rear of the car.

'She's hurt,' Hazel said. 'I think it's quite bad. She's covered in blood and she doesn't seem to be very with it.' She turned back to the woman. 'How long have you been here, lovey?'

'About…' She paused for a moment, clearly having trouble processing the question. 'About… Sorry, what time did you say it was?'

'Almost ten.'

'I think my Mum will…' The woman dropped her head again, her chin rested on her sternum and she muttered groggily, '…she'll be worried about me.'

Hazel stood up. 'Go and open the side door on the van, Jules.'

Julie hesitated. 'Is this a good idea? I mean…'

'Please. Just go and open the door.'

Although she looked distinctly unhappy about it, Julie hurried back to the van.

'Do you think you can get up, love?'

The woman raised her head a little and nodded. 'I think so.'

With Hazel's help, she got unsteadily to her feet. As she did so, a mobile phone slipped off her lap and dropped onto the grass. With one arm supporting the woman, Hazel carefully bent down, picked it up and slipped it into her pocket.

The woman was hobbling badly – a tear in her jeans beside the knee was sodden in blood – and she winced with every step she took, but with Hazel's arm looped around her waist, they carefully managed to make their way across to the van, where Julie was waiting beside the open side door. As they got there, Julie stood well back to give them plenty of room and Hazel helped the woman inside.

Sitting on the couch, she seemed to be a little more lucid.

'Can you tell me your name?' Hazel asked.

The woman nodded slowly. 'Sarah.'

'Do you remember what happened to you, Sarah?'

'A car ran me off the road,' the woman replied. She was still shaking. 'It was so dark and the headlights dazzled me. He didn't even stop to see if I was alright. I tried to call 999, but the line was dead.'

Hazel glanced at Julie, who was hovering in the open doorway. 'That sounds familiar. There's a first aid kit in the glove box, Jules. Can you grab it for me please?'

'Okay.' Julie nodded and went to get it.

'My friend's just going to get the first aid kit,' Hazel said. 'We'll clean you up a bit. Then I'll get you a blanket, you're shivering.'

'I can't find it!' Julie's voice called out. 'Where did you say it was?'

Hazel put her hand on Sarah's arm. 'I won't be a moment. Are you going to be okay?'

Sarah nodded slowly and lowered her head again.

As Hazel hopped out she saw that Julie was standing at the passenger side door, beckoning to her urgently.

Hazel walked over. 'What's the matter? I told you, it's in the glove box.'

'It's not the first aid kit,' Julie said in hushed tones.

'What then?'

Julie looked awkward. 'I'm sorry, but I'm really not comfortable with this.'

Hazel frowned. 'With what?'

'Helping this girl. I mean, I know we *have* to do something to help her, but what if she's got the virus? She's covered in blood, for Lord's sake.'

'Don't worry,' Hazel said. 'Just get the first aid kit and I'll attend to her.'

'But if she has got the virus *you* might catch it!'

'Please, Jules,' Hazel looked at her earnestly. 'You said it yourself, we have to do something.'

'Okay, okay,' Julie agreed, though she evidently still had reservations. 'Just don't say I didn't warn you.'

Hazel afforded her friend a wink. 'Duly warned.' She turned to go back. 'Oh, and there should be a packet of antiseptic wipes in the glove box too. Can you bring those too please?'

Hazel climbed back into the van. Pulling the mobile phone from her pocket, she squatted down in front of Sarah. 'Here you go, lovey. You dropped your phone.'

Sarah raised her head. There was definitely a little more life in her eyes now, Hazel thought.

'Thank you. The battery's dead.' Sarah took the phone from her.

Julie appeared with the first aid kit and the packet of antiseptic wipes. She set them down on the floor in the open doorway, and then backed off a few paces.

Hazel opened the box and pulled out a pair of latex gloves. Snapping them on, she smiled at Julie – 'It'll be fine.' – then turned to attend to Sarah. 'Okay, let's see if we can clean you up a wee bit. Let's get this off

180

first.' She helped Sarah to remove her jacket. Then, pulling an antiseptic wipe from the packet, she carefully began to dab away the dried blood from Sarah's face. 'You've got a really nasty cut,' she said as she gently parted Sarah's hair to examine her scalp.

Sarah winced at the sting of the alcohol in the wipe. 'I banged my head in the crash.'

As carefully as she was able, Hazel finished cleaning up the blood and stood up. 'There,' she said, smiling. 'Almost good as new.'

'Thank you,' Sarah said.

Hazel pulled down a blanket from the rack above the couch and tucked it around Sarah's shoulders.

She nodded appreciatively. 'Thank you.'

'Where were you heading?'

'I'm…' As she was about to reply Sarah broke into a hacking cough.

A look of dismay appeared on Julie's face and she took another couple of steps away from the door.

'Would you like some water?' Hazel said.

Sarah's face filled with horror. 'No!' she managed to splutter.

Slightly taken aback by the defensive reaction, Hazel stood up and picked up a bottle of water from the counter. 'It's okay, we've got plenty.'

At the sight of the unopened bottle, the fear ebbed away and Sarah nodded. 'Okay,' she said quietly. 'Thank you.'

Hazel unscrewed the top and handed her the bottle. She took a couple of small sips and then, apparently satisfied, followed up with a big mouthful.

'So where exactly are you headed?'

181

'I'm going to see my Mum.'

Julie stepped back up to the open doorway. 'But everyone is supposed to be confined to their homes. Nobody's allowed to see anyone, not even relatives.'

'I know,' Sarah said. 'It's just…' She paused.

'It's okay,' Hazel said, smiling at Sarah. 'We didn't want to stay locked up for a month either.'

'It's not that. My husband, Paul died from the virus right in front of me.'

Julie put a hand to her mouth. 'I'm so sorry.' Her face conveyed compassion, but she involuntarily stepped away again.

'It's fine. He was… I mean, we were… well, it doesn't matter. I called 999, but it just kept ringing and ringing. I kept trying and trying and I was about to give up when I actually got through. A man took my details and a police car came. There were two policemen, they took one look at Paul's body and said it looked like he'd probably been infected by the virus. They took a statement from me – they said I wasn't being accused of anything, it was just procedure – and then some men came in those radioactive type suits and took him away.'

Hazel frowned. 'Weren't they concerned you might have it?'

Sarah shook her head. 'No, it was weird. I thought they would have wanted me to go with them – for tests, you know, just to be sure I hadn't got it – but they said that wasn't necessary and that someone would be in touch about Paul soon. So I went to bed. I slept through the whole night soundlessly. I haven't slept that well for years.' She almost smiled. 'Shock I suppose. When

I got up I sort of went into autopilot and I cleaned the place top to bottom, I mean *really* thoroughly. But when I was done I didn't know what to do with myself. I was suddenly alone in the flat and I knew I just had to get out. I couldn't stay there. Not after...'

Sarah trailed off. She looked as if she was about to cry.

Hazel put a comforting hand on her knee. 'I understand. But what Jules said is right. No-one's permitted to leave their home. If you'd been caught out on the road you could have been in serious trouble.'

'I needed to be with my Mum.'

'Sure,' Hazel said. 'Does she know you're coming?'

'Before they said we had to stay in our homes I was due to go and visit her anyway. She's in a care home in Hartlepool. I tried calling them so many times, but they just weren't answering. I'm *so* worried.'

'I'm sure she's fine,' Hazel said. She hoped that she sounded more assured of that than she felt. 'There are all sorts of problems with the phone lines at the moment.'

'It's only 999 that...' Julie trailed off as Hazel gave her a hard look.

'Hey, listen,' Hazel said cheerfully. 'You say you need to get to Hartlepool?'

Sarah nodded and took another mouthful of water.

'We're headed to Ripon. We know some really nice people there and I'm sure one of them would be willing to get you to your mum.'

'Really?' Sarah smiled. 'You'd do that for me?'

'We'd be delighted, wouldn't we Jules?'

183

Julie grimaced and beckoned Hazel to the door. 'Don't you think we ought to be trying to get her to a hospital?' she said quietly.

'If it wasn't for the fact that we'd almost certainly be turned away, I'd agree. But…'

'No! I don't want to go to hospital!' Sarah's tone was adamant.

'It's okay, we won't take you to a hospital if you don't want to go,' Hazel said. 'Do you have any luggage with you?'

'Just a small suitcase.'

'Okay,' Hazel said. The blanket had fallen loose from Sarah's shoulders, so Hazel tucked it up around her. 'You stay here and keep warm, I'll fetch it.'

Sarah shook her head. 'No, I can manage. I'm feeling much better now.'

Hazel wasn't convinced. 'Are you sure? You still look very pale.'

'No, really, I'm fine.'

Still with the blanket draped across her shoulders, Sarah shakily stepped out of the van. Julie stood well back, giving her plenty of room.

Hazel peeled off the latex gloves and dropped them into a carrier bag, adding the blood-stained wipes. She tied a knot in the top and dropped it on the counter, to be disposed of later, then turned to see Julie in the doorway watching her.

'You're not seriously thinking of taking her with us?' Julie whispered with an undisguised hint of annoyance. 'She's just told us her husband died from the virus. Surely if he had it then she's got it too!'

184

Hazel too was getting annoyed now. 'What would you have me do? We can't just leave her here, she needs our help.'

'I really don't want to be the bad guy here, but isn't there something else we could do?'

Hazel frowned. 'Such as...?'

Julie shook her head. 'I don't know, I...'

'Exactly. It'll be okay. We'll be sitting up front, she can stay back here. We're going to be at Ash's in a few hours anyway.'

Julie nodded slowly. 'I know it's the right thing to do really. I'm sorry.'

Hazel smiled at her appreciatively. 'There's no need to apologise. I didn't mean to sound like I'm disregarding your concerns. I'm not that sure either. It's just I don't see what other option we have that would let me live with myself later.'

Julie smiled. 'I'll make up the bed.'

'Thanks, Jules. Just put a fresh sheet on, the duvet will be fine. I'll go check she can manage with that case.'

Hazel stepped out of the van and saw Sarah over by her car, struggling to get a large suitcase out of the boot. Hazel hurried over – 'Here, let me,' she said firmly – and as she took the case from Sarah she almost dropped it. 'Crikey, that's heavy. I thought you said it was a *small* case!'

'Sorry. And it's a bit heavier than I remembered. I packed quite a bit. I'm not sure I can bring myself to go back to that flat any time soon.'

'It's fine,' Hazel said.

She lugged the case back to the van and got to the side door as Julie stepped out. She gave Sarah a weak smile and went over and opened the passenger door. She picked up Pip from the seat and scrambled in, then with a last glance back at Hazel she shut the door.

'We'll be in Ripon soon.' Hazel slid the case in through the side door and climbed in. Making a little ooof sound she lifted the case onto the counter, but Sarah paused in the doorway.

'I, er…,' she started, then faltered.

'What's the matter?' Hazel asked.

'I hope I'm not being an inconvenience.'

Hazel smiled warmly. 'Of course you aren't. Now, come on, get yourself inside.'

Sarah stepped in. 'Only I can see your friend isn't very happy and I get the feeling it might be me.'

Hazel put a reassuring hand on Sarah's shoulder. 'Jules is just a bag of nerves about everything at the moment. It's understandable with what's going on. But we're more than happy to have you come along with us, okay?'

Sarah smiled.

'Right, let's sort you out some clean clothes.'

'No,' Sarah said. 'I'll sort myself out.'

Hazel unzipped the suitcase anyway and raised her eyebrows at the sight of the contents. There was a vast array of materialistic things inside but scarcely more than one or two pieces of clothing. She frowned. 'You didn't pack many clothes.'

'I wasn't thinking straight and, er… I didn't have anything worth bringing,' Sarah said unconvincingly. Of course, she hadn't packed the case the previous day

186

at all. It had been her emergency departure kit, secreted away at the back of the closet for several years. And as ridiculous as it seemed given the whole situation now, back then she genuinely hadn't considered clothing.

'Don't worry,' Hazel said. She pointed to a small closet. 'There are some clean clothes in there.' She laughed. 'They'll probably be a rubbish fit, but help yourself.' She gestured to the bed. 'Then you can lay yourself down for a bit and try to get some rest.'

'Thank you. You've been so kind,' Sarah said tearfully.

Hazel nodded, stepped out and closed the door.

When Hazel was gone, Sarah gingerly touched the back of her head and winced, sucking in air through her gritted teeth. Then she went to the closet.

Looking through, she selected a pair of jeans and a loose-fitting sweater. She held the jeans up against herself. They were a little long, but they would have to do.

She sat down on the bed, put the clothes beside her and started to unbutton her shirt.

The skies had turned dark and as Hazel jumped into the driver's seat and started the engine it began to rain.

'Come on, then,' she said to Julie, who was sitting with Pip on her lap. 'We need to get moving again. If we only stop off for a wee, we should make it to Ripon by this evening.'

CHAPTER 16

The faces of the people seated in the Downing Street boardroom reflected the evident black mood of the Prime Minister.

'Firstly, let me thank you all for coming in at such short notice.' For a man under immense pressure, Stirling was addressing his colleagues in a remarkably calm manner, but his grim expression spoke volumes. 'There has been a development,' he continued. 'I regret to inform you that the breach of confidence which we were able to shut down yesterday morning failed to seal the lid as we'd hoped. Damning information was leaked further and we were unable to intercept it in time.'

Professor Walsh listened with interest to what Stirling was saying. There was a muttering of worried voices from the other assembled men and women.

'It's all over the bloody internet now,' Stirling seethed through gritted teeth.

Simpson's eyes filled with alarm. 'Dear God, Prime Minister. What's going to happen to me?'

Stirling peered at the man with mild disdain. 'To *you*, Health Secretary?'

'Sorry, I mean to *us*.'

The equanimity returned. 'Nothing,' Stirling said. 'That's why I summoned you all here. I want to assure you that nothing has changed and we will get this under control.'

'But if our agenda is out in the public domain,' Simpson persisted, 'surely we'll…'

Stirling raised a hand to silence him. 'Our primary focus now is to eliminate these troublemakers. I have the best PR team available working on damage limitation protocols. It's not difficult to sell the public on the suggestion that any unsubstantiated information leak is a work of fiction, nothing more than the underhanded machinations of conspiracy zealots. Additionally I shall be broadcasting a message to the nation later which will further salvage the situation.'

Everyone around the table remained silent, but nodded their approval.

Simpson was still rattled. He stood up. 'But what about that man some of the tabloids reported on this morning? He'd been working from home for the past three weeks due to a knee injury. He hadn't been out of the house, yet he contracted…' – he made little air quotes with his fingers – '…"the virus". They're questioning how that's possible when he hadn't been in contact with anyone for weeks. How could we have made such a potentially dangerous oversight? How…'

Stirling sat watching him, patiently waiting for him to pause for breath.

But Simpson wasn't finished yet. 'And what about the children?'

'It's not aimed at children,' Walsh interjected.

'But what about that little boy, the one in Mile End?'

Walsh stroked his chin thoughtfully. 'He was obviously defective.'

'*Defective*?!' Simpson exclaimed.

189

'Precisely,' Walsh said. 'I forget what was wrong with him, but it's doubtful he'd have lived very long anyway. GX-23 just gave him a helping hand.'

Simpson looked at the other people seated around the table. 'Am I the only one concerned about this?'

There was no response.

'*Mr* Simpson!' Stirling's controlled façade slipped a little further. 'I've listened to you. Now you listen to me. I have said we will get the situation under control and that means *we will get the situation under control*. Have I made myself clear?'

Simpson glanced around the table again as if he was still expecting support. All the faces looked equally worried, but not one person met his eye.

Stirling was sat looking at his Health Secretary with a demanding expression on his face, impatiently waiting for compliance.

With undisguised reluctance, Simpson nodded and slumped back into his seat like a chastised child. 'Yes, Prime Minister.'

Stirling smiled at him. 'Good. We'll speak privately after the meeting, Michael.' He cleared his throat and turned his attention back to everyone else. 'Now, regardless of my confidence in our PR bods, I still think that prudence is of the essence.' He looked at Professor Walsh. 'David, you need to return to Cambridge and ensure that anything that might remotely make us appear culpable is secure.'

'There's nothing to worry about,' Walsh said calmly. 'Everything relating to GX-23 is safely under lock and key.'

'Good. If increasing the dosage as we discussed doesn't sort things out swiftly enough, the next step will be to roll out a vaccination programme and we'll simply infuse the vaccine with the GX-23 concentrate.'

Walsh smiled. 'An excellent idea, Prime Minister. But how can we be sure that people will be on board with vaccinations, especially after their reluctance in the past? There are a lot of anti-vaxxers out there.'

'Simple,' Stirling said, smiling confidently. 'Making it mandatory will take care of that.'

'How exactly will *that* work?' Simpson asked. 'You can't *force* people to have vaccinations!'

Stirling gave him a dismissive look. 'I think you'll find I can, Michael. One of the many benefits of not being answerable to Brussels for the past five years: I can do whatever I damned well want. God bless Brexit! To answer your question though, if we penalise any refusal to be vaccinated by removing people's freedom of movement – no travel, no leisure activities, no large gatherings in pubs, clubs, theatres – they'll be falling over themselves to get jabbed, you mark my words. We can even make it obligatory that workplaces dismiss employees who refuse to be vaccinated.'

Walsh nodded his head approvingly. 'Inspired.'

'Thank you, David. I think so too,' Stirling said as he turned to face Mathers. 'Now, you, General.'

The officer had a distinctly smug expression on his face.

Stirling brought his clenched fist down hard on the table. 'Get these *fucking* riots under control!' he exploded.

191

Not wishing to appear in front of the assembly as if this outburst bothered him, Mathers maintained a fixed smile. But his eyes betrayed the disquiet at the admonishment and the corner of his mouth twitched. He nodded politely. 'Immediately, Prime Minister.'

'Good.' Once again Stirling regained his composure and cast his eyes around the room. 'Any questions, ladies and gentlemen?'

There was no reply.

'Then that will be all for now.' Stirling looked at Simpson. 'Michael, we'll have that quick word now. The rest of you may leave.'

Stirling officiously shuffled the paperwork in front of him while everyone except Simpson got up and left the room.

As the door closed, Stirling let out a sigh, flopped back in his chair and cradled his head in his hands. 'Fuck.'

Simpson stared at the Prime Minister apprehensively, although the fact the cracks were beginning to show was the least of his concerns right now.

'I apologise for losing my temper with you just now, Michael. It's been a bit of a stressful start to the day, hasn't it?'

'I understand, Prime Minister.'

'It's that idiot Mathers who's really testing my patience right now.'

Simpson nodded. 'I concur he doesn't appear to have ring-fenced the riots at all. We can't accept ineptitude from our military.'

'Come.' Stirling stood up abruptly. 'Let's go to my office and have a drink.'

They left the boardroom in silence and went along the corridor and up a level to Stirling's inner sanctum.

'Close the door and take a seat, Michael,' Stirling said as he went over to the polished mahogany drinks cabinet behind his desk. 'Scotch?'

'Please.'

With a soft click, the door closed behind him and Simpson crossed to the window overlooking Downing Street where he settled himself in one of the twin merlot leather armchairs.

'Ice or water?'

'Water please.' Simpson chuckled. 'Provided it's bottled.'

Stirling smiled. 'Naturally.' He poured liberal measures of Scotch into two tumblers, added a splash of water from an unmarked bottle, then went over to join Simpson. Handing his colleague one of the glasses, he settled himself in the opposite armchair and put his own glass down on the table beside him. 'There's something we need to discuss, Michael.'

'If it's about what I said in the meeting…'

Stirling shook his head. 'It's more than that, Michael. I'm a little worried about you. I've been detecting the whiff of dissension for a day or two now.'

Simpson looked a little uncomfortable. 'Dissension, Prime Minister?'

'Tell me I'm wrong.'

'Not dissension. Just… well, concerns really. But I'd like to clear the air and if I got a little agitated just now I unreservedly apologise.'

193

Stirling held up a hand. 'Nonsense, old boy, don't give it another second's thought.' His piercing eyes watched as the Health Minister took a sip from his glass. 'The fact of the matter is that what you said in there a few minutes ago is correct. There are indeed scenarios emerging that weren't factored in to our initial plans. But we shall deal with them as we encounter them in a calm and discreet manner.'

Simpson took another sip of his Scotch. 'So now people are beginning to ask questions, we're able to provide acceptable answers, yes?'

Stirling smiled. 'In my 35 years in politics, Michael, I've yet to encounter a problem for which I couldn't find an answer. Come along, drink up and have another.'

As Simpson drained his glass, Stirling picked up his own and cradled it between his hands. 'Take the problem we were discussing with the GX-23 concentrate being markedly diluted as it's fed through the reservoirs.'

'Oh yes.' Simpson frowned. 'Malcolm got hot under the collar over the suggestion that upping the dosage to increase its efficiency would result in additional unnecessary fatalities.'

'Precisely. But who's to say what is and isn't necessary? Malcolm wasn't looking at the bigger picture.' Stirling relieved Simpson of his empty tumbler and handed his untouched one over. 'Here, take mine. I'll fix myself another.' He stood up and went back to the drinks cabinet. 'As I explained to him, in any campaign of this magnitude there is always going to be collateral damage. It's regrettable, of course, but if it solves a problem I believe it's defensible. Do you not agree?'

Simpson took a large draught from his second glass of Scotch. 'I'm not sure I do, Prime Minister.'

'Please, no formalities here. It's Cameron.'

'I mean, *are* additional deaths really justifiable? The whole point of our plan was to...' he paused and screwed up his eyes.

'Is everything alright there, Michael?'

Simpson opened his eyes again. 'Yes, sorry, Prime... I mean Cameron. I feel a little light-headed. Not used to drinking this early in the day.' He chuckled and set down his glass on the table. 'Better not have any more.'

Stirling squinted at his colleague. Leaving the empty glass on the cabinet he crossed back to his armchair and sat down. 'You see, as far as I'm concerned, there is nothing – and I mean *nothing* – that isn't justifiable if it achieves the results one seeks. Yes, this business about the fellow contracting the virus while working from home is a bit of a bugger, but all we need to do is give the media something more newsworthy to focus their attention on and it's a problem solved.'

Simpson's vision was beginning to blur and a sheen of sweat had formed on his forehead. 'You...' He coughed. 'You have something in mind to distract them, Cameron?'

'Indeed I do,' Stirling said quietly. 'Not going to finish your Scotch, Michael?'

Simpson's breathing had become laboured and his face had drained of colour. 'No, I'm sorry, Cameron. I really don't feel too well.'

'I must say you don't *look* well.'

Simpson's fingers scrabbled at his collar in an attempt to loosen his tie. 'It's so hot in here…'

'I'm very comfortable myself. Would you like to hear what my idea is?'

Simpson didn't reply. He appeared to be struggling to talk.

'Well, I'll tell you anyway,' Stirling continued. He picked up the half-consumed glass of Scotch and stood up. 'I was thinking we need a big story. Give the papers something to really get their gnashers into. Something that will make the public forget all about old Johnny knee injury in the blink of an eye.' He crossed to the drinks cabinet and set down the glass. 'We need a headline, of course. How does this sound?' He turned to face Simpson, raised his arms and made a theatrical sweeping gesture with both hands. "Virus Strikes Downing Street!"'

He looked at Simpson for approval. The man was slumped sideways in the chair, one arm hanging limply, the tips of his fingers brushing the floor. His eyes were closed, there were traces of pink foam around his lips and his body was twitching slightly.

'No?' Stirling frowned. 'No, you're probably right. It is a bit vague, isn't it? After all, a headline like that could be… what do they call it, clickbait? It could just mean one of the cleaners died.' He laughed. 'We need something much more specific. More *dramatic*. Something guaranteed to make all the doubting

196

Thomas's sit up and pay attention.' He walked to the window and looked out into the street. Pursing his lips, he thought for a moment. 'I've got it!' He spun round. 'You're going to like this, Michael, it's really good.' He raised his arms and repeated the sweeping gesture. '"ORACULTE Claims Life of Health Minister!" Now, *that's* what I call a headline; a 24-carat shocker. Just imagine the fear that will instil among the great unwashed. The man who's been trying to protect them from the killer virus has fallen victim to it himself!' His dark eyes glittering with excitement, he looked at Simpson. 'What do you reckon?'

Simpson didn't answer. The twitching was almost imperceptible now.

Stirling looked down at his colleague. 'If you can think of something punchier I'm open to suggestions.' He bent and leaned in close to Simpson's ear. 'Can you hear me, Michael?'

Simpson made a quiet, incoherent gurgling sound.

Stirling stood upright again. 'Of course, it's not down to me, but if it were I'd personally add a subheading, something along the lines of "Simpson Executed for Despicable Display of Cowardice". Although I suppose that would sound a bit vindictive, wouldn't it?' He chuckled.

There was no response from Simpson. His body had fallen still.

'It's going to be one hell of a story though,' Stirling said enthusiastically. 'Too bad you won't be around to read it.' Suddenly he screwed up his face and recoiled. He put a hand to his nose. 'Oh, for God's sake, man, have you soiled yourself? These armchairs were bloody expensive!'

Scowling, he turned away, walked over to his desk and picked up the phone. Punching a couple of buttons he spoke into the receiver. 'Pass this message through to Professor Walsh immediately: The efficacy of GX-23 in pure concentrate form is most impressive...' – he glanced contemptuously at Simpson's corpse – '...albeit a tad messy. And when you've done that send in someone to clean up my office.'

CHAPTER 17

Following the dramatic incident with Sarah, once they finally got moving again, Hazel and Julie hadn't encountered any more delays. In fact, Hazel had been surprised by just how few other vehicles there were on the road. She'd anticipated they would be flagged down and pulled over at least once, and later admitted to Julie that, despite her gung-ho approach to the whole trip, she wasn't sure how she would have handled it if they had been. Just the same, even with a mere two bathroom stops – and a quick check on Sarah, who'd been sound asleep on both occasions – it was almost dark as they hit the outskirts of the medieval city of Ripon.

They had been listening to the soothing sounds of Classic FM all afternoon – it brought a little bit of sanity back to the world, or so Julie said – and, as Debussy's "Clair de Lune" filled the cab an hour earlier, she had succumbed to sleep.

Now, as they drove past the entrance to Ripon's impressive Cathedral with its towering majesty brightly illuminated against the night sky, and the stirring notes of Orff's "O Fortuna" emanated from the radio, Hazel felt a little shiver go up her spine.

Julie was still dozing in the passenger seat with Pip curled up on her lap and she remained that way as they covered the last leg of their journey to the boatyard on the canal. The rain had persisted all day, but by the time they took a sharp turn off the main road onto a narrow, dirt track it had ebbed to a light drizzle.

The camper van crawled up the trail, squelching through the mud and puddles and nosing its way gently through a fountain of low-hanging branches.

They bumped over a ridge in the track and Julie's eyes flickered open. 'Sorry, I didn't mean to nod off.'

Hazel smiled. 'Don't worry about it.'

'How long was I gone for?'

'Not long. You missed the Cathedral though. It looked beautiful all lit up.'

Julie stretched and yawned and peered out of the window into the darkness. 'Where are we?'

'We're almost there.'

They eased round a bend in the track and the headlights fell upon a set of closed metal gates topped with barbed wire that bisected the road ahead.

'Scratch that. We're here.'

Hazel eased off on the accelerator and they slowed to a halt a few yards short of the gates.

Julie looked at her nervously. 'Are you sure we're in the right place?'

'One hundred percent. They've put new gates up since I was last here, but this is it.' Hazel picked up her mobile phone from the dashboard and turned it on. 'I won't be a moment,' she said. Leaving the engine running, she opened the door and got out. She walked up to the gates and located the keypad on the wooden post. Briefly consulting a text on her phone, she switched it off again, then reached up and punched a seven-digit code into the keypad.

There was an electronic buzz, followed by a metallic clanking sound, and Hazel stood well back as the twin gates jerked once and slowly parted, opening up to reveal a further stretch of gravelled track that snaked away into the inky darkness.

She climbed back into the van, slammed the door and deposited her phone on the dashboard. 'Right. It's only about another 400 feet. Onward.'

The van edged carefully forward and passed through with only a couple of inches to spare on either side, and the gates juddered noisily shut behind them.

They hadn't gone far before little dots of light became visible through the trees ahead. Hazel smiled at Julie. 'That's it. That's the boatyard.' No sooner had the words left her mouth than the headlights picked out a hunched figure bundled up in a coat and a beanie; whoever it was, they were strolling down the track towards the van. As the person came closer it became apparent it was a man. He raised an arm to shield his eyes from the dazzle of the headlights and Hazel quickly switched them to low beam. 'I think it's Ash,' she said excitedly.

She gently braked and the van came to a stop.

As Ash approached the driver's side, Hazel wound down the window.

'Watchya, little sis.' Ash stepped up close and pushed the black beanie back on his forehead. He was a good-looking man, but his weathered, freckled face and a full beard that looked as if it was overdue a trim made it impossible to age him with any accuracy. 'Been far too long,' he said.

'Well, aren't you a sight for sore eyes,' Hazel said. 'Lovin' the face fuzz, bro.'

Ash laughed and rubbed the beard vigorously. 'Ah, yeah. By special request.' He leaned forward and gave Hazel a peck on the cheek, brushing his beard purposefully against her.

'Ooh, I thought it would be all bristly, but it's lovely and soft,' Hazel said.

'Isn't it though?' His eyes looked past her and fell upon Julie. 'Who's *this* then?' he asked sternly.

Hazel rolled her eyes. 'You know *exactly* who it is.' She turned her head towards Julie. 'He's just messing with you. He knows you were coming with me.' She looked back at Ash. 'It's my friend Julie.'

Ash grinned. 'Hello to you, Hazel's friend Julie,' he said jovially. 'Got a bit fed up with this confinement lark, eh?'

Julie smiled. 'Somewhat. Very pleased to meet you, I've heard a lot about you.' She reached out a hand across Hazel and Ash took it in his and shook it. The grip was firm.

'Oh, have you now?' He winked. 'Nothin' good I hope?'

Julie laughed.

Ash's eyes dropped down. 'And who's he?'

Julie looked down at her lap. 'Oh, this little terror? *He* is a *she*. This is Pip.'

'Well, hello there young Pip!' Ash released Julie's hand and looked at Hazel. 'Come on then. It's brass monkeys out here tonight. Follow me and I'll show you where to park.'

202

He turned away and as he set off back up the track Hazel wound the window back up.

'He seems nice,' Julie said.

'Yeah, he's a good guy. It's really nice to see him again. Time gets away from you, and before you know it the months have become years.'

Fifty yards along, the track opened out into a small enclosure where several shabby-looking vehicles were parked up. The only light came from the glow of a single lamp, swaying gently in the evening breeze, hanging on a wooden pole.

Ash was stood on the far side of the enclosure and he waved his arms, gesturing Hazel over into the corner. With two attempts she managed to reverse the van into the tight space between a high wooden fence on Julie's side and a somewhat dilapidated-looking camper van on the driver side.

Shutting off the engine, Hazel climbed out. Somewhere in the distance there was the muffled sound of music and voices and raucous laughter. As Ash stepped over towards her, Hazel threw her arms around him and held him close. When she looked up into his face he saw tears in her eyes.

Ash took a step away from her. 'Come on now, what's with the waterworks?'

Hazel sniffed and wiped her eyes on the sleeve of her jacket. 'Sorry. It's been so long.'

Ash smiled. His eyes were wet too. 'Stop it or you'll set me off.'

'I meant to keep in touch more often, really I did.'

Ash put an arm around her shoulders. The embrace felt good. 'You'll get no judgement from me. I'm equally as guilty, if not more so. It's just... well, life I suppose. Gets in the way of stuff that really matters. It's a bit of a bugger, this life thing, isn't it?'

Hazel smiled. 'It is. But I really am sorry.'

'No apology necessary. I don't want to hear another word about it. We're here together now and that's all that matters.'

While Ash and Hazel were talking, Julie had got out of the van and was standing by the passenger side headlight, holding Pip and looking a little awkward.

Hazel glanced up and saw her and felt grateful that her friend was standing back to let her have a moment with Ash. She beckoned to her. 'Hey, come on, don't be shy. Come and meet my bro.'

Julie came over and stopped a few feet away. Ash stepped towards her with his arms open wide, but she took a pace back. Ash stopped. 'I don't bite.'

Forcing a smile, Julie said, 'Please don't be offended. It's this whole virus thing. You can't be too careful.'

'Nobody here's got a trace of any virus, I assure you.' He paused and frowned. 'Well, except for Big Martha. She has this permanent cold thing going on. If you ask me it's sinuses, but she won't be having it, insists it's a cold. A martyr to her ailments is Big Martha. You'll love her though. Salt of the earth.'

Julie looked unconvinced.

'Anyway,' Ash continued. 'Apart from her there's naught here in the way of viruses to go worrying yourself about.' He took a step forward. 'So come on, how about a hug?'

Julie took another pace away from him and held Pip tightly to her chest in a protective stance. 'Just a moment. How do you know *I* haven't got it?'

Ash stopped short again.

Hazel didn't say anything, but she was watching the scene unfold with amusement.

'Hmmm,' Ash said thoughtfully. 'That's a good point.' He looked Julie up and down. 'You don't *look* ill.' He frowned. '*Have* you got it?'

'No, of course not. But you didn't know that when you tried to…'

'That's good enough for me then,' Ash said breezily. Without giving Julie the chance to back away any further, he stepped briskly forwards and wrapped his arms around both her and Pip. 'Group hug!' he exclaimed.

Pip let out a little yap and Ash stepped back. 'Sorry, young lady, didn't mean to crush you.' He reached down and rubbed Pip's head. 'We might just have a few doggy treats laying around here somewhere. Sound good?' The little dog squirmed in Julie's arms and eagerly licked Ash's hand.

He leant forward and gave Julie a little peck on the cheek. 'Welcome to the Nuthouse. There aren't nearly enough attractive ladies here.'

Julie looked a little embarrassed, but she smiled anyway. 'It's, er… nice to be here.'

Even in the dark Hazel could see her friend was secretly rather flattered by her brother's display of bonhomie.

'Come on,' Ash said. 'You must both be gagging for a drink. Club Tropicana is fully stocked.'

205

Hazel's eyes lit up and she laughed. 'I'm assuming the drinks *still* aren't free?'

Ash stepped over and put his arm around her shoulders. 'Nope. And the sea's still missing.'

'The sea's missing?' Julie said.

Ash and Hazel turned to look at her. 'It's a joke,' Hazel said.

Julie looked bemused.

Hazel grinned. 'Club Tropicana? George Michael and Andrew Ridgeley? You know, Wham?' She sashayed her hips.

Julie shrugged and shook her head. 'I've heard of Wham, but I don't remember that song.'

Ash chuckled. 'It's one a lot of George Michael's fans – nutters, some of them, if you ask me – are still trying to forget! Anyway, all you need to know is *our* Club Tropicana is the finest watering hole in these parts.'

'Wait a minute, isn't it the *only* watering hole in these parts?' Hazel said.

'Stop splitting hairs, sis. The drinks are getting warm.'

As they started to walk off across the enclosure, Hazel faltered. 'Oh, hang on! We've got someone else with us. She's in the back of the van.'

Ash raised an eyebrow. 'Oh?'

'Yeah, sorry, I couldn't really let you know in advance,' Hazel said. 'It's a bit of a story really, but in a nutshell we came across an accident on the road near Blechnum this morning, a young woman on her own. She was in quite a bad way. I patched her up, and under normal circumstances I'd have taken her to a hospital.

206

But we shouldn't have been out on the road ourselves and when I actually mentioned hospital she got quite defensive, didn't want to know.'

Ash grinned. 'Well, go get her, see if she wants to join us for a pint. The more the merrier!'

'I'll fetch her,' Julie said.

Hazel gave her a look of disbelief. After all the fuss you made earlier, she thought.

Julie handed Pip to Ash. 'Here, would you hold her for a moment?'

'Delighted,' Ash said, taking the dog in his arms. 'She's a little darling.'

Julie hurried to the van and wiggled through the narrow space between the two vehicles. Opening the side door, she climbed in. She reached for the light and then changed her mind. 'Sarah,' she whispered. 'Are you awake?'

There was no reply.

Deciding not to disturb her, Julie stepped back out of the van and, as quietly as she could, slid the door shut.

Hazel and Ash looked up as she reappeared from between the two vans and walked over to join them. 'She's still out for the count,' Julie said. 'I didn't like to wake her.'

'Okay,' Hazel replied. 'But she's been asleep all day. Let's go have a drink and a bite to eat. We'll wake her up when we come back and make sure she eats something.'

Julie relieved Ash of Pip.

'Come on then,' Ash said. 'The bar's only open for...' – he turned towards the lamp to get a little illumination and glanced at his watch – '…another 24 hours.'

'Are dogs allowed in your clubhouse?'

Ash grinned and ruffled Pip's head. 'Only the attractive ones.'

Hazel sniggered. 'Do you realise how perverse that sounds?'

'Hmmm,' Ash said, shaking his head. 'It does too, doesn't it? Then let's say *everyone's* welcome at Club Tropicana, man or beast.'

The two women laughed and they all set off in the direction of the music.

CHAPTER 18

The music had been coming from the clubhouse, but it inside it was so loud that it was difficult to make out exactly what it was over the sound of people – upwards of 40 of them – chatting and laughing as if the past few days of draconian restrictions had no jurisdiction here. It was the first taste of relative normality that Hazel and Julie had seen for days.

'Looks like the party started without us,' Hazel shouted at Ash, trying to make herself heard over the hubbub.

'It's always like this,' Ash chortled. 'Everyone here works hard during the day, but at night they party even harder.' Surveying the room, he spotted an empty table in the far corner of the room near the fire escape. He took Julie by the arm. 'Come on, my lovely, let's sort you out somewhere to rest your buns.'

'I think it's a bit too raucous in here for me,' Julie said. 'I can't hear myself think. Maybe I'll go and wait in the van.'

Hazel grinned and gave her a gentle nudge. 'Aw, come on, Jules. Don't be a party-pooper.'

Julie nodded reluctantly and they pushed their way through the cluster of people and commandeered the corner table. Ash and Julie took a scat, but Hazel remained standing and dug around in her pocket for her purse.

'What are you drinking, bro?' Hazel asked.

'Lime and soda, please.'

Hazel gave him a look of disbelief. 'Sorry, for a moment there I thought you said lime and soda.'

Ash chuckled. 'You heard right. Shaun got me off the booze over five years ago and I haven't touched a drop since.'

'Well done Shaun for achieving the impossible!' Hazel exclaimed. 'I'm looking forward to meeting this fella of yours at last.' She looked at Julie. 'What would you like, Jules?'

'I'll have a pint of Pilsner, please.'

Hazel grinned. 'Of course.'

'I like a woman who takes her liquor by the pint,' Ash remarked, winking at Julie. 'Shows she's made of sterling stuff.'

'I'll leave you two to get acquainted,' Hazel said, and made her way through the throng to the bar.

As she approached she noticed an old chap propped on a stool at the end of the bar. He was surrounded by people who were chatting among themselves. Wearing a navy blue sailor's cap with the emblem of an anchor in gold stitching above the peak, the man was staring into space and nursing a glass of whiskey.

Hazel moved along the bar, stepping around a couple who appeared to be inebriated; the plump, curvy woman was muttering to herself and blowing her nose loudly – I wonder if that's Big Martha, Hazel mused – whilst the man, his head nuzzled sleepily in the woman's generous cleavage, was paying no attention to whatever it was she was saying.

Hazel reached the end of the bar and tapped the old man on the shoulder. 'Don't you ever go home? You were sitting in this self same spot the last time I saw you.'

The man shuffled round on his stool and looked at her quizzically for a moment. Then his face lit up and he burst out laughing.

'Well, bugger me. Can this possibly be young Hazel I see before me?'

Hazel laughed. 'Hello, Andy.' She flung open her arms and Andy stood up to give her a big hug.

He took a pace back and looked her up and down. 'Still looking as fresh as a daisy and as beautiful as a butterfly. Sit with me.' He patted the stool next to him.

'I can't,' Hazel said apologetically. 'I'm sitting over there with Ash and a friend.'

The barman appeared and looked at Hazel. 'What can I get you?'

'A pint of Pilsner, a lime and soda, and, erm…' – she thought for a moment – 'I don't suppose you have Cherry Pepsi do you?'

The barman smiled. 'We do indeed. Draught or a bottle?'

'Draught please.'

'A pint?'

Hazel nodded. 'Please.'

'Ice with the soft drinks?'

'Not in the Pepsi, but drop a couple in the soda please.'

Hazel turned her attention back to Andy. 'So how are you doing?'

'Never been better, my dear. The fresh air here keeps me young…' – he raised his glass – '…and a

211

splash or three of the holy water keeps me frisky.' He winked at her.

Hazel laughed. 'Nothing new there then!'

'But tell me,' Andy said. 'What brings you to this neck of the woods? Checking up on that ratbag brother of yours?'

'To be honest, with everything going on in this country at the moment, I had to get away for my sanity,' Hazel said. 'I brought my friend with me too. Turned it into a bit of a road trip.' She laughed. 'Mind you, it's been far more eventful than either of us bargained for. Anyway, it'll be nice to be around some normal people for a day or two.'

Andy chuckled and drained his glass. 'You'll not find too many normal people around here, m'girl.'

'Not anywhere right now,' Hazel sighed. 'But any abnormality here has to be preferable to what's going on everywhere else. The whole country's gone to hell in a hand basket and this is a great place to get away from all that craziness.'

'I'll drink to that,' Andy said, raising his empty glass. He pulled a face. 'Well, would you look at that!' He put down the empty glass on the counter. 'When did I finish that?'

Hazel smiled and rolled her eyes. 'Something else that hasn't changed! Can I get you another?'

Andy chuckled again. 'No, no, I couldn't possibly ask you to…'

'Alright then, I won't!' Hazel said abruptly, trying not to smile.

'However,' Andy continued, theatrically patting his jacket pockets, 'since I appear to have left my wallet back at the boat, if you were to absolutely insist…'

Hazel laughed. 'Of course I insist.' The barman was just setting down her order on a tray on the counter. 'Can I add one of whatever Andy's drinking to that order please?' she said.

The barman shook his head at Andy and rolled his eyes. 'You jammy old sod!'

Andy guffawed. 'Well I've never been known to refuse a pretty lady offering to buy me a drink before and I'm certainly not about to start now.'

Hazel opened her purse and looked at the barman. 'How much is that lot?'

The barman winked at her. 'Your money's no good here.'

'No, really,' Hazel said. 'How much?'

'Not a penny. Strict orders of your brother.'

'Young Ash!' Andy's eyes lit up. 'Never in all my days have I met a more generous young man as your lovely brother. You can make mine a double please, George.'

'You'll get a single and be grateful for it,' the barman said, rolling his eyes again.

Andy cackled. 'Can't blame a man for trying!' He turned back to Hazel, who was tucking her purse back into her pocket. He put a hand on her arm. 'You'll be safe with us. There'll be none of that rioting and looting nonsense here.'

'Thank God for that!' Hazel exclaimed. As the barman set down the tumbler of whiskey on the counter, Hazel gave Andy another big hug and picked up her tray of drinks. 'Catch you a bit later, Andy.'

Andy winked at her. 'I'm an easy catch, but way harder to keep hold of, m'girl.'

As Hazel walked away, Andy downed the whiskey in one, banged down the glass and slid it across the counter. 'George!' he exclaimed, grinning at the barman. 'A man could die of thirst in this place!'

When Hazel got back to the table, she saw that a muscular young man wearing a tight-fitting T-shirt had joined Ash and Julie.

Ash stood up to relieve Hazel of the tray and gestured to the young man. 'Haze, this is my partner, Shaun.' He put the tray down on the table and Julie took her glass of Pilsner.

Shaun stood up and pushed a comma of wavy red hair back from his brow. 'So, this is the little sister Ash has been bending my ear about.' He stepped forward – 'Incoming!' – and threw his arms around Hazel. 'I was away for a few days last time you dropped by, what… about five years ago?'

'Something like that,' Hazel said.

'Well, I'm cock-o-hoop to be meeting you at last!'

Hazel pointed to the front of Shaun's T-shirt, which bore the legend You've read my shirt... that's quite enough social interaction for today!. 'Does that mean I'm not allowed to talk to you anymore tonight?'

Shaun glanced down and laughed. 'Oh, pay no heed to that. I can be a bit of an antisocial bugger, I'll not be denying it, but I always make exceptions for family.'

Hazel smiled. 'In that case, what can I get you to drink?'

'That's kind of you, but I've already got one.' He pointed to a glass of lime and soda on the table, sat back down and patted the chair next to him. 'Plonk yourself down here.'

'Could you get some water for Pip, please?' Julie said. The little dog was curled up beside her feet.

'Oh, sorry, I should have thought of that.' Hazel made her way back over to the bar.

'That was fast,' George said. 'Back for more already?'

Andy chuckled. 'She's her brother's sister, alright.'

George looked at him. 'You mind your business. Ash hasn't touched the hard stuff in years and you know it. Furthermore, the young lady's drinking Pepsi.'

Andy thought for a moment. 'Fair point,' he said. 'I'll keep my clam shut.' He pinched his thumb and forefinger together and made a little zipping motion across his mouth.

George turned his attention back to Hazel. 'So what can I get you?'

'I just wondered if I could have a bowl of water for our dog please?'

'Of course,' George said. 'We've only got bottled though.'

'Bottled is perfect,' Hazel replied.

George reached under the counter and pulled out a small bottle of Highland Spring. 'Can't be trusting that crap coming out of the taps.'

'I couldn't agree more.'

'Back in a sec,' George said and disappeared through the door at the end of the bar.

Hazel turned to Andy. 'So are we going to be getting any of the infamous Andy karaoke tonight?'

Andy mimed unzipping his lips. 'You'll have to wait and see,' he said. He held up his glass and grinned. 'I may have to load up with a couple more of these Johnnies first.'

George reappeared carrying a dessert bowl and handed it to Hazel. Thanking him, she returned to the table to find Ash and Julie rocking with laughter.

'…and all the while,' Shaun was saying, gasping for breath and struggling to get the words out through his own guffaws, 'that steaming great cockwomble Stirling and his bunch of devious cronies are probably in and out of the Soho knocking shops shagging their pasty white arses off!'

Hazel put the bowl on the floor and emptied the bottle of mineral water into it. Pip got up and sniffed at it warily, then turned away and went to sit underneath Ash's chair.

'Looks like you've made yourself a new friend, bro,' Hazel said.

Ash bent down and ruffled Pip's head. 'Us old dogs have got to stick together.'

Shaun grinned. 'Except that one's quite cute and you're a mangy old mutt.' He leant over and gave Ash a little kiss on the lips. 'But you know I loves ya anyway.'

Hazel took a seat and picked up her glass. 'So come on then, tell all. How exactly did you two end up together?'

Ash exhaled loudly. 'Blimey o'Riley, now you're asking. It's been well over five years now. It's clichéd, I guess, but when I first met Shaun he was working in a cocktail bar…'

'Not as a waitress, I hasten to add,' Shaun interjected.

Hazel giggled.

'No,' Ash continued. 'He was performing. I first set eyes on him on stage singing "Reflections of My Life".' He rested a hand on Shaun's knee. 'It was love at first sight.'

'You, couldn't resist m'gorgeous Irish charms, could you?' Shaun winked at Hazel. 'He still can't, of course. It's sheer animal magnetism. A heavy burden, I don't mind telling you.' He sighed. 'But I've learned to live with it.' He saw the expression on Ash's face and gave him another quick kiss. 'I've got this brother of yours right where I want him.' He tapped the palm of his hand.

'He speaks the truth,' Ash said, smiling at Shaun.

Julie had been looking a little uncomfortable, but she made the effort to join in. 'So, are you two actually married then?'

'Not yet,' Ash replied. 'I've asked him a couple of times, but he's not too keen on the shackles of the marital knot. He's an advocate of free love.'

'Well I'm certainly not paying for it!' Shaun exclaimed, feigning indignance.

Much to Hazel's surprise, Julie giggled.

'Seriously though,' Shaun continued. 'I'd be the first to admit I used to be a bit of a free spirit, but my days of sowing the old wild oats are over. I said I've got Ash in the palm of my hand, but he's got me in his too.'

The two men smiled at each other affectionately and kissed again.

Hazel grinned. 'Oh, just go and get a room, for God's sake!'

Shaun picked up his drink and took a sip. 'So, what's the story with you two ladies then? Are you an item?'

Hazel laughed, but Julie looked distinctly flustered. 'Most certainly not!' She picked up her drink and took a large mouthful of the amber fluid to hide her embarrassment.

Shaun was about to say something else when a loud cheer emanated from the other side of the room.

They all turned to see Andy, clutching a microphone in one hand and a glass of whiskey in the other, stepping drunkenly up on to the dais in the corner. He selected a button on the karaoke machine, there was an eardrum-assaulting screech of feedback through the microphone, and then he launched into song.

'And now… the end is near… and I must face… the final curtain…'

'Oh no! Ash exclaimed. 'Frank Sinatra's at it again.'

Shaun winced as Andy hit a bum note. 'Frank Spencer, more like.'

Hazel could see that Julie still appeared to be flustered over Shaun's innocent remark. She leant over and whispered to her. 'He was only joking, Jules.'

'I don't think he was,' she whispered back. 'He obviously thinks we… well, you know.'

'I'm sure he doesn't. He was just asking. But it doesn't matter what he thinks,' Hazel said. 'It's great here. Just enjoy yourself.'

Ash was watching Andy with amusement. He nudged Shaun. 'When he's finished, you can get up and show him how it's done.'

'Only if the lovely Julie here will join me,' Shaun replied, winking at her. 'What d'ya say?'

'Oh I don't know about that,' Julie said nervously. 'I don't really sing. Certainly not in public.'

'Oh, come on with you, now,' Shaun said jovially. 'We'll do "Dead Ringer for Love". You can be Meatloaf, I'll be Cher."

All four of them burst out laughing, the little moment of awkwardness now all but forgotten.

'Actually,' Hazel said, 'can we save it till tomorrow? All that driving today has caught up with me. I'm bushed.'

Julie giggled. 'Who's being the party pooper now?' she said, draining her glass.

Even in the soft lighting of the clubhouse Hazel could see her friend's cheeks had taken on a distinctly rosy glow. She raised her eyebrows. '*Seriously*, Jules?'

'I'm pretty beat too,' Ash said. 'Come on, let's go back to the boat, have a quick bite to eat and get you some beds sorted out.'

'No need,' Hazel said. 'We'll get some zeds in the van.'

'You'll do no such thing,' Shaun said. 'We've got plenty of room in the boat, haven't we, m'darling?' He looked at Ash.

Ash nodded. 'And it's got to be warmer than the van.'

'And there's room for Sarah too?'

Ash nodded again. 'We can squeeze her in.'

'Okay then, thank you,' Hazel said. 'If it's alright with Jules too.'

'Of course,' Julie said, relishing the idea of a comfortable bed for the night.

As they finished up their drinks, Andy hit his crescendo – '…The record shows… I took the blows… And did it myyyyyyyyy way!' – and the room erupted in a cacophony of applause and whistling.

Andy took a bow. 'Any requests?' he asked.

Someone heckled him playfully. 'Yeah. Get off!'

Everyone laughed.

Andy grinned. 'Don't think I know that one,' he chuckled. He pressed a button on the karaoke machine. 'I think you'll all know this one though.'

'Not likely the way you sing!' the heckler shouted.

Andy ignored him. 'Feel free to join in.'

As the music started, Ash stood up. 'Time we were leaving. We'll wait for you outside while you go get your friend.'

'Don't forget your peejays,' Shaun said, winking at Julie.

They all made their way to the door, leaving the crowd to the mercy of Andy's warbling. 'When the moon hits your eye like a big pizza pie that's amore…' Andy put a hand to his ear.

'That's amore!' the crowd hollered back.

CHAPTER 19

Their arms linked, Hazel and Julie crossed the compound to the camper van. Pip was scampering along behind, trying to keep up with them.

'I feel all light-headed,' Julie said, sniggering. She was evidently a little tipsy.

Hazel laughed. She was pleased to see her friend unwind a little. 'I can't take you anywhere, can I? You only had a pint!'

'I know. I think it must be the cold air hitting me.'

'Well sober up. We can't keep Ash and Shaun hanging around outside the club all night. They'll get arrested for loitering.'

Julie laughed.

'Seriously though,' Hazel continued. 'We need to check on Sarah. I feel bad we're going to have to wake her, but we need to get her something to eat and sort out the sleeping arrangements.'

They reached the camper van, which Hazel was pleased to see was easily accessible now; the other van had gone. She slid open the side door. 'Sarah,' she said quietly.

Sarah didn't stir.

Hazel glanced back at Julie, who was holding Pip in her arms. 'Hang on,' she said, climbing into the van.

Sarah's leg was hanging out from beneath the duvet. Hazel reached down and gave it a gentle shake. 'Sarah…?'

She looked at Julie, who was now standing in the open doorway. 'She feels really cold. Something's wrong.'

'Oh, no...' Julie said quietly.

Hazel leant in close to Sarah's face and listened. 'I can't hear her breathing.' She turned to Julie, her expression showing panic. 'Go and get Ash quick.'

Julie set down Pip – 'Stay!' – and hurried off across the compound.

Hazel suddenly felt nauseous. She stepped out and leant against the side of the van, exhaling heavily. She pushed her hair back out of her face and looked down at Pip, who was sitting gazing up at her as if she understood that something bad was happening. 'You know, don't you?' Hazel said softly. Pip cocked her head. 'Yeah, you do.' She wrapped her arms tightly around herself to stave off the sudden shiver of cold that coursed through her.

A few moments later there was a sound of crunching gravel and Ash came sprinting across the compound. Shaun and Julie were hot on his tail. He skidded to a halt in front of Hazel. 'What's happened?' he asked breathlessly.

'It's Sarah, the girl we picked up earlier,' Hazel replied shakily. 'She's in the van. I think she's dead.'

'Okay,' Ash said, resting a comforting hand on her arm. 'Stay calm. Let me take a look.'

The others gathered around the open doorway and a deathly silence fell as Ash bent down beside the bed and gently rested two fingers on the side of Sarah's neck. Feeling some slight stickiness, he withdrew them.

Even in the dark he could see they were stained. 'Is there a light in here?'

'On the wall above the counter,' Hazel said.

Ash flicked on the light and Julie spotted the blood on his fingers. Putting a hand to her mouth, she turned away. Hazel put an arm round her shoulders and led her round to the front of the van.

Ash fished Sarah's wrist out from beneath the duvet and felt her pulse. Looking at Shaun, he shook his head. Then he gestured towards the front of the van. 'Can you go see they're okay?'

Shaun nodded. 'For sure.'

Shaun stepped out of sight and Ash peeled back the duvet. The blood on Sarah's neck was still slightly tacky and appeared to have emanated from a wound on her head. With care, he pulled the sweater away from her neck and his eyes fell upon a large black bruise streaked with claret that extended from the base of her neck across the top of her sternum. Lifting up the sweater from the bottom, his eyes widened as he saw that the bruise was huge; it curved over her shoulder and almost all the way down her left side, then inwards across her rib cage where the blackness turned into an ugly reddish-blue. Even to Ash's untrained eye, what he was seeing suggested the possibility of internal haemorrhaging. He shook his head and carefully pulled the sweater back down.

Standing up, he lifted the duvet high over Sarah and gently lowered it across her head. Then he climbed out of the van, slid the door firmly shut and walked round to the front, where Hazel was comforting Julie and Shaun was standing holding Pip.

223

'Sorry, sis. You were right. She's dead.'

'I'm really sorry,' Shaun said. 'Was she a good friend of yours?'

Hazel shook her head. 'No. We only met her this morning. She'd come off the road just outside of Blechnum.'

'Blechnum?' Shaun said, raising an eyebrow. 'I've heard a lot of stories about that place, a lot of bad things have happened there. I had an uncle who lived in the next village. I'm not superstitious, but if ever a place was cursed, Blechnum is that place, so it is.'

'She was going to see her mother in Hartlepool,' Hazel said. 'I promised her we'd try to help get her there. I knew she was hurt, obviously, but she was alert enough when I last spoke to her. I thought it was best she try and get some sleep. I should have known better, I should have insisted we get her to a hospital.' She was beginning to sob.

'Don't you be upsetting yourself now,' Shaun ventured. 'It's not your fault.'

Ash removed a handkerchief from his trouser pocket and handed it to Hazel. 'He's right. I only had a quick look, but she'd sustained a serious amount of body trauma. I'm no expert, but I reckon it could have led to internal bleeding. There's nothing you could have done, sis.'

'I still feel absolutely dreadful,' Hazel said, blowing her nose.

'It's my fault,' Julie said tearfully. 'I should never have left her here. When we arrived I thought she was fast asleep. If I'd checked properly…'

Ash shook his head. 'I don't think that would have made much difference.'

'Why not?' Julie said. 'We were in there...' – she pointed towards the clubhouse – '...drinking and joking around, and the poor girl's laying out here alone dying.'

'It's neither of your faults, my love,' Ash said. 'It's nobody's fault. I'm not a doctor, but I'd say she's been gone for... well, several hours at least. Some while before you arrived here, anyway. She's tucked up under that duvet, but she's cold as ice.'

'Poor girl,' Hazel said sorrowfully.

Ash looked at Shaun. 'I'll take care of things here. Can you see them down to the boat?'

'Of course,' Shaun said soberly. 'Come on, girls.' He looped one of his arms through Hazel's and the other through Julie's. 'I'll rustle us up some hot tea,' he said breezily. 'Take the chill outta your bones. Only thing worse than old bones is cold bones.'

Hazel knew he was making an effort to lighten the mood, but there was no disguising that the geniality they had been enjoying less than ten minutes earlier had dissipated.

'Do you like a nice toasty buttered crumpet by chance?' Shaun continued as he led them away, back across the compound. 'I must confess I'm rather partial to them m'self.'

The cosiness of the little kitchenette aboard Ash and Shaun's houseboat did little to alleviate the sombre mood.

Hazel, Julie and Shaun were sitting at a small, circular table drinking hot tea, but the plate of crumpets remained untouched. Even Pip, curled up under the table beside Julie's feet, was looking a little sorry for herself.

A clattering noise came from the stairwell and Ash appeared. Taking off his coat, he sighed heavily. 'All taken care of. For now.' He crossed to the sink and washed his hands.

Shaun got up and gave him a little peck on the cheek. 'You okay?'

Ash nodded.

'Would you like some tea? Kettle's only just boiled.'

'Please,' Ash replied. 'No, wait, I'll have a coffee actually. I could use the caffeine.'

Shaun squeezed past him to get to the counter to prepare the drink. 'Instant okay?'

'Sure, if you're all drinking tea it's not worth doing a filter just for me.' Ash dried his hands and sat down. Picking up a crumpet he took a big bite out of it.

'Thank you so much for letting us sleep here tonight,' Julie said. She still looked very pale. 'There's no way now I'd have slept a wink in the van.'

'Yeah, thanks, bro,' Hazel chimed in.

'You're welcome, you know you are.' Ash smiled. 'It's lovely to have some company, isn't it Shaun?'

'It is so,' Shaun said smiling. He handed Ash a mug of coffee and looked at the two women. 'I'll go make up the spare bed. I'm afraid we've only got the one.' She saw Julie glance apprehensively at Hazel. 'I hope you two ladies don't mind sharing,' he added with a mischievous wink.

Julie managed to muster a smile. 'That's absolutely fine.'

'Good stuff.' Shaun winked again and made his way through to the cabins at the rear of the boat.

'Here,' Ash said, bending to pick up a newspaper from the top of the small pile on the floor in the corner. 'Take a look at this.' He opened it, folded it once and slid it across the table for Hazel and Julie to see. He tapped the page. 'Yesterday's paper. If ever you were in any doubt there's something dodgy going on with this whole bloody ORACULTE epidemic, read this.'

The headline on the page read: **IT'S ALL LIES!**

Ash leant forward in his seat. 'I'll save you the time. Some independent doctor has been running tests involving a man who was diagnosed as having contracted the virus. Obviously he was one of the lucky ones, he didn't perish. But he'd apparently been pretty ill and was still showing symptoms. So this doctor – Edwards I think his name is, it's in the report – got five volunteers that he ascertained had no trace of the virus to help him conduct some tests. Now, it says in the article they all had pretty severe underlying health conditions and the clock was ticking for them anyway. But they allowed this guy, who was still clearly sick, to touch them, breathe on them, even cough on them.'

Julie screwed up her face. 'That's abhorrent!'

'Yes, but here's the rub,' Ash said. 'None of the volunteers got the virus. Not *one*. Think about that for a second.'

227

Hazel frowned. 'Then it's not transmissible through contact with someone who has it.'

'Exactly. This doctor told the papers that there is no evidence whatsoever to suggest it's viral.'

'So what is it then?'

Ash sat back. 'A couple of the guys who live here, Jake and Scarlett, went down to Trafalgar Square yesterday to kick the hornet's nest.'

'How did they manage to get to London?' Julie said. 'There's a lockdown.'

'How did *you* manage to get *here*?'

'We kept to the back roads,' Hazel said. 'Took it steady, made sure we didn't break any speed limits, avoided routes where it was likely there would be speed cameras...'

'There you go then,' Ash said. 'They went on Scarlett's motorbike – a beauty she is too, a vintage Kawasaki Z1 900. Man, she' so cool.'

Julie looked at him blankly.

Ash saw her expression and smiled. 'Trust me, it's a beast to die for. If I was a few years younger that's how I'd want to travel around. Anyway, the thing is they're also hooking up with a guy who claims to have evidence that the whole virus thing has been orchestrated.'

'There are a lot of conspiracy theorists around,' Julie said slightly dismissively.

'This is apparently very compelling evidence,' Ash said. 'Have you heard of a guy named Isaac Owusu? He did videos on Nu-Tube.'

'We heard on the radio yesterday he'd died,' Hazel said.

'Yeah, well I used to watch his stuff.'

'So did I,' Hazel said.

'He was no bullshitter. A hell of a lot of what he said made sense. Anyway, apparently the guy who has this evidence claims it was uncovered by Owusu. Jake and Scarlett are due back tomorrow, so I guess we'll find out.'

Shaun reappeared. 'Your bed is ready, ladies. Second door along.'

'Thank you,' Hazel said. She stood up. 'It's been a hell of a day. I think it's time to get some zeds.'

Shaun slipped his arm round Ash's shoulders. 'We'll try not to keep you awake,' he said with a wink.

Ash brushed away his arm and gave him a sideways look. 'Rein it in, eh? Not appropriate right now.' He looked at Julie. 'Sleeping on a boat takes a bit of getting used to. I can't really describe it, it just feels kinda different. But you go get your head down now.'

They wished each other goodnight and Julie and Hazel made their way through to the spare cabin.

The following morning, Ash, who had been up for almost an hour, was crunching on a piece of toast slathered in honey when a rather weary-looking Julie appeared, dressed in a loose-fitting sweater and jeans.

'Morning,' Julie said, stifling a yawn.

Ash put aside the well-thumbed paperback book he'd been reading and stood up. 'Morning. Can I get you some breakfast?'

'No, I'm fine at the moment thanks.'

'Well, when you're ready there's cornflakes in the cupboard above the sink and bread on the side if you want some toast.'

'I'll probably have something when Hazel gets up,' Julie said.

Ash politely waited for her to take a seat and then he sat down again. 'Still in her pit, is she?'

Julie nodded. 'I left her snoozing.'

Ash chuckled. 'Leopards don't change their spots, do they? When we were kids Mum and Dad tasked me with getting her up for school in the morning. Nightmare!'

'Have you seen Pip?' Julie asked, leaning to look under the table.

Ash nodded. 'She came trotting through while we were making breakfast. She obviously wanted out, so Shaun's taken her for a little walk. I hope you don't mind.'

Julie smiled. 'Of course I don't mind.'

'So how did *you* sleep?'

'Not very well to be honest,' Julie sighed.

'Oh?' Ash picked up his unfinished toast. 'Sorry to hear that.' He popped the last bite into his mouth and tried to wipe a smear of honey off his beard. 'Honey wasn't meant for people with chin-fuzz.' He rolled his eyes. 'Sorry. Going off at a tangent. Was the bed uncomfortable?'

'No, it was very comfy.'

'Okay, well, like I said, sleeping on a boat takes a bit of getting used to.'

'It wasn't that either.' Julie stifled another yawn. 'Just bad dreams.' She nodded at the paperback book. 'What's that you're reading?'

'George Orwell.' Ash picked it up and ran his thumb across the pages. 'It's "1984". It's really good and incredibly prescient. I've read it dozens of times. I like his "Animal Farm" a lot, but this has the edge.'

'I've not read it.' Julie stood up. 'Actually, I think if you don't mind I'll make a cup of tea.'

'Knock yourself out.'

'Would you like one?' Julie asked.

'No thanks.'

While Julie set about preparing her hot drink, Ash leaned back in his chair and stretched. 'So what's your take on all this virus business then, Julie?'

'What do *I* think?'

Ash nodded. 'Yeah.'

'It's horrible, obviously,' Julie said, putting milk and a teaspoonful of sugar into a mug.

Ash sighed. 'It certainly is that.'

'But after what you were saying last night,' Julie continued, 'I'm not sure I know what to think any more.'

'Yeah,' Ash said. 'About that. Don't you find it strange that some random contagion surfaced out of nowhere and spread so fast?'

The kettle started to boil. Julie frowned. 'Viruses mutate all the time. It's what they do. Do you know, I read once that every single time a cold does the rounds it's different than the previous one and the label "the common cold" is a misnomer. So, do I find it strange? No, not really.' She poured the hot water into her mug.

231

'This isn't a cold though is it?' Ash said thoughtfully. 'Let's not say strange then, let's say unlikely. At least insomuch as the effect it's had on our lives.'

'Maybe... I suppose... I don't really know.' Julie finished making her tea and sat down.

'Think about it,' Ash said. 'Who'd even heard of ORACULTE a few weeks ago? Nobody. Not even the Government.' He leaned forward conspiratorially. 'Or had they?'

'What do you mean?'

'Regardless of any evidence that might exist to prove its all been orchestrated – we'll see about that later today – you've only got to think about it for a minute and the cracks begin to show. Telling people that they're confined to their homes is a simple enough thing to do. That's just words. But to implement the distribution of food supplies to every household across the nation? The logistics are mind-blowing. It's the sort of thing that takes serious planning. Yet our esteemed leaders got it organised, practically overnight. I believe that they knew this outbreak was coming weeks, if not months ago. And if they knew it was coming, you've got to ask yourself *how* did they know?

Julie found herself captivated by what Ash was saying. Laid out so simply it suddenly seemed all too obvious, so why hadn't it even occurred to her before? 'That's a very persuasive theory,' she said. 'Why aren't people questioning it?

'Some are. All of us living here at the yard certainly believe that's the case.'

Julie sipped her tea. 'So supposing what you're suggesting is right, how *did* they know?'

Ash sat back. 'Well, that's the 64,000 dollar question, isn't it? There are a lot of theories about the hows and whys. Some are a little bit out there, I'll grant you. And unfortunately all that the extremists do is furnish the Government with ammunition to dismiss people with genuine insight as conspiracy theorists. And while the public are busy laughing at the wackier hypotheses, the rational ones – the ones that hold serious water – get quietly buried. Trust me, it's all about the two Ds: distraction and deflection.'

'What do *you* think?' Julie said, warming her hands around the mug.

'There are some guys who live on a barge just up the river a way. They're part of an alliance that's emerged in response to what's going on. I think you and Haze should meet them.'

Hazel, dressed in an oversize baggy T-shirt that finished at her knees appeared in the doorway. 'Meet who?'

Ash grinned. 'Morning, sis. Finally dragged yourself out of your pit then?'

'Actually I've been half-awake since Julie got up.' Hazel plucked the mug of tea from Julie's hands and took a swig.

'Oi!' Julie exclaimed. 'That's mine.'

Hazel laughed. 'Always tastes better when it's someone else's.' She raised the mug – 'Cheers, Jules.' – and drained the last of the tea. 'I'll make you another.'

'How did you sleep?' Ash asked.

'Like a log. It was really cosy.' She refilled the kettle from a bottle of water and put it on the hob. 'So come on, who are these people you want us to meet?'

Footsteps sounded on the stairwell and Shaun appeared carrying Pip. His cheeks had a rosy glow and he was slightly out of breath. 'For a little'un this hound of yours can't half shift. Gave a me a proper workout.'

Julie stood up and took Pip from him. 'I hope you've been a good girl,' she said, hugging the little dog close. Pip twisted her neck and lapped at Julie's chin.

'She's been good as gold, so she has.' He reached out and ruffled Pip's head.

'Tea?' Hazel asked.

'No thanks. I had one before I went out.' He sat down next to Ash and lowered his voice. 'I bumped into Youseff. He said to tell you he's going to take the van and get the lady's body to the hospital this morning.'

The reminder of the previous evening's tragedy cast a doleful silence over the kitchenette.

CHAPTER 20

It was a beautiful morning and the golden fingers of sunlight glittered through the line of fir trees dividing the towpath from the fields beyond.

Ash and Shaun, followed by Hazel and Julie, emerged from below deck.

'What a beautiful morning,' Julie said, inhaling deeply. 'Look at that sky.'

The others looked up. The sheen of blue stretched out as far as the eye could see and there wasn't so much as a trace of cloud.

'Told you it was idyllic here,' Hazel remarked.

'I don't mind telling you, it's not so much fun when it's pissing down,' Shaun said. 'But when you get up to a morning like this, there's no place on Earth I'd rather be.'

'Seconded,' Ash said. 'Wild horses couldn't drag me away from this place.'

They walked down the gangplank onto the towpath.

The name painted in bold green letters on the hull of the houseboat caught Julie's eye: PIRATES' BOOTY. 'I didn't notice that last night,' she said. 'Shouldn't a boat bearing that name have a Jolly Roger fluttering on the flagpole?'

Shaun chuckled. 'Sure, we've had a few of those aboard haven't we, Ash?'

Ash gave him a feigned look of disgust. 'Cold shower for you later!'

'Promises, promises!'

'Can you just stop it!' Hazel exclaimed.

'Sorry, sis.'

'Truth be told,' Shaun said, 'we named her that because we're a couple of salty seadogs at heart...' – he reached down and patted Ash's bottom – '...with nice firm booties!'

A little way up the towpath, a man reading a newspaper was stretched out in a deckchair that was lodged at an awkward angle on the bank where a distinctly dilapidated-looking vessel was moored. As the group approached, he peered over the top of the paper. 'Ah, good morning, good morning, lads and lasses!' he exclaimed, standing up and stepping out onto the path in front of them.

'Morning, Andy,' Ash said. 'You survived the hecklers last night then.'

The old man guffawed. 'Hecklers, m'boy? I'll have you know that's my adoring fans you're talking about!' He frowned. 'I'll concede it was a tough crowd last night though.'

'Maybe you should change your repertoire,' Shaun suggested. 'Mix it up a bit, you know? Throw in something that wasn't recorded a hundred years ago.'

Andy laughed. 'Cheeky bugger!' He smiled at Hazel and Julie. 'Pardon my French.'

'We'll see you a bit later,' Ash said.

'I certainly hope so,' Andy said with a broad grin. He stepped off the path to let them pass, eyeing up Julie, who smiled at him politely. He looked down as Pip scuttled past in her wake. 'Awww, what a little cutie!'

Further along the towpath a long barge came into sight. Hazel immediately noticed a flag with a red, five-pointed star embroidered on it, flapping gently in the breeze.

Two muscular, shirtless men in their mid-to-late-20s were busily loading goods aboard. Both of them had an earthy look. The darker of the two had impressive dreadlocks and was squatting on the edge of the deck, while the other – parading a long, auburn mane that cascaded down around his shoulders – was stood on the bank passing up crates to him.

Shaun's eyes lit up. 'Wowzer! Davey and Jas are looking exceptionally fit this morning,' he said. His eyes widened and he theatrically put his hand over his mouth. 'Lordy, did I say that out loud?'

'Down, tiger,' Ash said, affording him a slightly withering look.

As they got nearer, a young woman with her arms full of placards and tins of paint emerged from below deck. Clad in cut-offs and a T-shirt with an image of Che Guevara emblazoned on the front, she was a striking woman with long, wavy, sun-kissed locks and strong-looking arms bedecked with colourful tattoos. She paused as she spotted the group coming along the towpath. 'Ay-up, guys. We've got visitors.'

The two men looked up simultaneously and acknowledged the approaching group with a friendly wave. The one called Jas plonked himself down on the side of the barge with his legs dangling over the edge.

The woman set down the things she'd been carrying, stepped around Jas and came ashore down a rickety looking gangplank. Pip scurried towards her, a few yards ahead of the others and she dropped to her knees to greet the little dachshund. 'Hello,' she said chirpily. 'Who are you then, eh?'

'That's our little Pip,' Julie said.

Pip stood on her hind legs, put her front paws up on the woman's bended knee and started eagerly licking her arms.

'Easy, I've already had a wash this morning!' the woman exclaimed. 'You'll lick my tattoos off!' She stood up. 'I'm Bex,' she said, extending her hand.

Julie shook her hand. 'Julie.'

'Pleased to meet ya, Julie!'

Hazel stepped up alongside her. 'Hiya, Bex.' The two women embraced.

'Long time no see, my love,' Bex said.

'Too long,' Hazel replied.

Davey approached Ash and offered his hand for a high-five. 'How's it going, guys?'

'Pretty good,' Ash replied.

Shaun nodded. 'Likewise. How about yourself?'

'Same.'

'You've met my sister, I think?' Ash said, gesturing at Hazel.

'I believe we met at the Club, but that was…' – he sucked in air between his teeth – 'five years ago if it's a day?'

Hazel nodded and smiled. 'Hi, Davey.'

'And this is our friend, Julie,' Ash continued.

'Pleased to meet you,' Davey said with a welcoming smile. He patted his chest. 'Apologies that we're only half dressed. We're just loading up and it's baking out here already this morning.'

238

'Loading up?' Ash said. 'Going somewhere?'

'Yeah. We're shipping out on a little trip tomorrow. We're gonna be hooking up with a few others.'

'Good luck,' Shaun said.

Davey smiled at him. 'Cheers, dude.'

'Listen,' Ash said. 'I've been telling Hazel and Julie about the alliance.'

As Jas, who had come down the gangplank unnoticed, stepped up alongside him, Davey's eyes narrowed. He brushed his long hair back out of his face. 'Have you now?' he said solemnly.

Almost as if someone had flicked a switch, Hazel felt the genial mood change, and she saw the look of suspicion on the two men's faces.

'Oh, don't worry,' Ash said hastily, as Bex joined her friends. 'It's all cool. They're of exactly the same opinion as all of us over what's going down at the moment. I wanted them to hear your take on it.'

For a moment the three of them stared at Ash in silence. Then Davey broke into a smile. 'How long have they got?'

'Give them the short version.' Ash grinned.

'I'll leave you to it,' Bex said, as she climbed back up onto the deck of the barge. 'I've got a bunch of banners to prepare.'

'The short version, eh?' Davey chuckled. 'Okay, short version coming right up. We believe the whole country is being taken for a ride by a charlatan governing body playing out a sordid game of natural selection. Cleansing. Streamlining. Decreasing the surplus population. Call it what you will, it all boils down to an act of genocide. And it's survival of the

239

fittest. We don't think this ORACULTE is a virus at all. We believe it's an engineered toxin that they're manipulating to dispose of the weak and the helpless, moulding the remaining populace to conform to their grand design.'

Julie looked aghast.

Even Hazel appeared to be a little shaken by what she was hearing. 'What do you mean by grand design?'

'Grand design,' Jas echoed. 'Your modern day equivalent of the Master Race.'

'And *that's* your short version,' Davey said. He wasn't smiling any more.

Ash looked at Hazel. 'Told you these guys were worth listening to. Some of their ideas are a bit radical, even for me, but I'm pretty sure in many respects they aren't so far off the mark.'

'So what you're saying is that you think the Prime Minister – our *elected* Government officials – are directly responsible for the death of thousands,' Hazel said. 'Not because of their incompetence to deal with it, but by *design*?'

Davey nodded. 'Pretty mind-blowing, I'll grant you.'

'You're likening Cameron Stirling to Hitler then?' Julie said.

'Too damned right we are,' Davey said. 'Not all Nazis are swastika-brandishing, goose-stepping, gas chamber fanatics, you know.'

'Tell them about the alliance,' Ash said.

'There are a lot of people who think the same way we do. And I mean a *lot*. More than you'd probably think. There are pockets of resistance all over the country and the cogs are turning. Slowly, unfortunately, but nevertheless turning. All of us realise that if we don't make a stand soon, before long we'll all be slaves to a corrupt regime for the rest of our days. Trust me, it's been a long time coming, but we're on the eve of resurgence. The tide is turning!'

'What do you think of this?' Bex called out. They all looked up to see she was holding aloft a placard with two words painted on it: JUDGEMENT DAY!.

'Nice!' Jas exclaimed. 'One down, thirty to go.'

Bex gave him a filthy look. 'It would get done a lot quicker if you got your arse up here and gave me a hand.'

Jas chortled. 'Just get on with it, woman!'

'I'll give you a hand if you like,' Julie said. 'I did art at college.'

Bex exchanged glances with Davey. 'Cheers, that'd be cool,' she said. 'It doesn't have to be anything flash though, just some simple slogans.'

Hazel stepped forward. 'We can do simple, can't we Jules?'

Julie looked slightly disappointed that her artistic skills were going to be superfluous, but she nodded. 'Sure.' She scooped up Pip, who had been circling her legs.

Hazel saw the expression on her friend's face. 'Alright, Picasso, come on, let's make some masterpieces.'

Julie smiled.

'*Two* volunteers,' Davey said. 'Quick, Bex, grab them before they change their minds.'

Bex watched Hazel and Julie cautiously ascending the gangplank to join her on deck. 'I need all the help I can get and I'm sure whatever you design will be a heck of a lot better than mine.'

'Yo!'

The voice came from off up the towpath and everybody turned their heads to look.

In the distance, two men and a woman were coming down from the boatyard.

The other men hung back as Shaun strode purposefully towards the new arrivals.

Hazel and Julie watched nervously from the deck.

As Shaun got closer he recognised two of them. 'Sure, it's okay,' he called back. 'It's just Jake and Scarlett.'

Bex relaxed and carried on painting. Julie and Hazel also turned their attention on the protest banners.

Davey and Jas resumed loading the crates of supplies onto the barge.

'How ya?' Shaun said as he reached out his hand to the young man wearing jeans and a camouflage jacket.

Jake took his hand and pulled Shaun towards him in a shoulder bump. 'All good bro, all good.'

'What's with the fat lip?' Shaun asked.

'Oh, some gung-ho plod swung at me with his batton,' Jake replied, gingerly touching the swollen cut on his mouth. 'It was carnage. Cops with shields and water cannons, totally heavy handed.'

Shaun smiled at the woman, who was dressed similarly to Jake. She immediately came over and hugged him. 'You're a sight for sore eyes,' she said.

'Hi guys,' Ash said as came over to join him.

Shaun eyed up the young man accompanying Jame and Scarlett. 'And who's this?' he asked suspiciously.

Dressed in an immaculate pinstripe suit, the man was anxiously examining the spatters of mud that had accumulated on his expensive-looking loafers.

'This is Rory Hopkins,' Scarlett said. 'He followed us back from the smoke.'

Rory stepped forward. 'I struggled to keep up with them on that bike,' he said, offering his hand to Shaun. 'Gave my Picanto a workout, that's for sure.'

Shaun hesitated for a moment, then smiled and took hold of Rory's hand with his usual strong grip. 'Ah, Rory! Sure, you're the chap with all the dirt, right?'

'You could say that,' Rory replied. 'And not just on my shoes.' He grinned and pulled a USB flash drive from his inside pocket. 'I was just going to give this to Jake, but I've heard so much about you guys and this place that I had to check it out for myself.'

Shaun slapped him hard on the back. 'Well come on then, son. Come and meet the gang.'

As Bex came down the gangplank, Shaun led Rory towards the barge.

Jake and Scarlett followed along and Bex ran up to greet them with a hug. 'How was it?' she asked. 'I've seen loads of stuff on TikTok and Twitter. Looks like it got quite heavy.'

'It was crazy,' Scarlett said. 'We started in Trafalgar Square and it was pretty peaceful. I mean there were a few idiots climbing on the statues, but mostly it was all under control until the fuzz piled in wearing full riot gear and it all kicked off. Jake got walloped and they had me on the ground at one point. Honestly, Bex, it

243

was like a full on dog-fight down there. Fucking mental!'

'Hi, I'm Rory,' the young man said, smiling at Bex.

She returned his smile. 'Great to meet you.'

Jake held out his hand and Rory dropped the flash drive into his open palm. 'I don't reckon you'll be needing all those banners now,' Jake said pointing towards the pile of placards on the deck of the barge. 'This little device holds enough information to bring down that genocidal maniac Stirling and all of his corrupt cronies with him.'

Hazel looked up to see Jake was holding the small USB aloft like a miniature trophy 'This, my friends, is the key to unlocking our freedom and overthrowing that bunch of dystopian Nazis for good!' He passed the USB to Ash. 'There you go, my friend.'

Ash took it from him and examined it. It resembled a packet of chewing gum. 'Where did you get this exactly?' he said, addressing Rory.

'It comes to you courtesy of the late Isaac Owusu,' the young man said gravely. 'I worked with him pretty closely, he called me his go-to guy for all matters internet. He told me about that stick a couple of days ago – the night he was murdered – and I was able to retrieve it from his flat.'

'Okay, let's go see what we've got then,' Ash said. 'Then after we've had a good look-see, we'll take you over to the Tropicana.'

Rory looked unsure. 'Where's that?'

'It's just the clubhouse here at the yard,' Shaun said. 'You can wet your whistle and meet some of the others.'

Rory glanced at the expensive-looking expanding link-chain Rolex on his wrist. 'It's only 10.15. Isn't it a little early to be drinking?'

Ash fixed him with a stern look.

'Now you listen to me, young man. If you want to fit in here you're going to have to understand it's never too early for a pint or three of the hard stuff.'

Rory smiled, but it wasn't a confident one. He wasn't sure he *did* want to fit in here. 'Er, yes, of course,' he muttered.

Everyone burst out laughing.

'It's okay, I'm messing with you,' Ash said. He slapped Rory on the back. 'It'll be soft drinks all round. You can even get a coffee if that's your poison.'

Shaun looked back towards the barge. 'You guys with us?'

Hazel and Julie were coming back down the gangplank.

Davey ran a hand through his hair. 'Jas and m'self will help Bex clear up and we'll join you shortly.'

CHAPTER 21

Cameron Stirling sat cradling a tumbler of whiskey in one hand and studying the morning paper laid out flat across his desk.

From the moment he had awoken, he'd had a feeling of dread, something that was quite unfamiliar to him. He wasn't one to dwell on such things and there had never before been a problem too big for him to overcome. Yet in his 25 years of politics he had never felt so incensed at the lack of commitment and dedication from his team as he did this morning.

The plans that he had single-handedly devised were perfect in every way and he had every faith in their implementation. He had handpicked his team and had felt no concerns about their allegiance – until now. Cracks were starting to show; not within the strategy or Stirling's belief in the end goal, but within the stronghold of his associates. His feckless and frankly shoddy colleagues had let him down and he was not impressed.

Simpson had been the biggest disappointment; a man Stirling had known since Eton and worked alongside for most of his political career. He sighed as he recalled the moment he had taken care of the treacherous Simpson, but even so there was an unmistakable glint of satisfaction in his eyes.

He glanced at the paper and swigged his whiskey. A photograph of a riotous crowd being held back by the army emblazoned the page. Stirling frowned. Mathers had also proven to be a poor choice. A well-decorated and dedicated soldier, but when tasked with maintaining control over the British people, he had failed miserably. Riots, destruction and downright disobedience flew in the face of everything Stirling had envisioned. The people were out of control and this simply was not on. If they can't be controlled, they can't be ruled. And without rule, what is there? They can't just be allowed to roam free, he thought to himself, doing whatever they like. They can't spout off about civil liberties and revolution. No, that simply will not do. People with freedom and a voice are dangerous, a threat to the regime – people like Isaac Owusu – and they need to be silenced. Mathers couldn't even manage that small task efficiently. True, Owusu wouldn't be spreading his revolutionary ramblings any more, but the General and his incompetent team were careless and thanks to their failure to sweep Owusu's home properly, everything Stirling and Walsh had worked on was out there, loose in the hands of rebels. And speaking of Walsh, had he spent a bit more time vetting his own team, there would have been no information *to* leak.

Stirling put the glass down and let out a big sigh. 'I'm surrounded by idiots,' he said out loud.

A feeling of sadness washed over him as he studied the Artex swirls on the ceiling. His election as Prime Minister after the exit of his predecessor beneath a cloud of disgrace had been a proud moment and he knew it would take something groundbreaking and radical for him to make his mark in the history books. GX-23 and the rebirth of mankind had been his golden opportunity to make Britain great again and the shambolic efforts of his team had now made it untenable. All he could do now was try to separate himself from the whole sordid affair and ensure his record remain unblemished.

Having heard first thing that the lab had been raided by police and that Walsh and the rest of his team had been marched off in handcuffs, it was in Stirling's best interest to let them take the blame and deny any knowledge. He had already been forward thinking enough to plant evidence in Simpson's office; evidence that would implicate him as the sole conspirator and the man pulling all the strings to orchestrate a heinous plan that would see him become the leader of a new world order.

Stirling stood up. His bags were packed and the traps were set. A chartered plane from an airfield in Essex would take him to a private island owned by a close friend, where he would simply disappear and leave his treacherous acolytes to face the music alone.

Casting a final glance out of his office window at the teeming rain assailing Downing Street, Stirling picked up his briefcase from the desk and walked across to the door. He paused and turned to survey the room.

'This isn't goodbye,' he said. Even now, with the cloud of a lifelong prison sentence hanging on the horizon, the gravity of what would become of him should he ever return to the United Kingdom appeared not to trouble him; the vanity of the irretrievably deluded. 'More a case of à bientôt, I think,' he added with a thin smile.

He opened the door and his face froze.

'Good morning, Prime Minister.' The man wearing the sodden overcoat and mopping the rain from his face with a handkerchief took a pace forward. 'What a foul morning.'

Stirling didn't reply. He stood in the open doorway with a blank expression on his face.

'My name's Detective Chief Inspector Conrad. I wonder if I might have a word with you, please?'

Still Stirling said nothing.

Two men holding automatic rifles were positioned a couple of feet behind and to either side of Conrad.

'May I?' Conrad repeated.

Stirling stepped back into the office and the two guards accompanied Conrad inside, closing the door quietly behind them.

*

The previous evening, with a single keystroke on a laptop in a houseboat in Ripon, the truth about ORACULTE had been released to the world's media. Thanks to the courageousness of the late, never to be forgotten Damian Gardner – a former employee at a laboratory near Cambridge, and without whose intervention the Government would have gone on to expedite the deaths of countless thousands more citizens – the nightmare was over.

On the lunchtime news an awestruck populace had witnessed live footage of the Prime Minster, Cameron Stirling, being escorted at gunpoint from Downing Street with a blanket over his head.

The Internet had immediately burst into life, reporting the known facts behind ORACULTE and GX-23. The headlines became increasingly outrageous, and within hours the substantiated truths had become corrupted and littered with conjecture and falsehoods. But it didn't matter. As Ash observed, 'Let the wolves have their day. They deserve it.'

Ash's favourite headline, which appeared on the home page of one of the more disreputable British tabloids, was **WAT-ER W**KER!**, although Shaun was a little put out, claiming to have said it before it ever appeared online.

The mood at the boatyard that afternoon was one of jubilation, and the alcohol was flowing at Club Tropicana, where, for the first time since it had opened, the drinks really were free.

Hazel had been standing at the bar talking to Bex for some while. Now, clutching a Cherry Pepsi, she pushed her way through the partying crowd to join Ash, Shaun and Rory at the corner table.

Pip was on Shaun's lap. He was making a fuss of her and the little dog was lapping up the attention.

'Where's Jules?' Hazel said as she took a seat. 'I haven't seen her for ages.'

'Did you not see her dancing with Andy?' Ash said.

'Yes, I did,' Hazel replied. 'But that was half an hour ago.'

Shaun beamed at her. 'I saw them leave together.' He wiggled his eyebrows mischievously. 'From what I could see the old bugger was getting a bit handsy too.'

Hazel's mouth dropped open. 'What?! Julie would never…'

250

'Never say never,' Shaun interjected. 'She seemed to be rather enjoying it. If I know Andy – and trust me I do – they'll be back at his boat making tidal waves as we speak.' He guffawed.

Hazel smiled. 'Well, Jules deserves a little bit of happiness. Thanks for making her feel so at home here, guys.'

'Come on then, sis,' Ash said. 'Now it's all out there and that parasite Stirling and his cronies have finally been taken down – what do you think will happen next?'

'Things will return to normal pretty quickly, I reckon,' Hazel said. 'Be it good, or bad, or whatever constitutes normal. But the main thing is, Stirling's agenda was psychotic. Alongside the physical act of poisoning the water, the age-old ploy of divide and conquer was playing out under our noses and he almost triumphed there, instilling fear into the meek, riling people strong enough to question what was going on, pitting them against each other.'

Ash nodded his agreement. 'Precisely,' he said.

'Divide and conquer,' Hazel repeated. 'Take away our basic freedoms. The simple pleasures of attending a football match or a concert, going to the cinema or out for a meal, every leisure activity that we used to enjoy completely denied us. Ban us from socialising with our friends. Separate us from our loved ones. Stop people seeing their children and their grandchildren. Get us frustrated to the point we turn on one another, causing so much segregation and unrest within communities that nobody knows which way to turn and everyone ends up falling on bended knee before the Government,

251

begging for a solution to the very problem they designed and orchestrated.' She took a sip of her drink. 'If we had ever allowed them to break our spirit, we would have become their perfect pliable puppets.'

'She speaks a lot of sense,' Rory said.

Shaun and Ash nodded.

'But I don't think anything even remotely like what they were half way to achieving will ever be permitted to happen again,' Hazel continued. 'It's probably a stretch too far at the moment to imagine Britain as an autonomous collective, but I don't think it's beyond the realms of possibility.'

'I'll drink to that,' Shaun said.

'Me too,' Ash said.

As they raised their glasses, Shaun pointed towards the door. They all turned to see Andy and Julie standing at the edge of the crowd. They saw Andy whisper something in her ear and give her a peck on the cheek before disappearing into the crowd.

Julie came over to join them at the table. She was smiling and her cheeks were flushed. She sat down alongside Rory.

'You didn't?' Hazel said, her eyes wide.

'That's for me to know and you to never find out!' Julie replied. She laughed.

Before Hazel could respond, the room filled with the sound of cheers and applause and Andy appeared on the dais with a microphone in his hand. 'Some of you might know this one. Some bloke called Shakin' Stevens did it. Waste of time, he was though. I do it way better. I'm not naming names, but I dedicate this to a very special lady. She knows who she is.'

Andy pressed a couple of buttons on the karaoke machine, the music started and he began to sing.
'Whoa, whoa Julie,
If you love me truly,
If you want me Julie,
To be, to be your very own...'

Shaun guffawed. 'Lucky he made it clear he wasn't naming names!' he exclaimed.

Ash lifted his lime and soda. 'To liberation, my friends.'

They all picked up their drinks and clinked glasses. Julie didn't have a glass, but she nodded in agreement. 'And to good friends and lifelong friendship.'

'And let's not forget sappy old buggers singing love songs really badly,' Shaun added.

'Long may they all continue,' Hazel said.

Pip barked and they all burst out laughing.

And for just a short while everyone put aside their worries and enjoyed the simple pleasure of each other's company.

Hazel glanced around the room at the sea of happy faces. She smiled and, as she blinked, a single tear trickled down her cheek.

She was home.

POSTSCRIPT

Julie was awakened by the sound of frantic yapping and she sat bolt upright in bed.

It had been almost three months since the end of the awful ORACULTE ordeal and the memories were still very much fresh in her mind. Every little sound put her on edge and she often found herself fending off attacks of anxiety, and having to tell herself repeatedly that the threat was over and life had now gone back to normal.

The yapping continued. Julie glanced over at the clock beside her bed. 'Oh my!' she exclaimed, throwing off the duvet and quickly stepping into her slippers. She hurried downstairs, grabbing her dressing gown as she went.

Through the frosted glass of the front door, Julie could see the outline of someone on the step outside. As she got closer, she could see the figure was moving on the spot in a jerky fashion. Trying hard not to trip over Pip, whose tail was thrashing about like a little bullwhip around her ankles, she put the safety chain across, gingerly opened the door and peeked through the gap.

'Hurry up woman! I'm breaking my neck for a wee!' a familiar voice said.

Julie smiled and unlatched the chain. 'Hazel!' she exclaimed. 'How lovely to see you.'

Hazel pecked her quickly on the cheek and pushed her way past, making a desperate dash up the stairs to the bathroom.

Pip scurried excitedly up behind her.

Julie stood in the hallway a little bemused and her face broke into a big smile as Hazel's voice echoed down the stairs, 'Do you mind?!'

Pip had evidently accompanied her into the bathroom.

'Pip,' Julie called out. 'Let Hazel be for a minute will you?'

The overexcited dachshund rushed down the stairs, her back end almost catching up with her as she slid down the steps like a slinky.

Julie walked into the kitchen and flicked the switch on the kettle. Pip was circling her feet and panting with excitement.

'Alright, you, don't trip me up,' Julie said sternly as she crossed the room to open the back door.

Pip shot out into the garden and squatted, barely giving herself enough time to finish before she darted back up the concrete step and into the kitchen.

'Phew! That was a close shave,' Hazel said as she hung up her coat in the hallway.

Pip hurtled towards her and Hazel scooped up the little dog in her arms. Pip's tongue flicked out and she slavered all over Hazel's face.

'Hello, Pip! I've missed you.'

Julie handed her friend a cup of tea and smiled. 'Well this is a pleasant surprise.'

Hazel put Pip down. 'I was in the area and I couldn't pass by without dropping in on my best friend,' she replied, stepping forward to give Julie a hug.

'It's wonderful to see you, but you could've given me a warning, I've nothing in and I'm … well, I'm still in my pyjamas!'

'Yeah what's with that?' Hazel asked sarcastically. 'You're usually up and at 'em before the sparrows.'

Julie picked up her mug and took a sip, hoping her tea would hide her embarrassment. 'Well, truth be told, I've not been sleeping too well. I sit up all night watching trashy movies on the TV and usually pass out in the chair. Then I get woken by a stiff neck at 2am and hoist myself up to bed, but I just lay there, tossing and turning. I don't know what's wrong with me.'

Hazel smiled warmly. 'There's nothing wrong with you. You've just gotta get back into a normal routine.'

Julie half smiled. 'I don't feel like anything's normal any more.'

Hazel looked at Julie with concern.

The pair were startled by a sudden shrill yap. Pip was looking up at Hazel with her tail wagging.

'What's this?' Hazel asked playfully.

Pip yapped again.

Kneeling down to pick up a small rubber bone from the floor, Hazel let out a groan. 'Ooh! The old back is giving me jip. Maybe I could stay with you for a few nights. A proper bed will straighten me out.'

Julie smiled. 'Of course, you're welcome anytime, you know that.'

Hazel waved the bone at Pip. 'What do you reckon, little legs? Is it okay if I stay for a few days?'

Pip yapped excitedly.

Hazel gave her the bone and ruffled her head. 'Yeah. I think that's okay,' she said, giving Julie a wink.

Julie smiled broadly. 'That's settled then.'

'I'd better fetch some stuff from the van,' Hazel said.

'While you do that, I'm going to pop upstairs and get myself dressed.' Julie patted her hip. 'Come on Pip.'

Hazel watched her friend climb the stairs with the little dachshund scampering up behind her and she smiled. Quickly downing her tea, she went outside and retrieved her belongings from the camper van. As she slid the side door shut, she glanced across to the garden outside the late Mrs Parkinson's house. The grass was overgrown and already full of weeds. There was an estate agent's board up with the words **FOR SALE** on it. Hazel frowned. 'They didn't hang about!' she said out loud to herself. Picking up her duffel bag, she made her way back into the house.

Julie, now dressed, was in the kitchen washing the mugs in the sink.

'I see the old girl's house is up for sale,' Hazel said, putting her bag down beside the leg of the table.

Julie sighed. 'Yeah. That went up yesterday. It's a shame.'

'You see, it doesn't take long for things to return to normal,' Hazel said reassuringly.

'Yeah. I s'pose. I just hope the new neighbours will be quiet. You never know who you might get.' Julie said anxiously.

'Jules, you worry too much. I'm sure whoever buys it will be lovely. If not, there's always a spare bunk in the camper.'

Julie laughed. 'I've really missed you.'

Hazel's eyes fell upon a stack of 2-litre water bottles sitting on the floor beside the fridge freezer. 'Are you stocking up for a war?' she asked, pointing at the pile.

Julie followed Hazel's finger. 'Ah, well... after all that happened, you can't be too careful.'

Hazel chuckled. 'I never thought I'd see the day you were stockpiling bottled water. There's enough there to last you all year!'

Julie suddenly started to sob.

Hazel hurried over to her. 'I'm sorry, lovey. I was only pulling your leg. Please don't cry.'

'It's not that,' Julie replied, struggling to hold back the tears.

Hazel pulled a tissue from her pocket, unfolded it and handed it to Julie. 'What's up, Jules? Talk to me.'

Julie looked at her. 'Oh it's silly really.' A tear trickled down her cheek.

'Come on, let's sit down. Whatever it is, it's not silly if it's making you this upset.' Hazel gently led Julie into the living room and the pair sat down on the sofa.

Pip quietly followed and, as if sensing the sorrowful mood, she slunk off to her basket with her rubber bone.

'Oh, I feel so silly,' Julie sobbed.

Hazel held Julie's hand and rested it on her own knee. 'What's up?' she asked.

'It's this whole virus thing and what the Prime Minister did. I just can't seem to get it out of my mind. I've been having nightmares.' She paused to blow her nose. 'I keep thinking, what if it happens again? And if I died, what would happen to little Pip?'

The dachshund looked up at the mention of her name and wagged her tail slowly.

Hazel gripped Julie's hand. 'It won't happen again. They've got him now and all his crazy cronies.'

Julie sniffed. 'Yes, but...'

Hazel cut her off. 'No buts. They've *got* him. This whole thing has really shaken up the establishment. We've not seen an overturn like this since the days of Oliver Cromwell!'

'But what if he gets out? He's the Prime Minister, I'm sure he can wriggle out of this.'

'He won't be wriggling out of this, lovey. No way. That man is staying behind bars for a long, *long* time. And if there's any justice in this world he'll get some of what that evil professor got!'

Julie looked at Hazel. Her face red and her eyes wet. 'What happened to him?' she asked weakly.

'Didn't you hear?' Hazel looked surprised. 'It's been all over the news.'

'Oh I can't watch that right now,' Julie replied. 'What happened?'

Hazel took a deep breath. 'Some of his fellow inmates waterboarded him.'

Julie frowned. 'What does that mean?'

Hazel considered her reply carefully. Her friend was clearly very anxious and too much information could tip her over the edge. 'Let's just say, he got what he deserved. What goes around comes around.'

Julie glanced across the room. Pip was sat upright in her basket looking at Julie with a worried look on her little face. Julie smiled at her and she instantly hopped out of her basket and bounded towards them.

Julie bent down and picked up Pip. 'I'm sorry bubba. Don't worry, mummy's alright.'

Hazel leant across and scratched Pip behind her ear. 'Hey, look. It's a lovely day today,' she said. 'How about we take Pip for a walk over to the park and get some lunch at the little café by the pond?'

Julie smiled. 'That sounds lovely!'

Hazel lifted her friend's hand and kissed the back of it. 'We might even have room for an ice cream too.'

Pip jumped down onto the carpet and the pair stood up.

Julie threw her arms around Hazel. 'I'm so glad you're here!'

Hazel beamed. 'That makes two of us.'

Acknowledgements:
The authors would like to thank Sue Hards and Sara Greaves.

Rebecca would also like to thank
Ray, Dave, Tony and Huwey for keeping it real.

Cover photography and design by Rebecca Xibalba.

Also from Rebecca Xibalba and Tim Greaves:
Misdial (2020)
The Break (2021)
The Well (2021)
Available from Amazon, for Kindle and in paperback.
Misdial is also available in Audiobook format from Audible and iTunes.

Printed in Great Britain
by Amazon

23451690R00152